The Phantom Sleuth

The Phantom Sleuth

A Fantasy About Cats

CONNIE CLIFFORD

*Dedicated to my great granddaughter
River Demi Angstadt*

Copyright © 2021 by Connie Clifford.

Library of Congress Control Number: 2021900980

HARDBACK: 978-1-954673-38-0
PAPERBACK: 978-1-954673-37-3
EBOOK: 978-1-954673-39-7

All rights reserved. No part of this publication may be reproduced, distributed, or transmitted in any form or by any electronic or mechanical means, without the prior written permission of the publisher, except in the case of brief quotations embodied in critical reviews and certain other noncommercial uses permitted by copyright law.

Ordering Information:

For orders and inquiries, please contact:
1-888-404-1388
www.goldtouchpress.com
book.orders@goldtouchpress.com

Printed in the United States of America

THE PHANTOM SLEUTH

GRETCHEN DANDRICH is a young, happy socialite and sometimes writer who happened upon an unusual situation. Along with her best friend KRISTIN, who owns an antique shop, she sets out to solve a mystery she unwittingly becomes entangled in while having dinner with her attorney husband HARLEY DANDRICH, a quiet bespectacled, intense young man given more to realism than his wife's excursions into past lives and fantasy. Gretchen and Harley were having a quiet dinner at SHAMAN'S PUB, a noted eatery in the small town of Ridgecrest, Connecticut—a replica of an Olde Irishe Pub—when they are approached by one of Shaman's customers, PROFESSOR IPSWITCH and his new invention—guaranteed to keep the young youthful and the old contented—and sold by Kristin in her antique shop—until he tangles with Gretchen and her alter ego—a white Persian cat —that introduces Gretchen into the cat world.

SHAMAN, a bartender of some notoriety, fashioned his Pub reminiscent of an Olde Irishe Pub. The ambiance of Shaman's Pub—and his two Siamese cats, Ming and Einstein—makes it a favorite watering hole among youthful adults as Shaman regales his customers with stories about past lives, legends of Ireland and the little people with whom he seems to have an intrinsic acquaintance. No one knows how many years Shaman has been on earth. Many suspect he's been a fixture for centuries as no one can remember him as a youth—or remember a time before his arrival.

THE PHANTOM SLEUTH is a trilogy for cat-lovers—a mystery adapted to the superior senses of cats, an ability unattainable by mere mortals. Add to that a cat's ability to understand people—and an inability to answer them, combined with an ability to slip into tight places virtually unobserved—makes sleuthing fun. Don't expect a clear-cut solution to the mysteries for, like life, nothing is ever what it seems.

> *The law of life is change. Nothing continues in the same way for any length of time. Happiness becomes unhappiness, and in time becomes joy again. The past also is seldom far behind us, but often in front blocking the way. The future trips over the past, whenever we think the road ahead is clear. —Olde Irish Faerie Tales*

THE PHANTOM SLEUTH

By Connie Clifford

Gretchen, an ordinary housewife, out for a night on the town with her husband, Harley Dandrich, runs into unusual problems. The couple meets Professor Ipswitch having a drink in a local pub. The professor asks Gretchen if she would like to participate in his new invention—a new potion he assured her worked wonders on the white rats in his laboratory at the university. He believes his serum ready for further testing on humans, explaining to her that the potion would extend youth in young women—lasting well into their eighties—a youth serum he calls *Resurrection*.

When Gretchen reneges on his proposal, he sneaks a few drops into her glass. Not noticing any difference in taste, she drinks the wine. Later that evening, feeling a trifle woozy, she leaves the Pub and crawls into the back seat of Harley's Daimler. Hours later, she feels someone or something, tugging at what she believes to be her bed covers, but awakens to find her entire world turned topsy-turvy. Cat eyes surround her, and when she checks her own situation, is surprised to find herself no longer a person, but a beautiful white Persian cat.

The motley array of felines who surround her, claim they rescued her from a fate worse than death. Accepting her altered state, Gretchen and her new feline friends embark on a mission to determine how her transformation occurred. Now able to converse with cats, as well as understanding *humanoids*, as her new friends call them, she enlists their help to search for answers. Their search for an antidote to Gretchen's metamorphosis takes them into situations and scenes she has no desire to witness, but her adventures develop within her a strong sensibility to the wisdom of the feline race.

ABOUT THE AUTHOR

CONNIE CLIFFORD was born Constance Mildred Carrier in Rapid City, South Dakota, the second child of an English mother and an American father. A late-in-life graduate of the University of Texas at El Paso, majoring in business and education, she began writing in her spare time. Semi-retired from civil service at Biggs Air Force base, where she met and married WWII bomber pilot, Howard Clifford, she taught Creative Writing to other retired seniors, a class sponsored by the local community college.

CONNIE'S first novel, **Then There's Murder!**, completely fiction, is supported by actual headlines from the El Paso Times during the 80's. It investigates the effects of a rising drug culture on the sleepy village town along the Texas-Mexico border and offers a political theory about our neighboring government plotting to take over Texas from the inside.

CONNIE'S yet un-published trilogy, **Out of the Ashes**, charts her own heritage following her mother, the mail order refined English bride taxed with raising three daughters during the Depression in America; the "witch," Martha Carrier being burned at the stake for "speaking her mind" and other colorful "mystics" in the family tree who influence Connie's writing and current psychic abilities

Forever independent and perfectly content living alone in Texas with her three cats, all of whom served as the inspiration for this book, Connie finds herself quarantined in assisted living in the middle of the 2020 Covid-19 pandemic while celebrating her 97th birthday. She expects to be watching from the *Netherworld* what her actress daughter, Denise Pence, does with her books.

PART 1

HEAVEN SCENT

TRILOGY ONE

HEAVEN SCENT

To imagine is everything, to know is nothing at all.
— Anatole France

Roscoe crossed the road, looking both ways before darting between the cars. He'd promised Gretchen he'd be at their favorite lunch spot behind the Fisherman's Wharf. He'd met Gretchen quite by accident one day, and had never completely recovered from the shock. Roscoe, a large, varicolored cat with glossy green eyes, had been engaged in his usual skullduggery under the overpass. He and his cronies had been rooting through the garbage debris vagrants left behind, when he stumbled on a tightly bound sack.

"Hey, fella's," he called out. "Can any one of you help me with this sack. There's something in there. I can smell it." He waited until the alley cats crowded around the sack, eager to see what had attracted Roscoe. Each one grabbed a corner in his sharp teeth and pulled at the worn gunnysack. As the bag started to rip, a fluffy white tail poked out, tickling Roscoe' nose.

"By God, it's one of us," Roscoe said. "Who do you suppose tied her up, and dropped her off here? Is she dead?"

"No," answered Einstein, a Seal Point Siamese, and self-appointed leader of the alley cats. "She's moving. Get back and give her some space." The cats gather around and watch as the gunnysack comes to life. A strange, white cat pokes a pink nose out and struggles to speak.

"Damn that devil! What's he done to me?" Gretchen closes her eyes, shakes her head, and tries to concentrate. She looks around at the curious cat faces surrounding her. "Where am I?" She looks down and sees hairy paws instead of hands, and turns in time to see a long, white, fluffy attachment flipping back and forth over her back with no effort on her part.

"What's happened to me? I'm not a cat." The motley crew stares at her in disbelief. "Am I?" The newcomer glared at Roscoe. "Did you do this to me?" she asked.

Einstein watches the scene in disbelief. Instead of being pleased at being rescued, this cat is mad. Roscoe tries to step in, but the white cat takes a swing at him.

"Did you? You filthy feline." Roscoe ducked and hissed until Einstein came to his rescue. He jumps on the white cat, and holds her down.

"Calm down, Matey," he advised. "Roscoe, here, is a gentleman. Whoever did this to you is not one of us, but one of those unreliable creatures we call *humanoids*."

"What do you mean? You're not a cat?" Roscoe shakes himself off and glares at the intruder. "What do you call yourself? You look like the rest of us, even if you do have blue eyes and long, white hair. And, what's that silly chain doing around your neck?"

"You could hang yourself with that, you know, if you're not careful." Einstein cautioned. He'd selected himself advisor *extraordinaire* to the Cat Monger's League, and prided himself on getting his entourage through some rough scrapes. *What's one more cat? And this one looks sadly in need of my services.*

"You apologize to Mr. Roscoe," he instructed Gretchen, "Or it's no dinner for you tonight." The white cat ignored him. The onlookers watched. The newcomer had an accent like the people they avoided, but they understood her.

Einstein sits back on his haunches and observes the white feline. "You're a cat," he decided, looking at the confused intruder. "You're complaining?"

"Yes. I'm not a cat, that's for sure," the white metamorphosis said.

"What do they call you?" asks Roscoe, smoothing the fur she'd ruffled, with his rough pink tongue. "You do have a name, don't you?"

"I'm Gretchen, and I'm a person." She looks at her paws, and adds, "At least, I thought I was." Gretchen pushed herself back into the gunnysack as though seeking some kind of solace, and stares at the puzzled cat faces around her.

"Honest," she tells them. "I really don't know what happened to me. The last I remember, there was this weird-looking cat—oops, I'm sorry —I mean chap in the Pub. He bought me a few drinks." She drops her head on her front paws, and looks up at them, her eyes welling with tears. "That's all I remember—and I wound up here."

"What were you drinking? Some of that stuff they throw out here can really curl your hair," said Roscoe.

"Maybe you should give it a rest," Einstein advised. "Try not to remember everything all at once. Let it come back gradually. If you are a person, as you say, and you were tossed over the side of the overpass, you're not supposed to be alive. Luckily, you landed on your feet. The question is, 'When did you become a cat?'"

Yes, how did I suddenly change into this beautiful white Persian cat? Vaguely, she remembered an odd-looking guy at Shaman's who promised to take her by his laboratory. *Did I go?* Gretchen closes her eyes, the better to concentrate, and to keep out the staring eyes of those strange felines surrounding her. *Oh, Harley, where are you when I need you?*

These cats, what do they want from me? Einstein appears to be the leader—he with the sleek dark fur and intelligent face, but what's a Siamese cat doing out so late at night? I thought they were pampered pets—too precious to roam streets and alleys after dark. Einstein seemed like a king on his throne and the other cats, his subjects.

That big black cat with the cold green eyes, I know him. He lives down the street from me, and is forever chasing Amber, my dog. He seems to be the friendliest cat here, although he looks mean. And the one they call Roscoe—he's large and muscular like a Maine coon cat—but seems a likable pet, too. I don't know the other three—they seem to wait for Einstein to make their decisions for them.

"Oh," said Einstein, "I suppose I should introduce you. I'm forgetting my manners. He extended a graceful paw in the direction of the black cat. "This cat's Julius," he said. "Roscoe is the cat that found you, and these cats," his paw swept toward the remaining three, "Are Methuselah, Antonio, and Kristin."

Gretchen blinked at the three she didn't know, acknowledging Einstein's introductions. Methuselah, a quiet, playful Ragdoll, Antonio, a gray tabby who looked very much like Einstein; and Kristin, a short-haired, British tabby watched the proceedings in silence, happy to be part of a group.

HEAVEN SCENT

Chapter One

*Spirit whose breath is in the four winds breathe,
breathe on me.*

Gretchen Dandrich puts the finishing touches on her new novel in preparation for sending to her publisher. Her best story yet—even **Harley**, her husband, agreed. Usually he never wanted to read her stories, but this time he took her manuscript to work and read it from cover to cover. She wondered about his sudden interest in this particular story, but decided not to investigate too deeply. Enough that he read it. Nevertheless, today being Friday—her weekly luncheon engagement with **Kristin Sanders**—she closes up her desk and takes off for **The Brass Ring**, her friend's antique shop. She couldn't wait to tell her about her new novel—how her fictional phantom sleuth had uncovered an espionage plot that had successfully eluded the FBI for years. Her college friend, **Lauren Calloway,** worked for the FBI in Washington, D.C. and had been her advisor in setting up the plot. After feeding her cocker spaniel, she pats Amber on her head and says "Take care of the place for me while I'm gone, Amber." Amber barks her assent—as well as her indignation at being left behind—and Gretchen bounces down the well-trodden path to meet Kristin. They were having lunch at **Shaman's Pub.**

Shaman, a recent immigrant from Ireland, purchased **Grumman's Bar and Grill** from Mr. Grumman's heirs when the old man died. His sons had no desire to continue in the food business, and Shaman purchased the restaurant shortly after his arrival. Missing the cordial camaraderie of hometown Irish pubs, Shaman had restored **Grumman's** to an attractive replica of an ancient Irish pub. He kept the name because of its past *good will"* value, but the establishment unofficially became known as **Shaman's Pub.**

Shaman added his own touches, and the Pub achieved a certain distinct ambiance. He'd tossed out bar stools, but kept a brass rung that served as a footrest for customers—*to discourage women from drinking at the bar,* he'd tell customers. Instead, he served wholesome meals at charmingly arranged tables in a crisp, immaculate dining room. Winters, he kept a roaring fire in the huge stone hearth, where Ming, his Siamese cat, yawned and stretched for her public. Ming, his seemingly ageless Siamese, seemed entirely too wise and knowing for an ordinary cat, and talk of her being a witch's *familiar* made the rounds of speculation.

Shaman's own rotund self also defied age designation, as he could be anywhere from 50 to 100, and some of the tales he told customers caused them to believe he had lived for centuries. Usually an amiable bartender, with twinkling blue orbs and ready smile, he could turn indignant in a moment if he suspected mischief in his Pub. Gretchen had introduced Harley to Shaman, the Irish bartender at her and Kristin's favorite watering hole, and Harley had adopted the attractive Irish pub as his second home. He and Shaman had developed a congenial rapport, Shaman regaling Harley with tales of past lives in his Irish homeland.

Today, Gretchen breezed along the sidewalk this brisk October morning intent on her purpose and unaware of what lay ahead of her before the day's end. The tall, willowy New Englander turned heads wherever she went, although she pretended to be unaware of this ability. She still thought of herself as a shy, gawky teenager—all arms and legs—worried about acne, and her sudden thrust into popularity during her college years presented a challenge to her earlier—almost puritanical—upbringing. Sometimes, she often felt as though she had a foot in two oddly contrasting worlds. Today, though, she believed she's conquered her two worlds and is now at peace with her life.

Her worldly college roommate Kristin helped her overcome her shyness, and introduced her to all kinds of new and exciting adventures. Kristin's upbringing had been considerably more indulgent than Gretchen's —she took profound pleasure in experimenting with the new and the untried. "That's what college is for," she'd assure Gretchen. "So you can make sane choices for your future lifestyle unencumbered by social mores." Gretchen envied her friend's liberal British approach to life, in sharp contrast to her own restrictive Quaker roots. Kristin shocked the staid Connecticut College where the two were thrust together as roommates. Anyway, they connected, as each found in the other what they lacked in their own lives.

Today, Gretchen reveled in the crispness of a beautiful New England autumn day as she breezed along the tree-lined street leading to Kristin's antique shop. The three college friends had maintained contact after college despite diverse lifestyles—Kristin, an entrepreneur, Lauren, a professional, and Gretchen, married to her attorney-husband Harley, happy in her role as a Connecticut housewife and filling her spare hours writing mystery novels.

Gretchen met Harley when he helped her settle the complexities of her mother's estate. They hit it off immediately—like soul mates who'd known each other in previous lives. They each shared a common belief in the complexities of reincarnation. She'd had the same feeling of *déjà vu* when she met Kristin, but unlike Harley, Kristin thought her belief of reincarnation crazy—a sort of wishful thinking or product of a vivid imagination. But Harley understood. They both believed it so natural—a solution to all those questions King James never answered for them.

Gretchen loved this attractive old town, one of the oldest in America, with its elm trees and well-kept shops. Recently, huge trucks had begun using Main Street as a short cut from the Parkway to the

Interstate, and the pavement, unused to heavy traffic, had begun to crumble in spots—keeping town officials busy making repairs.

"Ready for lunch?" she asks the young, vivacious British shopkeeper as she enters **The Brass Ring,** her friend's antique shop. The young woman facing her carried herself with distinction, her short stubby hair bristling with energy as she caressed the stock she so lovingly maintained. Gretchen realized that Kristin had deep affection for all this old furniture and ancient bric-a-brac that cluttered every available inch of her attractive little enterprise.

A new display on the countertop caught Gretchen's attention. "What's this, Kristin? I don't remember seeing this display before. Is it new?"

"Yes, it's a new line I'm trying out. My gift area seems to attract teenagers. They're some of my best customers." She laughs as she shrugs into her English mackintosh and slaps a snazzy brown fedora on her shaggy curls. "You know how they are—they love intrigue. It's all in fun, but they seem to hunger for the mystic." She picks up one of the bottles, and hands it to Gretchen. "This particular bottle is called *Heaven-Scent,* a love potion created by a professor at the University, and one of our best sellers. Would you like it?"

"Really? And the kids fall for this?" Gretchen reads the verse on the tag attached to the potion. "*Spirit whose breath is in the four winds breathe, breathe on me.*

"Not only kids. I sold some to Shaman over at the Pub," Kristin chuckles. "Plans to give it to his wife. Sure hope it works for him—might change his disposition."

"Why the old coot," Gretchen smiles, "but, hey, if he believes in it..." She reads the label. "What's the secret ingredient?"

"I've no idea," says Kristin, her eyes twinkling. "But it does add to the intrigue, doesn't it?" She appraises the tall, slender blonde with the sparkling blue eyes—eyes as blue as a summer sky—an intelligent person, but slightly gullible, a characteristic Kristin found intriguing at times. *Imagine, believing in reincarnation!*

"Ever hear the legend of Magus?" she teases, hoping Gretchen will bite, and she does.

"Magus? No, who is he?" asks Gretchen.

"You remember the Magi, don't you?" Kristin asks. "You sing about them at Christmas time—the visitors at the Manger of the Christ child. In its singular form, Magus means Wise Man or Clever One. Today, he'd be your *shrink*."

"Really? I've heard that England is full of stories about witches and ghosts. Does Magus deal in any of that?" She pockets the love potion Kristin offered her. *If she sells it, it's got to be safe.*

"Sure, according to legend, Magus had good spirits and bad spirits around who appeared to him as men," Kristin says, amused by Gretchen's sudden interest in the occult. She slips on her gloves and heads for the door. "There's a third kind of spirit we call *ghosts*—spirits separated from the body, but still roaming the earth. There the legend becomes very complicated and murky—dealing with sorcery and witchcraft. But everything begins with Magus and his magic drum."

"Aha—a magic drum—of course." Gretchen wonders if she's being teased, but Kristin looks totally serious, so she continues. "And pray tell, how did Magus make use of his magic drum?"

"Why to exorcise fiends who roamed the four-corners of Heaven, my dear. How else?" Kristin checks her watch, turning the sign in the window to read: OUT TO LUNCH—BACK AT 2 PM. "Let's go, Gretchen. We're running late. The **Pub** will be crowded." Locking the door behind her, the two exit the shop.

Kristin hurries Gretchen into the crowd of hungry workers heading to one of the many scenic cafes dispersed among a proliferation of antique shops along Main Street. On reaching **Shaman's Pub**, she steers Gretchen to a table already occupied by a husky, good-looking redhead. Gretchen's eyebrows raise, and she looks questionably at Kristin.

"I asked Roscoe to save a table for us," she explains. "Gretchen, this is Sergeant Gregory Baggette, an old friend of mine from my days in *Merrye Olde England*. Roscoe, this is Gretchen," she tells the man in the blue cop's uniform. "From my college days."

Kristin...? A cop? I can't believe it. Gretchen recovers from shock in time to acknowledge her introduction to the handsome cop. "What a surprise," she said. "How long has this been going on?"

The friendly face spreads into a mischievous grin, his freckles struggling to stay in sight among crinkling laugh lines. His steel-blue eyes denoted a humor he had difficulty hiding. A slight man at first glance, his biceps and pectorals tested the seams on his police uniform, and belied any frailty a casual observer might envision. "Since I visited an antique shop for a desk she had advertised," the hunk answered. "Imagine my surprise to find Kristin in charge."

"I like him," decided Gretchen, noting Kristin's pleased expression. "But why *Roscoe*?"

"A high school nickname," Kristin informs her. "Can't quite get used to calling him Gregory, or Greg—or Sergeant Baggette for that matter. He's always been Roscoe."

"You knew each other in school?" Gretchen asks.

"Yes, in Britain." Kristin's cop friend laughs as he tells her, "She's an Army brat whose parents thought an English education would be good for her."

"When they shipped me off to college in America before I became too British, he followed me," Kristin teased

"I got an opportunity to work here after college," he explained, appraising the attractive blonde facing him. "Didn't expect to run into Kristin, but rather glad I did. I meant to call her as soon as I got settled."

"So you say," Kristin tells him, then turned to Gretchen. "There's nothing mysterious about our knowing each other. We've more or less kept in touch all through college."

Gretchen noticed that Sergeant Baggette had the same delightful English accent so much a part of Kristin's appeal. Toasted by the wine, the ambiance, and the company, she warmed to Kristin's friend who seemed genuinely fond of Kristin. A sudden draught from an open door startled the group as a chill wind blew into the room. Their attention turned to the door as a strange man enters and heads for the bar. A second stranger, sneaking in through the open door, heads for the warm fireplace and curls up on the hearth alongside Ming.

"Oh, look," Gretchen said. "Ming's found a new friend. Isn't he beautiful?" The three glance at the hearth where two matching Siamese cats share space. As Shaman approached the table, Gretchen asked about the new feline.

"He be hangin' around the Pub, and don't seem to belong to no one, far's I can tell, so I sort'a adopted him," he tells them, glancing at the hearth. "I call him Einstein, he's that smart. Little devil—comes and goes as he pleases—doin' his own thing, so to speak." He looks at the two affectionately. "Ming seems to have taken a shine to 'em."

"He's a beauty, Shaman," agreed Gretchen, feeling the same strange eeriness with Einstein that she felt with Ming. *No wonder Shaman calls him Einstein.* The cat turns and locks eyes with Gretchen. "He seems almost human."

"That he does—wise beyond his years, he is," Shaman agreed, picking up a few of the dirtied dishes on the table. "You be wantin' more wine?"

"We're on our way back to work, Shaman," Kristin says. "Another time, but we'll be back. The food's delicious and the service superb." Gretchen gives a parting glance to the pair on the fireside hearth as she leaves.

Chapter Two

The source of the existent and the non-existent is but one.

Professor Ipswitch clutched his notebook close to him as he headed for the campus laboratory. He considered the day he bailed **Jake Dunbar** out of jail, and earned his friendship, to be his luckiest of days. Yes, Jake had surpassed all expectations during his later incarceration when he perused the prison library and read up on little known facts. His research uncovered an item of immense interest to the professor—a remarkable recipe—obtained from a colleague presently residing at the Connecticut House of Corrections.

Professor Ipswitch had also managed to secure a position at the local university—not as a professor *per se,* but as an assistant to a legitimate professor in the chemistry lab. And what an interesting place that turned out to be, especially when he discovered he had access to laboratory facilities after hours. One of his jobs included cleaning up after students left for the day. He'd even managed to befriend one student who gave him access to paraphernalia he needed for his own personal research. Then, he had the good fortune to meet that young antique dealer, **Kristin,** at **Shaman's Pub** and the pieces fell into place.

The recipe Jake found in the archives of the prison library helped him concoct a potion that proved quite popular among the younger crowd. Kristin, a terrific marketer of the unusual, agreed to sell his product in her gift shop. She called the potion *Heaven-Scent—a Love Potion,* and assured the Professor that that name alone would attract any teenager's love for mystery.

"It's all in the marketing," Kristin convinced the Professor. "We can expect to gain considerable profit if it's marketed correctly. I'll have my attorney friend draw up an agreement." Her attorney friend, **Harley Dandrich,** assured them there would be no problems.

After that little venture, Professor Ipswitch accepted the moniker of *Professor*—as the students dubbed him—without guilt. They were exceptionally successful in maintaining discretion as no one bothered to investigate the source of his product—a harmless scent.

Today, slipping into the laboratory, he sees **Morgan** already hard at work. Morgan, a short, ugly, gnome-like man—who looked for all the world like one of the Seven Dwarfs that so beleaguered Snow White—had been a find for Professor Ipswitch. The professor had kept Morgan pretty much out of sight—in the woods behind his cottage.

He'd been thoroughly vexed when he entered **Shaman**'s last evening, and saw Morgan sitting at the bar listening to one of Shaman's Irish tales. Morgan knew how dangerous it could be for him to be seen in public. Professor Ipswitch could only hope that no one would remember him, but that seemed highly unlikely as Morgan's strange appearance made an indelible mark on most minds. Morgan merely said—n*ot to worry*—that he could make himself invisible if the need arose.

"Humph, a lot of *malarkey*," the professor huffed. "I'll need proof before I believe that far-fetched story." He knew Morgan to be a chap full of unbelievable tales—like Shaman and his weird tales of past lives in Ireland. The professor marveled at the ease with which Morgan silently came and went, as though walls didn't deter him. He claimed to come and go at will—from this world to the next—whenever he pleased. He did seem to disappear into thin air at times, a worry to the professor as he needed some kind of contact with him—a phone number, an address or something—but Morgan merely said he'd pick up his messages without the inconvenience of a telephone.

Morgan claimed to have met Jake Dunbar in prison—the thief Harley Dandrich sent up the river—claiming Jake introduced him to the prison library where he'd discovered a recipe that when taken promised entry into the *Netherworld*. The professor didn't believe him. Morgan didn't elaborate. He refused to use Jake's recipe claiming his own version vastly superior. Thus, the professor allowed Morgan to create his own concoction, and kept Jake's recipe in reserve—in a place no one knew of except himself.

Professor Ipswitch entered the laboratory to find Morgan already hard at work on his latest invention. His test tube bubbled and foamed as Morgan peered and sniffed, stirring his concoction with deep concentration. Kristin intended to market this one as *Resurrection*, a youth potion created to extend the aging of young women far into their mid-eighties. The professor envisioned riches beyond all expectation.

"What do you have there?" the professor asked him. "Anything interesting?" Morgan turned slowly and looked at the professor with his catlike yellow eyes, blinking his disapproval at the unexpected interruption. *The man seems almost catlike in his demeanor, even speaks a sort of guttural sound that's hard to follow.* Morgan, working on a new product—one he says will far surpass *Heaven-Scent* and revolutionize the world—disliked interruption.

"Time to test," groaned the gnome-like little man. He turned to face Professor Ipswitch. "Your job." He slides down from the high stool at the lab table, hands the professor a tube filled with a liquid solution, and uttered his last remark. "Done." He shuffled from the room. The professor watched his department from the building from a window until he disappeared into the forest—not to reappear until next the professor willed him—then only at his discretion.

Professor Ipswitch took the vial Morgan left with him to his cottage at the entrance of the University, and called Kristin to ask for her assistance in bottling and marketing the new product. She agreed to his terms, but first wanted assurance the potion would do no harm. "You need to test it," she tells him.

"Do you have any ideas?"

"I suggest an animal test," she replied. "If the animal survives, the substance is harmless. Otherwise..."

"What kind of animal do you suggest?"

"Any animal—maybe a cat, or a monkey—then I'd have no qualms about marketing your product, but I refuse to be responsible for consequences that may develop from inadequate testing."

Professor Ipswitch hangs up the phone. "Damned female," he grumbled. "I need something larger than a cat." He looks at the vial in his hand. "Shaman has a cat, and that place of his is always good for an evening of entertainment. Maybe I'll find me a willing *guinea pig*." He slips the small vial in his pocket and leaves the cottage. "Yeah, that's what I'll do," he decided.

Chapter Three

Imagination is the eye of the soul.
--Joseph Joubert

Harley had consumed his first glass of wine by the time Gretchen arrived at **Grumman's Bar and Grill** that Saturday evening. She'd met him there after he left the office, walking the few blocks from their home on Main Street. He'd struck up a conversation with a strange-looking gentleman at the bar, but when Gretchen arrived, he leaves the bar and joins her at a table near the fireplace.

"An interesting man, that Professor," he tells Gretchen as he helped her off with her coat. "Does a bit of experimental work in his laboratory at the University. Seems he's made up some concoction that he sells to shops here, and it's going over big."

"I know, I have some," Gretchen said, pulling out the bottle Kristin had given her from her coat pocket. She reads the inscription to Harley. "Catchy, isn't it?"

"Let me see that." Harley takes the bottle from her and reads the label. "What's the secret ingredient?" he asks.

"It's a mystery. Why don't you ask the Professor?"

"Later," he said and slips the potion into his pocket.

When Shaman approached to take their order, Harley asked him, "What do you know about that fellow at the bar? Is he for real?"

"I'm not one you should be askin'," he said. "Seems a likable enough chap. Pushin' his latest snake oil, methinks." More than that he refused to say, leaving them to arrive at their own conclusion.

"Doesn't seem to think much of the professor's creation, does he?" Harley commented. "What does Kristin say?"

"She feeds into the mystery—tells me old English tales of Magus, magic drums—old wives' tales,' Gretchen answers.

"You believe her?"

"I'm a writer. I don't discount anything. Introduce me to him, then I'll decide."

After they had eaten, Harley takes Gretchen to the bar and introduces her to the eminent, **Professor Ipswitch**. She thought him a weird-looking chap with his big owl eyes framed in huge octagon-shaped spectacles—giving him the appearance of a big hoot owl. Even his hair—chopped short and gelled into spikes—emphasized the oddity. Harley couldn't remember ever having seen him before, but Shaman seemed to know him so he must be an okay guy.

"I'm associated with **Brohaugh's Conservatory of Arts and Science**," the professor told them. He ogled Gretchen over black-rimmed specs, and attempted to entice her. "You'd make a terrific prototype for my new invention."

"Really?" Gretchen's eyebrows made a definitive arch. "What is it?"

"A youth potion, one I call *Resurrection*, for want of a better name," the professor said.

"What does it do?"

The professor glanced at Shaman before answering, but Shaman appeared busy with another customer. "Guaranteed to resurrect the aged, and keep them young for decades to come. Are you interested?"

"Who wouldn't be?" Gretchen smiled. Harley watched, amused. "Is it dangerous?"

"No more dangerous than most experiments," the professor replies. For just a flash, Gretchen registered a chilling glimpse into his ice-cold eyes, and pulled back.

"I don't think so," she said. The professor shrugs. Gretchen turned to Harley. "I'm a pussy cat when it comes to taking chances. He should try Kristin."

Harley laughed and the two returned to their table, Gretchen forgetting her glass of wine. The professor brought it to her, and joined them at their table. The three talked into the evening. Harley seemed mesmerized by the professor's plans. Eventually they've delved into patents, marketing, etc. Gretchen tried to concentrate, but the room felt stifling. She needed air.

"Harley," she said. "It's too warm in here. I'm going outside to the car and cool off."

Harley looked at her. "You do look rather flushed. Take a walk outside and cool off. I'll join you shortly." Gretchen remembered her last thought as she went through the door—*once a lawyer, always a lawyer.*

The memories of the Dandriches stopped at that point.

* * *

Harley Dandrich pulled into his driveway about two o'clock that morning. He vaguely remembered stopping off at **Grumman's Bar and Grill** after he got off work. Maybe he'd only dreamed it, but he could have sworn he met Gretchen there. His memory seemed pretty fuzzy, but he hadn't drunk any more than usual. Two glasses of wine, that's all he ever had, but he remembered Gretchen consuming the entire bottle of Kriter's Brut de Brut that weird young man brought to their table. *Did Gretchen leave alone, or did she go with that chap?* He tried to clear the cobwebs from his brain. *Damned if I can remember.*

"Called himself a professor," Harley vaguely remembered. "... Professor Ipswitch from **Brohaugh's Conservatory of Arts and Science.**" He promised to take Gretchen by his laboratory and show her how innocent combinations of supposedly mild elements could produce the strangest results. Gretchen appeared fascinated. *Had she gone?* Harley literally crawled up the stairs to his and Gretchen's room. He didn't see Gretchen. *Is she mad at me?* His brain failed to cope. Feeling drugged, he fell across their king-size bed. Sleep came immediately and he drifted into a frightening nightmare. Usually his dreamlike sojourns crept into some wilderness of his reveries and he survived them, but tonight he discovered Gretchen acting in a most peculiar way—more like a house cat than a housewife.

Harley wasn't a strange person, as people go, but he did have strange ideas—like believing in ghosts and the hereafter, reincarnation and time travel. Most of his friends thought him crazy when he advised them to shape up in this lifetime or run the risk of returning as one of their archenemies. Sometimes in his dreams he'd see Julius, the young chap who lived down the street from him, in the form of a big black cat. He didn't know Julius and seldom saw him, but he could have sworn that big, black cat he'd seen Gretchen feeding some mornings was his spitting image. *Julius reborn? But that couldn't be. Could it?* Harley tossed and turned. Gretchen attacked him. He feints. *What's wrong with her?* He slept on.

Chapter Four

For whatever purpose a man bestows a gift For that same purpose, he receives in his next birth…its reward.

Shaman was in his cups. It had been a long night at the Pub, and he'd drunk more than usual. The Dandriches, Gretchen and Harley, were there—along with that crazy Professor Ipswitch. Now there was a character.

Shaman didn't know if he really were a professor or if he tagged the name on himself to bolster his self-esteem. He never seemed to have a class at the University, but kept talking about his experiments. If his experiments really did what he claimed they did, he'd turn the world upside down.

Shaman had felt as though his head would split. *Why did I take that last drink?* He knew he shouldn't drink in front of customers—but that night he'd broken his own rule. Why? Was it that gnome-like little man who'd come in near the end of the evening? *Where have I seen him before?* He'd been in the middle of his latest Irish tale when the man entered, sat at the opposite end of the bar from the Professor, and proceeded to drink heavily, glaring at Shaman as though he knew him.

The gnome-like little man reminded Shaman of a tale he'd once told —that is, until the tale became too personal and kept him awake nights—a tale of his boyhood in Old Ireland, of cats he knew who talked to people—of tales of the *Netherworld,* and where Morgan moved easily between the two worlds of life and death. *Could he be* **Morgan**—*his arch enemy of many centuries ago?*

That night when he'd tested too many of his weird concoctions and told too many of his weird stories, Ming spoke to him—as plain as day. He hadn't had a drink since. That is, until the night when Morgan, a gnome-like little man, appeared out of nowhere in his very own Pub—a message right out of his past. *What's he doing here?* He'd stumbled into the back room where he kept a couch for just such occasions and falling on it, drifted into an uneasy sleep.

* * *

He is a child again in Olde Ireland and his nanny sends him out to play. He loved to wander through the woods behind his house, and listen to the songs of the different birds—or watch a spidery web spill from dew-soaked vines. There were animals in his world, too—graceful cats that sprang from limb to limb and wolves that howled taunts at animals out of their reach. Every day the scenery changed. He never knew if they were the same spiders or the same animals, but that was the wonder of it all. Every day he watched the spidery webs grow and flowers bud—then burst into bloom. He'd learn and study the ways of the forest—until one day when darkness came to his young world. His mother died, and his father remarried. He no longer had a nanny, and his stepmother barely tolerated him.

One day, he left that home behind, doubting very much if they'd even miss him, and made his home in the forest with his animal friends. He talked to the little people in the forest and they took care of him. He became skilled in locating animals in the trees, and snakes in the grass. He knew how to find help, which plants he could eat, and which he could not. When he believed his education finished, he moved on to prove his worth in the outside world.

During his wanderings he discovered the Feast of Shaman in progress. He'd heard about its wonders from the little people—how only a door separated his world from the Netherworld—and how the doors would open during the Feast of Shaman, and allow people to wander back and forth between the two worlds. Curious about this custom of Shamanism, he decided to attend, and arrived at Tara, the castle of the little people, in time to join them and partake of the feast. As he wandered among the guests, he learned how they performed this feat—how some people could wander through the two worlds and glean Wisdom on the other side. Shaman wanted Knowledge and Wisdom more than anything else, and really believed that if it were possible for one to see into the past, one could surely see into the future. Not many were allowed this privilege, and he wanted to be one of them.

The night of the Feast of Shaman, he meets Fionn, an Irish laddie who claimed to have lived centuries ago. Fionn had eaten of the Tree of Knowledge, and told Shaman he would teach him all he knew if he would return to the Netherworld during the Feast of Shaman every year. Shaman agreed, and every year thereafter he would return with Fionn to the Netherworld during the Feast of Shaman to gain more knowledge.

After one Feast, Fionn takes him far into the Netherworld. "You have until morning when the Feast of Shaman ends, to find your way back to your world. I have taught you all I know. If you can do this, you will gain the knowledge you desire. Otherwise, you must remain in the Netherworld until the next Feast of Shaman," he tells Shaman and departs. Unknown to Fionn, Morgan had followed the pair into the Netherworld, hiding behind a tree until Fionn departed.

Shaman stirs restlessly in his sleep as he relives his encounter with Morgan. *He wanders along the river until he sees a fisherman fishing along the banks of the River of No Return. He does not know that the fisherman is Morgan who has gotten there ahead of him.*

"What are you fishing for?" he asks the old man.

"I'm fishing for Wisdom," *the old man tells him, looking around at Shaman.*

"How long have you been fishing?" Shaman asks.

"Forever," the old man answers. "You see I must fish until I find someone worthy of eating of the fish I catch. Are you worthy?"

"I want Wisdom more than anything else in the world," Shaman answers him.

Morgan pauses in his fishing and turns to Shaman. "I am weary of seeking someone worthy of Knowledge, but I cannot stop fishing until I find him."

The fisherman reminded Shaman of Father Time, with his wrinkled and worn face, his aged, red-rimmed eyes sunken in a haggard face, and his hair drooping in strings beneath his cap "I'm running short of time," Shaman tells the old man. "I must return to my world before morning or remain until the next Feast of Shaman."

"I understand. If you are the one worthy of Wisdom, you will have time," the old man assures him. He points to a path behind him. "Do you see that cottage there in the woods? Go there and build me a fire. The flesh of the Fish contains the Wisdom you desire."

"How can that be?" Shaman asks.

"It is so," the fisherman tells him. "From a Sacred Bush overhanging a secret pool in a sacred place. The Sacred Bush overhanging the secret pool drops its berries into the water and they float on the river. The fish eats of the berries and becomes wise beyond all things. If you are the one, the fish will be ready when you are."

"Why not eat of the berries of the Sacred Bush?" asks Shaman.

"The berries can only be eaten by the fish," says the fisherman.

"We wait for the fish," agrees Shaman and wanders down the narrow path towards a thatched cottage nestled among the trees. He gathers twigs to build a fire, and looks inside the cottage for a pan for roasting—all the while watching the fisherman fishing on the banks of the river. He lights the fire and works to keep it burning, wondering if he will be found worthy of the Wisdom that eludes so many.

"Will I ever be wise enough to learn all the answers to all the questions everyone asks? Can Wisdom really be absorbed into the flesh from eating a fish? Will I learn why some people are happy and some people are not?

Why the moon comes up at the same time every day? Why people fight, and men make war? Will the old man catch the fish because I am here and have built a fire?"

The fire burns brightly, and Shaman can almost taste the flesh of the fish. The fisherman continues to fish, and Shaman becomes anxious. "Time is running out. I must return to my world. I cannot wait another year to gain Wisdom." As Shaman waits for the fisherman to return, he falls asleep by the fire.

When the fisherman catches his fish, he returns to the cottage and places the basket near Shaman. "Look in the basket," he tells Shaman when he awakens.

Shaman looks in the basket and sees a huge fish. He cleans the fish, and bakes him in the roasting pan. The fisherman refuses to partake of the fish. "How can I thank you?" he asks the fisherman. Shaman eats his fill of the truculent flesh.

"There is no need," the fisherman says. "You are late, and must remain my guest 'til next Feast of Shaman.

"Oh, no!" Shaman cries. "You've cheated me. Where is Fionne?"

"He is gone." As he speaks, he strips off his disguise and stands before Shaman, his hunchback in evidence and his cruel lips curled in a sneer. "I am your old friend, Morgan. We'll see how far your Wisdom takes you."

Shaman leaves the cottage—his hopes shattered. He meets up with a small tiger that listens to his tale of woe. "Morgan does not know all exits," the tiger assures Shaman. "Come with me. I will lead you home."

"How can I trust you?" asks Shaman.

"You must. I will guide you home. Close your eyes and repeat after me. Spirit whose breath is in the four winds breathe, breathe on me. *Shaman did as the tiger requests. "Trust me. It is so," the voice continues. "When you open your eyes, you will be home."*

Shaman does as the tiger requests, repeating the phrase over and over as if in prayer until he sees Fionne in the distance. "Tell Fionne you have accomplished your mission," the tiger says.

As he approaches, his friend Fionne says to him. "Morgan deceived you. He has been captured and will spend many centuries across the River of No Return."

"Thank you for your help, Fionne. Will I see you again?"

Fionne's voice floats off in the distance. "When next you need me," the voice floats back. "When next you need me…"

***

Shaman felt a paw tapping his shoulder as Fionn's voice floated off in the distance. The tapping paw becomes more urgent as Ming hesitantly attempted to awaken him.

"What is it, Ming?" he asked, stroking the Siamese affectionately. He opened his eyes and groaned—surprised to be in the back room of his Pub and trying to remember why.

Didn't I go home last night?

"Mirreeow," Ming wailed.

Then Shaman hears a scratching sound at the front door of the Pub, and gets up to investigate. Opening the door, a shadow darts between his legs. He turned in time to see a cat—the spitting image of Ming—parking itself beside her on his hearth.

"Where did you come from?" he asked the intruder. The two bookends stared silently from their place on the hearth. Puzzled, he asks, *am I still dreaming*? As he stares at the two cats watching over him, an overwhelming sense of peace and tranquillity enveloped him. He returned to his cot and immediately falls back to sleep.

Chapter Five

In as much as body is not the self...
it is impermanent—so is it with feeling.

Gretchen's head ached. Her world had turned upside down. She needed to fill in the blanks, and tried to remember. *What happened! It's all so frustrating, and I'm too tired to think.* Gretchen laid her head on her paws and considered her plight. She'd dreamed of being home in her own bed—a dream so vivid, she swore she heard Harley growling in his sleep beside her. But when she awakened, her cat body remained—still there. Tears roll down her cat face, and she brushed them aside with her paw.

"I want to go home," Gretchen said to her new friends. "I'm hungry."

Einstein took over. "It'll be daylight soon," he informed the cats. "Can one of you take Gretchen home with you, and get her something to eat?"

"No," said Gretchen. "I'm going to my own home. I know where the food is."

"Do you think that's wise? Houses are locked up during the day when owners are at work." Einstein looked at Roscoe. "Take her home with you, Roscoe. She's not used to scrounging, and could run into trouble. We really shouldn't leave her alone until she becomes oriented to dangers associated with living in a people world."

"No," a determined Gretchen said. "I can handle it. I've a doggy door for Amber. She knows me. She'll let me in."

"I live down the street," Julius piped up. "I can watch out for her."

"It's settled, then," Einstein said. "After you've eaten—and napped—we'll meet behind the Fisherman's Wharf." Einstein looked at Gretchen. "Try to remember how you spent your last hours as a person, Gretchen. We need a lead of some kind."

The motley crew drifted apart, Einstein keeping watch until the cats all safely crossed the road. Then, he trotted nonchalantly toward the last place Gretchen could remember—**Grummans Bar and Grill**—popularly known as **Shaman's Pub**. *Maybe Ming knows what happened the evening past.*

* * *

Einstein had made the acquaintance of a certain feline wonder of his own ilk—her moniker, Ming. Ming resided at **Shaman's Pub**, and could always be depended on to keep Einstein up on the latest village gossip. *Maybe she knew what inhumane sorcerer wreaked his magic on an unsuspecting humanoid.*

Shaman had sort of adopted Einstein, since he hung around the Pub so much and seemed to enjoy his hearth and companionship with Ming. Einstein had complete freedom to roam the village green, while Ming, being a female, stayed close to hearth. Shaman didn't believe males—being the scavengers they are—should be so confined. Besides, he suspected Ming and Einstein had a romance going.

Einstein found Ming curled up on the hearth at **Shaman's Pub**. He nuzzled her until she awakened. "P-s-s-t," he whispered into her twitching ear. "I've a job for you." He stood by as Ming stretched the length of the hearth, yawned sleepily, and with half-closed eyes put out a paw to meet Einstein's. The two curled up close to each other on the fireside. An outsider would believe them asleep, but they were passing messages between them.

"I've need for your powers of observation," Einstein began. "An odd occurrence took place this evening past in this sanctuary, and I'm wondering if you happened to observe an odd-looking gentleman seated at the end of the bar, buying drinks for a good-looking young lady with husband in tow."

"I saw them," answered Ming. "A gentleman with glasses and spiked hair—I wonder how he does that? I prefer my hair smooth so I can clean it easier. What do you suppose is wrong with these *humanoids*?"

"I don't know. 'Ours is not to wonder why...'" Einstein says... then remembers himself. "Did anything strange occur? I mean, what did this gentleman do?"

"Why, nothing that I saw. Why should he? He's the eminent Professor Ipswitch from the University. He's working on some new potions to revolutionize disease control," Ming informed him. "The pretty blonde and her husband seemed most interested. In fact, he promised to take her back to his laboratory to pick up some youth potion he'd invented—guaranteed to eliminate aging in beautiful young women."

"She fell for that old line?"

Ming looked at him, her ears back, tail twitching in anger. Einstein backed off. "How dare you?" she hissed. "We women do whatever it takes to stay young and attractive to the opposite sex." She sniffed in disdain. "Certainly, men fall for it every time, so what's a girl to do?"

"Well, she certainly won't age anymore," said Einstein. "In fact, he's given her nine lives to play around with."

"You mean she's a cat now?" asked Ming, turning to look at Einstein, her eyes wide and alert. "How can that be?"

"That's right. She's one of us, and no one seems to know how it happened—or why. Certainly, she'd prefer to turn back into a female, if she only knew how." Einstein put his head down on his paws and opened one eye, the better to observe Ming's reaction. But Ming is distracted. She sits upright—her attention focused on the entrance to the Pub. Einstein followed her gaze.

The Pub door opened, and Professor Ipswitch entered. His eyes dart around the room as though looking for someone. He ordered a drink from Shaman, and asked, "Has Gretchen Dandrich been by today, per chance?"

"No, Matey," said Shaman, noting the man's nervousness. He shoved a Rob Roy in front of him. "She's not much for comin' in on Saturdays. Why? You be needin' of her?"

"She's supposed to meet me here." The Professor took a swig of his Rob Roy, his feet tapping an irritating rhythm on the brass rail. He checked his watch, and tossed Shaman some change. "Can you let me know if you should see her?" he asked Shaman. "It's very important I contact her." He gulped down the rest of his Rob Roy, and headed for the exit.

"Sure," said Shaman to the departing back as he continued to mop the bar top, intending to forget the matter. Something about the Professor bothered him. "What's he up to?" He mumbled something that sounded like, "Does he think I'm his bloomin' secertary."

Einstein turned to Ming. "Something's amiss," he told her. "And I think I know what it is. You keep a lookout here. I'm going to follow the Professor—see if I can find out something about that drink the Professor gave Gretchen. Evidently, it's backfired."

Einstein slipped out the door between the feet of incoming customers in time to see the professor climb aboard his motorcycle. He raced down the street following the sound of the fast disappearing machine. One good thing about being a cat, you didn't have to follow the roads. Einstein leapt across yards and over fences, following the sound of the motorcycle. It headed towards the University, but instead of continuing toward the institute of higher learning, the professor stopped at the caretaker's cottage located inside the university grounds.

Einstein located a comfortable spot under the surrounding shrubs outside the cottage, and watched as the professor enters the cottage. He hears the professor speaking on his cell phone.

"Something's gone awry," Einstein hears. "I know it. She was supposed to meet me at Shaman's, and didn't show." The professor listens. "You never told me there were possible side effects.... Some sense of humor, you have.... What form...? You don't know, but you think some type of animal? Well, I've got to find her, whatever shape she's in." Einstein wished he knew whom the professor had called.

"There's fifty-million animals in this town," the professor informed his listener. "And we haven't a clue which highly intelligent animal lurking around is Gretchen. I can't go around talking to all the animals in town. They'll throw me in the loony bin."

Professor Ipswitch hangs up the phone, but Einstein has heard enough. He figured he has the winning hand because he knew the animal concerned. He races back across the housetops, and slips in beside Ming.

"There's someone else in on this," Einstein tells Ming. "I have to find out who."

Ming merely raises her cat eyebrows. "You mean, the professor may have a partner?"

"It's a likely possibility," Einstein says. "And I need to find out who it is."

"What do you want me to do?" Ming asks. "The Professor may be back. It's Saturday night."

"If he does, get as close to him as you can, and keep your ears open. I've got to find Gretchen, and tell her what's happening. Maybe somehow, it will jog her memory," Einstein says, and slips into the night.

Ming stretches the length of the hearth, yawns, turns around twice, and resettles—tail curled around her body and ears in alert mode. She catnaps, waiting.

Chapter Six

There is a superstition in avoiding superstition.

Einstein has positioned himself outside Professor Ipswitch's window. He hears the professor talking to someone. The only indication of another presence in the room was the rhythmic creaking of a rocker. The professor faced the open window.

"Which are the smart animals?" Professor Ipswitch asks his companion.

Einstein considered it indelicate to drop into the room uninvited for a better look. He had no yearning to face the consequences of a surprise visit. His desire to learn the identity of the professor's cohort did not surpass his cat sense. So far, he didn't have a clue.

"Who in the devil is he talking to?" Einstein wonders. "I wish he'd turn around."

"Oh, yeah! Cats!" he hears the professor say. "You mean Shaman's stray Siamese that hangs around the Pub? That the one you mean?" Einstein strains to hear, but the man only mumbles.

"Yeah, there were two of them today—sleeping on the hearth. The female's been there for years. The stray couldn't be Gretchen. He's a male."

(Mumble, mumble, mumble, came from the chair.)

"You may be right," the Professor agrees. He leans back in his chair as though contemplating his cohort's latest words. "Yeah, that's right. The stray may lead us to her—she'd be bait." He placed a slim, elegantly slippered foot on the coffee table. "We'll wait 'til the male leaves—he prowls all night—and we can move in on the female when Shaman's too busy to notice."

(Mumble, mumble, mumble, came from the chair.)

"Okay, you go after that stuff for the formula. I'll grab the cat." The professor picks up his helmet and looks around for a sack. He leads his cohort to the back door, then heads for his trusty Honda. Einstein faces a dilemma. *Follow the professor or his partner—or stick around and look for the Professor's formula?* He sends a mental message to Ming warning her to keep out of sight as she's about to have a visitor of the nastiest kind—a catnapper.

As the Professor's motorcycle roars away and the stranger exits the back door, Einstein tails him at a safe distance. The man shuffles off in the direction of the university building—*to the laboratory?* No, the man veers right, slipping into shadowy shrubbery surrounding the main building on campus. As swift as Einstein considered himself to be, he couldn't outpace this stranger. Before he could get far enough ahead to catch a glimpse of his face, the stranger vanishes into thin air. Einstein sniffs with his keen nose, but the trail ends short of the forest.

Baffled, Einstein returns to the cottage, slipping into the room through an open window. Keeping one cat antenna on Ming back at the pub, and the other on instant alert in the cottage, Einstein looks around the room, wondering where to start first. *Might as well see what's here—I'll figure out what to do about that guy later.* He creeps his way among the papers on the table nosing one piece of paper this way and another that way. *Amazing what clutter these humanoids live in.*

A book falls off the desk and onto the floor. Einstein jumps down beside it, trying to interpret the title, but to no avail. "Gretchen needs to see this," he decides. "I can't read it, and that picture on the cover means nothing to me."

Grabbing the book in his strong jaws, Einstein jumps out of the window, and heads for the overpass, hoping Julius and Gretchen have returned, but the place is deserted. Sitting on the small book he carries with him, he falls fast asleep.

* * *

"Einstein," a soft voice whispers in his ear some time later. "We're back. What have you learned?" Einstein opens one eye and sees Gretchen and Roscoe watching him. He stretches his long legs and curls his tail back over his body, shaking off the fatigue that threatens him.

"A-h-h-r," Einstein purrs, fully alert and facing his two friends. "I found something on the professor's desk, but I don't know if it's what we're looking for." He pushes the book toward Gretchen. "If it isn't, I'll have to go back."

"Let me see," said Gretchen, sitting on her haunches and attempting to read the book. "Roscoe, you hold the book down on your side, and Einstein, you hold down the other side. I can't do this alone." She studies the book, while the two cats attempt to hold it steady.

"You mean this may be it?" Einstein asks, his tail flipping in anticipation. He holds the book down securely on his side, while Roscoe struggles with the other side. Gretchen steps back from the book.

"Hold it up a little more, would you? I can't read if it's too close," she said. "I don't seem to be far-sighted, anymore." She begins reading. Einstein and Roscoe watch her, impatient for a verdict. "This isn't it." Gretchen said, hitting the page with her front paw. "This is a recipe for clam chowder." She turns a page. Then, she turns another page, looking up from the book to the two waiting cats. "These aren't lab notes," she determines. "This is a cookbook."

Einstein and Roscoe look at each other. "But why would he have a cookbook on his desk?" Einstein asks, puzzled. "He looked at this book when he talked to the stranger. Are you sure that's all it is?"

Gretchen glares at Einstein, fur bristling, her tail twitching. "I may look like a cat, but I can read. Why should I lie to you?"

"It's okay, Gretchen," Roscoe said. "I'm sure Einstein didn't mean it. Maybe there's something else in the book." He picks it up, and shakes it. Something falls out from between the leaves. "Oh, my! Oh, my! What's this?" he asks, dropping the book and nosing a loose slip of paper toward Gretchen. "There's some writing on it, Gretchen. What does it say?"

Gretchen purrs with pleasure, pushing the paper smooth with her paws. "This is it, the formula. But look at those ingredients. I've never heard of some of them."

"What are they?" Einstein asked. "Do you know where to find them?"

"They must be in the professor's laboratory, else how could he have mixed the potion?" Roscoe asked. Occasionally, Roscoe came up with real insight.

"You're right, Roscoe. They must be in the lab. We'll have to go back there. Gretchen, you read out the ingredients and I'll memorize them," said Einstein. "Help me remember, Roscoe. We have to return this book to Professor Ipswitch before he finds it missing."

Gretchen begins to read. *Transmogrification, sole property of Erichtho of Lucan.*

"What's that?" Roscoe interrupts, "And who's Erichtho of Lucan?"

Gretchen tries to explain. "He's the Devil. Quit interrupting. Who else would have a recipe like this? And Transmogrification is . . . Oh, no!"

"What is it, Gretchen?" Einstein asks. "What is it about transmogrification that scares you? Isn't this the antidote?"

"What if this is what the professor already gave me? I might turn into some other kind of weird animal."

"Didn't he call the potion, *Resurrection?*" Einstein asks.

"Oh, that's right. This has to be the antidote." She continues to read the incantation, and as she reads, Roscoe and Einstein repeat the ingredients after her, concentrating as hard as they can to remember.

Mingle together to confect a charm,
The bloods of black animals, in a remote, solitary place.
Burn entrails, feet and claws, the head, the skin or feathers.
Except, a black cat.
Scatter some ashes far and wide and others in a quart of wine.
Roast over a slow fire,
or on charcoal embers 'til air is full of smoke.
And in its midst
Set a pristine bowl of crystal clear water before the fire.
Gaze into the water as you drink the wine and cry out the words,
Boil and bubble, toil and trouble.
Spirit whose breath is in the four winds, breathe breathe on me.

"Ugh, gross," comments Gretchen. "How can we do this? Surely there's a better way."

Einstein and Roscoe look her in bewilderment.

"We do this all the time. Are you going to be a squeamish female?" Roscoe asks. "How else do you plan to be transformed, Gretchen?"

"Course if you're beginning to have second thoughts . . ." Einstein says.

"Yeah," says Roscoe. "If you prefer being a cat…"

"No," says Gretchen, shuddering. "I have to get back to my original form." She looks at her two accomplices with affection. "Let's go." And the three race back to the Professor's cottage to return the book. No sooner do they replace the book than Einstein hears the roar of the Professor's motorcycle. He scoots out of the cottage to join Gretchen and Roscoe. Leaving them at the cottage to spy on the professor, Einstein races over the housetops to check on Ming. He finds her safe and sound, sleeping with one eye open, invisibly taking in the activity in the Pub.

"Did the Professor ever come by, Ming?" he asks.

"He did, but I joined Shaman behind the bar. He didn't dare make a move on me," Ming answers, shifting her cat body to give Einstein space to curl up beside her. "Einstein, I just remembered.

Gretchen left alone, that night. Harley and the professor didn't leave 'til after closing time."

"You're sure?" Einstein mewed.

"Of course, I'm sure," Ming snaps, "I wouldn't say so otherwise."

Einstein puts his head on his paws, and looks up at her. "That puts an entirely different slant on the project," he says, and closes his eyes to reflect.

Chapter Seven

Such as we are made of, such we be.
-Shakespeare

Harley Dandrich returned home that evening disappointed. With Gretchen's car still in the garage, he knew she hadn't been home. He'd tried all weekend to find her, certain she would contact her best friend, but Kristin hadn't heard from her either. The cops allowed Gretchen forty-eight hours to return before Harley could file a "missing persons" report. After all, Gretchen was an adult and in full charge of her faculties.

"She'll show up when she's ready," a burly, disinterested policeman told Harley, and that's the best Harley could do.

He looked around, thinking there might have been activity around the house since he'd left early that morning, but except for the stray cat he found on his doorstep, nothing seemed out of the ordinary. He tried to shove the wayward animal aside, but the cat hissed at him, determined to enter the house. Alarmed at the cat's ferocity, Harley hesitates, and Gretchen slips between his legs and into the house.

Harley reviews the situation. *Maybe it's best I make friends with this cat.* He pours the cat a saucer of milk, and sets it on the kitchen floor. The cat drinks the milk eagerly, and Harley settles down with his newspaper. Having finished the milk, the cat jumps on Harley's lap and begins to purr. She snuggles up on Harley's warm chest.

"Don't let him know you can speak, or that you understand him," Einstein had warned her. "Until we know what happened to you, we need to take all necessary precaution."

"But it's Harley—my husband. We can trust him," she said, but Einstein insisted. Gretchen knew he was right. She'd say nothing until they knew for sure what had happened to her—*if they could only find that antidote.*

Harley watches the cat purring peacefully, kneading her furry paws into his chest, and has a change of heart. Normally a cat hater, he actually begins to stroke the intruder rather fondly, thinking her unusually friendly despite having hissed at him. Then it happened. Harley begins to sneeze—and sneeze—and sneeze. He couldn't help it—and he couldn't stop. He picks up Gretchen, strides to the door, and tosses the puzzled cat out onto the front yard. Brushing cat hairs from his dark suit, he remembered why he hates felines. They make him ill.

"Damn cat," he grumbles. "That'll teach me. Can't get near the damn things." He returns to his comfy easy chair, and begins again to read his paper. He has no trouble being around the cats at **Shaman's Pub**, but then he never touched those cats. This one insisted on jumping on him. He couldn't have that.

Gretchen grooms her ruffled fur, disgruntled at being dumped so unmercifully, when the phone rings. She perks up her ears, moving closer to the window by the telephone. *Why couldn't that happen when I was inside?* Not being able to hear through the thick pane of glass, she moves towards the patio door that Harley opened when he came home, and pushes close against the screen in time to hear him say, "A cat? You think she's a cat? Well, I admit, there were times... Oh, you mean, literally." He listens. "Look, Professor, that's impossible." He shakes his head. "You're crazy," and hung up.

Harley resumes reading his newspaper—thinking over what the professor said. Then it registers. He throws down his paper, walks out on the patio, and calls to the cat, "Here, kitty, here, kitty. Come to Papa. I'm sorry I put you out." But Gretchen had heard enough and has disappeared.

I think I know who called Harley. Thank God, he tossed me out in time. I need to talk to Einstein before Harley finds out who I am. Somehow I have to convince him Harley can be trusted. We need his help.

She finds Einstein sitting with Ming occupying their usual spot on the hearth at **Grumman's Bar and Grill**, and hisses at him from the protection of the kitchen door. Shaman watches Einstein leave Ming when he catches sight of Gretchen by the door, and muses about cats and their strange behaviors. Outside, Einstein asks, "Where's Roscoe? You're not supposed to be alone."

"I know. I went home to see Harley," Gretchen tells him, adding in a plaintive voice, "Einstein, we can trust him. He can help us."

Einstein shakes his head. "No, not yet, Gretchen. We need to find the ingredients for that potion before we start adding accomplices."

"I nearly told him, but his allergies hit, and he threw me out. I can't stay a cat, Einstein. Harley's allergic to me," she says, nearly in tears.

Einstein felt empathy for Gretchen and her peculiar plight. "Maybe you're right. I'll think about it. Where will you spend the night?"

"At home. I've a nice comfortable chaise lounge on the patio. I'll stay there," Gretchen decides. "Don't worry about me."

Einstein hesitates, then he agrees. "All right. I'll have Julius look in on you," he says, intending to return to the fireside and Ming. Gretchen, about to return home, spies Harley's car pulling into the parking lot.

"Einstein," she tells him. "Harley's here. That must have been the professor on the phone. Is he inside?" Gretchen asks.

"No, but maybe they're meeting here. I'd better warn Ming." And Einstein disappears into the Pub.

Gretchen chills when she sees the professor arriving from another direction, and join Harley at the entrance. She watches the two enter the Pub. *Maybe Einstein is right. I can't trust Harley. Not yet, anyway.*

* * *

"Evenin' fellas," Shaman greets the two new arrivals. "What'll it be? The usual?" and places a Rob Roy in front of the professor—a beer in front of Harley. "World treating you right, is it?" He follows the professor's gaze in the direction of the fireplace, noticing that Ming and Einstein have disappeared.

"That cat of yours," Professor Ipswitch begins. "He ever display any unusual characteristics?"

"The cat's a *she*," Shaman informs the professor.

"Sorry," says Professor Ipswitch. "Does *she*?"

"Not unless you want to call bein' a witch's *familiar* an unusual characteristic," Shaman said, his eyes sparkling as he chuckles.

"Huh?" asked the Professor, white knuckles grabbing the edge of the bar. "What did you say?" You know witches?" Professor Ipswitch had nothing against witches, but they charged a horrendous fee for their services, and the Professor, already indebted to one witch, had no desire for the assistance for another.

"Can't you tell a joke when you hear one?" Harley says to Professor Ipswitch, who then relaxes. "Is she a witch's familiar?" he asks Shaman.

"No," Shaman said. "Ain't nothin' unusual about my cat that don't apply to every other cat. Why?"

"Shaman, we got a problem," Harley begins. "Remember when we were here last Friday night, and the Professor had some kind of *youth potion* he gave my wife?"

"Yeah?" Shaman stops in mid stroke of cleaning the bar to glare at the two. "What happened to her?"

"She's disappeared," Harley said. "We think she may still be under the influence of that potion. The Professor needs to check her reaction, but we can't find her."

Shaman chuckled. "And you think she might 'ave turned into a cat? And 'tain't even Halloween. You guys been drinkin' yer own potions, ha' ye?"

The professor and Harley look at each other, feeling foolish. Professor Ipswitch has heard about *Shamanism* and knew it to be an old religious belief in an unseen world inhabited by gods, demons, and ancestral spirits. Ming, sleeping on Shaman's fireplace, seemed to fit right into that scenario. *I can't accuse Shaman of even knowing about such things because of his name, can I?*

Finishing their drinks, the two leave the bar, and are surprised when they are faced by a front of six cats barring their way—one of them the cat Harley remembers petting in his home living room just hours before. He points to her.

"That's the one, Professor," he said. "That's Gretchen. I know it is." As he approaches her, Gretchen hisses and the other cats circle around her.

"She's gone from your world," the Professor tells Harley. "And she seems to have found allies to protect her. Leave her be."

"But I can't leave her here," Harley insists.

"Look, we can't bring her back. My formula has disappeared. Maybe that old hag I bought it from will return Halloween night to redeem her just dues," the professor says.

"You mean it's not even your invention? You experiment on my wife with a potion you bought from a witch? How dare you!" Harley said to the Professor, taking a swing at him. The Professor ducks.

"I didn't know," the Professor defends himself. "Not 'til after I went back to find her, and couldn't—not until Halloween, anyway." He shuffles his feet, his hand deep in his pockets. "There's something else you need to know," he said.

Harley sits on the curb, holding his shaking head in the palms of his hands, and ignores the professor. Gretchen and four cats watch the pitiful sight unable to understand what made Harley flare up like that.

Einstein, hiding behind the shrubbery, listens intently, but the professor says no more. *What else does the professor know that Harley needs to know?* He watches them leave, Harley in his Daimler, and the professor roaring out of the parking lot on his Honda—scattering rocks in all directions. He joined the other cats.

"You did good, tonight," Einstein tells the group. "We've got the recipe for the potion, and we are the only ones who can help Gretchen return to her world." He looks at Gretchen, pity in his blue eyes. "Although why she wants to is more than I can figure out." He turns his back on them, and returns to the Pub.

Chapter Eight

Nothing is so strong as gentleness, and nothing so gentle as real strength.
--Saint Frances de Sales

Gretchen snuggles down onto the patio chaise behind her home on Market Street. She'd always loved her garden and looks around it now from a new perspective, a position of quiet solitude. Fall blooms were in a dazzling array of nature's colors—amber, gold, rusts—intermingling with a scattering of brilliant red and yellows.

The cat Gretchen could wander through those plants, brush against them, sniff the aromas at close range, absorb the moisture of morning dew, and nibble at her late blooming strawberries. The adult Gretchen had to bend to be this close to nature, and Gretchen realized she seldom did that. Tonight, she listened to the chirping of crickets in the night air, watched the flickering of fireflies dancing before her eyes—swatting at them with her paw when they came close.

An evening breeze chills the October air, but Gretchen doesn't feel the cold through her heavy, white fur coat. Lazily, she rouses and takes a few licks at a burr she'd picked up during her travels that day. She thinks about Julius, the black cat down the street, and wonders what he's doing tonight. Instinctively, she knows he faces danger as a black cat on Halloween. Tonight, he and Einstein were hoping Professor Ipswitch would lead them to his lab so they could sneak in and await their chance to find ingredients for her antidote. Gretchen knew the errand Julius and Einstein undertook would benefit her, but she didn't know that Julius had plans of his own for the drug. So Gretchen dozes in peace, secure in the knowledge that her problems will soon be over. Soon she would be with Harley.

Julius told her he had been a *humanoid,* and *morphed* into a cat the same way she had, but Gretchen was skeptical. If that were true, why couldn't he read the way she could? Approaching footsteps interrupt her thoughts, and she springs up, alert and ready. She jumps from the chaise and scurries into the bushes in time to see Harley enter the garden and head for the storage shed.

What's Harley doing in the garden this late at night? She watches him enter the shed and return to the garden with a spade. He takes the spade into the garden Gretchen had planted in early May, and begins to dig up one of her strawberry plants. He retrieves a plastic-wrapped article out from under one of her prized strawberry plants, places the object on the patio table, and returns the spade to the shed.

Gretchen comes out of hiding when Harley take the retrieved object into the house. She jumps onto the window box and peers through the kitchen window as Harley opens the odd-shaped plastic packet. A revolver tumbles out onto the counter, and Harley proceeds to clean it.

"So that's what happened to my protection," Gretchen muses. "He told me he sold it—that he had no more use for it." Then she begins to worry. *Is he in trouble? Why does he need a gun?* She remembered the last time she had seen that particular gun. Harley had bought it for her the time he prosecuted a scam artist who threatened to get even with Harley. The client claimed Harley reneged on a deal he'd made with him, and fearing Gretchen might be vulnerable, he'd purchased the gun and given it to her for protection. When the scam artist went to prison, Gretchen gave it back to Harley. *Why did he tell me he'd sold it when he didn't?*

The phone rings. Harley stops cleaning the gun and picks up the phone. "Yeah," she hears him say, "I found it (pause). Seems in pretty good shape considering its long sleep (pause). Yeah, about thirty minutes. Okay, see ya." He hangs up, and continues cleaning and polishing the revolver on the kitchen counter.

Gretchen ponders. Tomorrow is Halloween, the night of witches and goblins. First, she feared for Julius. Now, she fears for Harley. *Who is this mysterious partner—and why the gun? Is it because of her disappearance from the people world?*

"O-o-h, we've got to create that antidote before tomorrow night," she says to no one in particular as she races across backyards toward the Pub. Einstein and Julius had already left—chasing the Professor to the University, and Ming refused to leave the Pub. Not knowing what to do, Gretchen heads for the overpass. Maybe Roscoe will be there. She stubs her paw on the curb in her rush. "Ouch," she complains. *This running around on cat's paws tires me. And they say all a cat does is sit around and sleep all day. Hah! I've had so-o-o little sleep since I became a cat.*

She sits down and licks her bruised paw, then takes off again, running as fast as she can, leaping fences and gardens until she reaches the underpass. Gretchen crawls behind some shrubbery near the concrete underpass, and waits for one of her cat friends to return. *Maybe I should have gone by the Fisherman's Wharf. I might have found Roscoe there with Kristin. He seems to spend an awful lot of time with her.* She stretches out her long, agile cat's body, wary eyes scanning the nearby parking lot. She listens to night sounds, enjoying the silence of the night. A car drives into a deserted lot across the road. It's lights shine brightly for a moment, then disappear and all is quiet.

Gretchen dozes as she waits. She had discovered that being a cat is tiring and required frequent catnaps. Minutes later, she senses movement nearby. Her antennae sail into full alert mode. Hearing voices, she slips deeper into the shrubbery. The voices become angry, disturbing her solitude. She peeks out from behind her secluded spot. Then it happens. In one quick movement a figure pulls away, and Gretchen sees the flash of a knife and hears the muffled sound of a body dropping to the ground.

A car drives by, its headlights flashing on a scene close by Gretchen. The man with the knife panics. He ducks under the overpass—tossing his weapon into the shrubbery—barely missing Gretchen as she scrunches behind a bush and against the concrete. She closed her eyes—afraid the killer might detect her presence—then opens them as she hears footsteps running toward the parking lot.

A couple walking across the bridge lean over and shine a flashlight on Gretchen. Blinded, she scampers away and the light follows her. "Only a cat," a voice said, and the couple continues their journey. After they leave, Gretchen hears footsteps running towards the parking lot. A car door slams, and an engine roars. The lone car in the parking lot departs. Gretchen races to investigate.

"Please, God," she prays, "Don't let it be Harley." But she'd never seen this man before. *Maybe Einstein knows him. He meets a lot of people at Shaman's.* Gretchen races for home. She had to be sure Harley wasn't the other man. *What if it is Harley—and the man he called is the dead man? Oh, dear, I don't know if I can stand being a cat much longer. It's so-o-o frustrating!*

Gretchen finds Roscoe and Kristin rummaging in an overflowing garbage can behind the cats' favorite restaurant. As soon as Gretchen approaches, Kristin takes off.

"Did I scare her off?" asks Gretchen.

"Nah, she has to go home. Time to watch *Tom and Jerry* with the kids."

"What?" *H-m-m, there's more to this cat business than I realize.* She looks at Roscoe. Compared to Gretchen and her immaculately maintained self, Roscoe's rough, untidy fur could never be termed *slick* no matter how much grooming it got. Tonight was no exception. He looked scruffy. *No wonder Kristin left.*

"Roscoe," Gretchen informs the raggle-taggle Tomcat, "I witnessed a murder tonight."

"Oh? Did you recognize the killer?" he asks, pausing over a delectable portion of leftover salmon he silently thanks some generous customer for leaving. Roscoe eyes her with suspicion, chewing the piece of salmon in his jaws. He believes Gretchen to have a terrific imagination—also exceptionally acute senses. Maybe having been *humanoid* did that to cats. He decides to go along with her fantasy.

"No, but I'm on my way home. I want to be sure Harley isn't involved."

"What do you want me to do?" Roscoe asks, wondering if she had plans to track the killer.

"Would you help me rescue the knife?" Gretchen asks. "I pushed it into the bushes to hide it, and it's too heavy for me to carry. I need your help."

"Me?" Roscoe asks. "You ask for my help?" He eyes her with suspicion.

"Yes." Gretchen's eyes tear. She sits down to wait. Roscoe watches her.

"Really, you're entirely too polite for a cat," Roscoe mews around the salmon clutched in his paws. "You must be more aggressive. All us cats are, you know."

Gretchen ignores his comment.

"Well, at least, let me finish my salmon." He motions towards the salmon. "Aren't you having any?" he tempts her, pushing a piece of salmon in front of her. "It's delicious."

Gretchen looks at the salmon. She hadn't eaten tonight. "Well," she concedes, "Just a bit while I'm waiting. We can't afford to waste time." She tastes the morsel Roscoe pushed towards her. "H-m-m, that is good—a delectable flavor. Wonder what seasoning the chef uses?" The two greedily finish off the salmon.

Half an hour lapses before Gretchen remembers the knife. "Oh, my goodness, Roscoe, we've got to hurry. What if someone's already found it?"

Roscoe pulls himself away. "I'm sorry, Gretchen. We should have saved the knife first instead of being so greedy. Let's go."

"It's probably already too late," admits Gretchen. "Poor Harley!" The two cats head back towards the overpass.

"What do you mean, poor Harley?" Roscoe meowed, trailing along behind Gretchen. "Is he one of the men you saw?"

"I don't know, but he has a gun," she informs Roscoe.

Roscoe stops and looks at her. "We're looking for a knife," he says, confidently. "Isn't that what you said?"

Gretchen stops running, her front paw poised in midair. "Oh, that's right. It couldn't have been Harley, could it? Unless…"

"Unless what?" asks Roscoe.

"Nothing," she mewed. "Let's hurry. Damn you and your salmon dinner!"

"Me? Seems you enjoyed it pretty much, too," Roscoe says, stopping to pull a plastic bag free that had blown against the fence. He locks the sack in his jaws. Then, leaping in tandem, the two cats scamper away to the scene of the crime.

They find the knife where Gretchen hid it. After a few failed attempts, the two succeed in bagging the knife—Gretchen holding the bag open with the help of a nearby rock, and Roscoe nosing the knife into position and into the bag. Julius and Einstein, having failed in their mission to locate ingredients for the potion, spy Gretchen and Roscoe at the foot of the embankment, and rush down to investigate.

"Einstein," Roscoe brags to the Siamese. "Look what we found."

"A knife? Collecting souvenirs, are you? What do you plan to do with it?"

Roscoe shifts the blame to Gretchen. "It's her idea. She seems to think it's important."

Einstein turns to Gretchen. "Why do you need a knife, Gretchen? Last time I looked, you were still a cat." Gretchen looks at Roscoe in disgust. He ignores her. Suddenly, a shout is heard from the bridge. All the cats go into alert mode. Someone has discovered the body. Einstein and Julius race to investigate, while Gretchen and Roscoe are left to drag the knife back to the safety of the bushes. Gretchen nears panic stage.

"Let Einstein handle this, Gretchen," Roscoe tells her. "He'll know what to do." Einstein returns, and faces the two cats. "You two know something about that body someone found up there?" he asks.

Gretchen looks at Roscoe. "Meow," she says.

"Don't look at me," Roscoe answers. "I was only helping."

"Gretchen?" Einstein accuses. "Where did you get this knife, and why are you hanging onto it when it is obviously the murder weapon?"

Gretchen confesses, giving Einstein a hasty description of her adventure under the overpass. "I witnessed the murder, and found the knife, Einstein. But I can't let the police find it 'til I know for sure Harley is not involved." Her blue cat eyes well up in tears. "Please, Einstein. It may have his fingerprints on it."

Einstein makes a hasty decision. He looks at the sack containing the evidence, nods to Julius, and they grab the sack. Between the two of them, they toss the knife into the Cat Monger's cache of memorable keepsakes. Relieved, Gretchen races for home, hoping to find Harley tucked in their bed fast asleep—unaware and innocent of Gretchen and her excursions.

* * *

A nearly full moon lit the path as Gretchen sneaks home, her heart pounding, afraid Harley would not be there. She passes the hole in her garden where she'd seen Harley digging up the gun—a gun she thought he'd sold years ago—and gave it a cursory glance before entering Amber's doggy door.

Once inside she listens for noises or movement. Amber, asleep in his basket, opens one eye, then goes back to sleep. Hearing nothing, Gretchen moves farther inside the house, racing upstairs. She creeps into the bedroom —their bedroom—where Harley now slept alone. She jumps on her dresser. Seeing a sleeping Harley in bed, she suppresses a desire to crawl in beside him.

Her cat eyes penetrate the darkness. That's when she sees the bottle on her dresser—set on a sheet of white paper with writing on it. Jumping on the dresser, she recognizes the incantation that fell from the cookbook Einstein found on the Professor's desk. Moving in closer to better read the prescription on the bottle, she believes it to be the antidote that will reverse her undignified existence in the cat world. *Did Harley kill for this bottle?*

She puts out one paw, and tries to pick up the bottle, but only manages to upset it. She thought about knocking it off the dresser, and rolling it down the long steps, but didn't want to awaken Harley. She leaves the bottle on the dresser and jumps down onto the carpet. *Finding the gun and getting rid of it is more important than facing the impossible task of opening a bottle with only cat paws. I might break the bottle and all would be lost—the potion worthless.*

Gretchen races downstairs—looking in all the places Harley might possibly have stored the gun, but couldn't find it anywhere. Frustrated, she resumes her spot on the chaise lounge knowing she won't sleep much that night. She contents herself by keeping an unrelenting vigil over the garden—particularly the disturbed plot of ground where Harley dug up the gun. Occasionally, she catnaps welcoming the opportunity to rest her eyes.

Sensing movement, she opens one dilated, blue eye in time to observe Julius moving stealthily along the garden fence. She watches him creep along the garden fence and marvels at the symmetry of his movements—like a cat dancing to an unheard melody—then silently jumps off the fence onto the chaise beside Gretchen.

Gretchen transmits a mental question. "You hear what happened?" she asks.

"I did," transmits Julius.

"I found the potion," she purrs silently. "Where is it?" he purrs back. "On my dresser, in my bedroom."

Gretchen turns to look in Julius' green eyes. *He's really quite handsome; that is, if I were really a cat.* "I left it there. I'm more concerned about the gun. I can't find it"

"You didn't take any of the potion?" Gretchen swore he actually smiled when he asked that. "Getting to like being a cat, are you?"

"Cool it, cat. That'll be the day." She sniffs her displeasure.

"Then, why?"

"Afraid, I suppose. What if it works? How could I explain what's been going on?" Gretchen lays her face on her front paws. "We've got to find the gun. No one's safe until we do. Besides…" she raises her face and turns to Julius. "How can I be sure the bottle of potion and the recipe are the same?"

"Probably isn't," Julius answers. "Halloween's tomorrow. Didn't the Professor say he wouldn't have it 'til then?"

"I know." She turns to the black cat, concern in her blue eyes. "Halloween. Julius, you know how dangerous that day is for black cats. What will you do?"

Julius' eyes twinkle. "I plan to take a certain white cat to the witch's coven for protection—a sort of good-luck charm, so to speak."

Gretchen stretches to her fullest and glares down at Julius. "How dare you!" she hisses, and slaps at him with a sheathed claw. "I'm not your Lady Luck."

Julius catches the paw and pulls her down. "Oh, come now," he purrs. "Admit it, we could make beautiful music together—you and me."

Gretchen shivers. The night has suddenly turned chilly.

* * *

Chapter Nine

A likely impossibility is always preferable to an unconvincing possibility.
-Aristotle

Poetics

Gretchen and Julius are awakened by the sound of someone opening the garden gate. In unison, they jump from the chaise and hide under a lilac bush by the side of the house, peering in the direction of the sound. A man enters the garden, walking directly to the hole Harley dug in the garden, and retrieving the gun that had miraculously returned to its original hiding place.

No wonder I couldn't find the gun in the house, Harley put it back in the garden. Pulling something from his jacket pocket, the man drops an object into the hole. Using his hands, he replaces the disturbed strawberry plant, tapping the soil firmly around the plant. When he finishes, he quietly leaves the same way he arrived. Julius and Gretchen immediately go into conference mode, hoping to contact Einstein, but he is out of range.

"What do we do?" asks Gretchen of Julius aware they are on their own.

Julius thinks a while. Then he says, "There are two of us and one of him. I could follow the interloper and you could retrieve the gun."

"We don't know if it's a gun he dug up, Julius. Let's follow the guy. We can worry about what he planted later. It won't go anywhere."

Julius looks at her with pride. "I knew your brains would come in handy, " he comments. "Come on, let's go." And the two flew out the garden gate tracking the fast disappearing lights of a pickup truck.

"Julius, I can't go much farther," Gretchen implores a few blocks away. "I don't have your stamina. Maybe you better go on ahead." She sits on her haunches to rest. "I'll go back and wait for you."

Julius slows for a moment, transmitting his sympathies, when the truck stops at the only stoplight in town. Julius and Gretchen catch up and the two cats scramble onto the truck bed.

"No sense running when we can ride," Julius says as the two cats struggle to catch their breath.

The run affects Gretchen most, not being as used to exercise as Julius. The two position themselves under the cab window, Gretchen to the right, and Julius to the left. Gretchen recognizes the driver first. "Oh, Julius," she says. "It's Shaman." Julius looks skeptical. "Look in the back window, if you don't believe me." Julius did.

"Why on earth would he be digging in your garden?" he asks.

Shaman catches Julius peering in through his rear view mirror. He continues to drive down the darkened lanes towards his home. Musing at the versatility of animals in hitching rides, a thought hits him. *Could one o' them cats be the one Professor Ipswitch be alookin' fer? Might be a bounty on it. I'll give 'im a call.*

On reaching home, he pulls the truck into his open garage, and immediately hits the button to close the garage door. Julius, realizing what is happening, jumps from the truck bed and scuttles under the door before it closes completely. Gretchen—tired and not as alert as Julius—takes a second too long to react and gets caught in Shaman's garage.

Shaman grabs at the white cat, intending to bag her until he can contact the professor. He picks her up by the scruff of the neck rendering Gretchen helpless. That's when Shaman feels the chain around her neck.

"What's this?" he asks, examining the collar around the cat's neck. "Well, b'gorra, what do you know. I do believe they be real diamonds."

And for the second time in her short cat life, Gretchen finds herself tied up in the limited confines of a gunnysack. She puts her head on her paws, and weeps real cat tears. Gretchen did not make it home that night.

* * *

Roscoe, partaking of his favorite pastime—eating—is interrupted in the middle of a delectable dinner of crab pasta by the appearance of Kristin. Kristin, a British tabby who complicated his bachelorhood, expressed disapproval of his recent interest in Gretchen. She cornered Roscoe behind the Fisherman's Wharf, and snarled at him.

"Look," Roscoe explains to Kristin. "She's a people cat. I've no interest in her at all. I'm merely trying to help her get oriented to living in the cat world. She doesn't know how to avoid *humanoid* pitfalls."

"I should warn her about you, then," Kristin counters, nosing at a piece of crab that has slipped from Roscoe' mouth as he turns to defend himself. "You've never been a good judge of character." She mouths another morsel of crab as she continues to pick at Roscoe and his shortcomings.

"Kristin," Roscoe consoles her, "You know Gretchen means nothing to me. Surely you understand. She'll return to her own way of life some day, and our lives will return to normal."

Kristin melted somewhat. Roscoe could always do this to her. Ever since she'd met him, his raggle-taggle totally British countenance attracted Kristin as had no other cat. Certainly not Einstein with his snooty ways, nor Julius—an alley cat if there ever were one. No self-respecting female was safe from his catting ways. He had absolutely no respect for decent felines.

"She's disappeared, you know," Roscoe informs Kristin.

Kristin stops eating. "She returned to the people world?"

"Don't know. If she's become a *humanoid* again, we'd have no way of knowing," Roscoe surmises. "She was last seen with Shaman. Maybe he dumped her somewhere."

"Good riddance," says Kristin. "She's entirely too consumed with herself and her own welfare. Even Julius fell under her spell." *Ah, retribution, how sweet it is.* A sudden thought strikes her. "If Einstein and Julius find the antidote and discover the potion, we may all be subjected to the *humanoid* world. I know you wouldn't resist becoming a *humanoid,* if you had a chance." She turns to look at him, and realizes her stab in the dark bears some validity.

Roscoe stops eating long enough to face his antagonist. "Don't tell me you wouldn't be the least bit curious, my dear Kristin," he says snuggling cozily against her. "Bet you'd make a honey of a female, *m'cherie,*" he says, using a favorite word for his *femme fatale.*

"H-m-m, maybe," Kristin agrees.

* * *

Meanwhile back at the Pub, Shaman checked out the gun he'd dug up from Gretchen's strawberry patch. Harley had concealed it in a plastic cover after cleaning it. *Exactly what I need. So nice of Harley to find this for me. Strange, all he wants in return is a signed picture of Professor Ipswitch and his partner. Wonder why? Ah, well, none of my business.*

He digs into the gunnysack exposing Gretchen's head and ties the sack firmly around her neck with a piece of string. He removes the collar from around the neck of the helpless cat, and checks the validity of the stones on a piece of glass. *Ah, that's what I thought—real diamonds.* He unties the string and drops Gretchen back into the gunnysack—places the necklace in a small jewelry box, and tosses the sack in the back of his pickup. Once at the Pub, Shaman dumps the sack in the back storeroom and heads for the telephone. For the second time in her short cat life, Gretchen finds her nightmare repeated. She struggles to get out of the sack, chewing the heavy burlap with her sharp teeth trying to break through while all the time sending cat messages to Ming, Einstein, Julius—anyone who would listen.

* * *

Julius watches Harley leave for work early the next morning, then scampers through Amber's doggie door. He races upstairs. The bottle is still on the dressing table, but Gretchen is nowhere to be seen. Julius worries. *Where is she?* Racing back downstairs he heads for **Shaman's Pub**. *Maybe Einstein knows.* Ming hadn't seen him, but she did give Julius some interesting information.

"If you look in the back storeroom, you'll find your white cat," she tells Julius. "You'll have to hurry. Professor Ipswitch is on his way here to pick her up."

"You sure?" asked Julius. "Why would Shaman turn her over to the enemy?"

"I'm not sure the professor is the enemy," Ming says. "Isn't he the one with the potion to return her to her own world?" She looks closely at Julius. "You're smitten with her, aren't you? You want to keep her in the cat world."

Julius had to admit Ming's guess hit close to his heart. He hadn't realized how fond he'd become of Gretchen. "How do I get into the storeroom," he asks Ming.

Ming shrugs her cat shoulders, and shakes her head. "If you must," she says. "Follow me." She takes a quick look at Shaman behind the bar, and says, "Meet me at the back door. I'll let you in from there. We'll look too suspicious if we trail through the Pub together."

Julius departs through the customer door, turns the corner and waits by the back door where Shaman's white truck is parked. A few minutes later, Ming pushes the door open from the inside, and Julius enters.

"Follow me," she says, leading Julius by a circuitous route that ends in the Pub storeroom. Ming has her own secret path into the storeroom without having to go through the Pub. The two find Gretchen still struggling to bite her way out of her gunnysack prison.

"Oh, no, not again, Gretchen. Is that you in that sack?" Julius scolds. "Can't leave you alone for a minute, can I? You get yourself all tied up again. Haven't you learned yet? You can't trust *humanoids*?"

"It isn't my choice," Gretchen sputters between bites. "Shaman steals my necklace, and dumps me here. I don't know what he plans to do to me with me. My opinion of him is slowly disintegrating."

"Shaman?" asks Julius as he gives the last rip to free Gretchen. "Why on earth would he steal your collar? Is it worth stealing?"

Gretchen tumbles out on the floor of the storeroom, shaking herself and licking at her ruffled fur. "The crazy nut thinks they're real diamonds." She looks around her. "Where am I?"

"In Shaman's storeroom," Julius answers automatically, his mind still on the necklace. "Are they real diamonds?" he asks.

"Impossible. Harley gave me that necklace for my birthday. He can't afford diamonds." Gretchen continues grooming her white fur coat as Julius watches.

"Well, whatever," he says. "We have to get you out of here. Shaman has already called Professor Ipswitch to tell him he's found you. He'll be looking for you." He leads Gretchen outside by the same circuitous route Ming led him in, but instead of following Ming into the Pub, Julius leads her out the back door and into the alley.

"Getting tied up is sort'a becoming a habit with you, isn't it?" Julius asks, as the two scurry home to safety.

"Sort'a looks that way, doesn't it?" she purrs, her blue eyes shining their gratitude. Once home, Gretchen jumps onto the chaise and turns to face Julius who has jumped up beside her. She places an appreciative paw on his. "Anyway, thanks for the rescue."

"It'll cost you," Julius purrs lasciviously, as the two cats cuddle down for a well-deserved nap—a portrait in black and white.

* * *

Later, awake and rested, the two scoot through Amber's doggie door and tear up the stairs at full speed. The bottle Gretchen had seen still sits on her dressing table. The two eye the bottle from all angles trying to decide how best to accomplish the task at hand.

"I think we can handle it," Julius says, looking over the situation. "But you'll need to use your mouth for something more than complaining."

Gretchen glares, ignoring his snide comment. "It's too heavy," she tells Julius. *How can such a kind, considerate cat, be so sassy at times?* "I tried, and merely succeeded in upsetting the bottle. We need something to wrap it in—then we can drag it."

Julius concedes, and Gretchen looks around to see what's available. Her eyes fall on a make-up pouch on her dresser. "This might do it, Julius. Help me dump it out."

Julius shakes his head. "Too flimsy," he decides. We need to pad the bottle—that is, if we want to get it across town in one piece."

"You're right." Gretchen jumps down and heads for the bathroom. "This should do it," she says dragging back a monogrammed guest towel, and dropping it in front of Julius for his approval.

"Mighty fancy," Julius comments, "Now, how about a little help. I can't go it alone."

Gretchen jumps up on the dresser. "Tell me what you want me to do," she says.

"Okay. You take hold of the pouch on your side and I'll take hold of the pouch on this side—and when I say *dump*, you pick up your end and I'll pick up mine. Ready?"

"Ready," purrs Gretchen and simultaneously the two dump her make-up onto the top of the dresser. They stuff the guest towel inside the empty pouch, and then tackle the bottle. Julius pushes it close to the pouch.

"Oops," he says as the bottle starts to roll.

"Careful," Gretchen admonishes. She pushes the open pouch at a different angle so the bottle will roll into the pouch rather than off the dresser. Julius is successful the second time in nudging the bottle into the pouch with his paws. Mission accomplished, they pull the drawstring with their teeth.

"So far, so good," Julius breathes. "The hard part is over—now to get it off the dresser without breaking or spilling it. Any ideas?" In answer, Gretchen jumps off the dresser and runs to the bed, pulling at the feather pillow on her side of the bed. She grabs a corner, her teeth tearing the cover.

"Hey, okay. Can you handle it alone?" Julius asks from the top of the dresser. Gretchen flips her tail in response. *Amazing how expressive a tail can be.* Dragging the pillow off the bed, she maneuvers it close to the dresser while Julius noses the make-up pouch slowly off the dresser in the vicinity of the pillow. "Catch," he says, as the pouch drops from the dresser, hits the pillow, and rolls off onto the floor.

Julius jumps down, and the two cats grab the pouch by its drawstrings —bouncing it down the long, carpeted staircase, through the doggie door and into the backyard—hiding the pouch behind a lilac bush to be retrieved later. Then they head for a meeting of the Cat Monger's League.

Chapter Ten

All Hallows Day is an important time of the year for cats, a time to pull together to ensure a safe Halloween for all. The cats organize the Cat Monger's League so that all cats, regardless of breed or color, have an equal chance in the world of *humanoids*. All year long they collect their arsenal of precious items to ensure their safety on Halloween Night—when the night goblins and ghosts are free to roam the earth. Sometimes the cats have to buy their way out of weird situations in order to survive another year.

Tonight, Einstein listens to Gretchen and her tale of woe—her escapade in the gunnysack, her stolen collar, and her rescue by Julius. "You were supposed to look after Gretchen," Einstein chides Julius. "Why did you leave her alone in the truck? She hasn't yet acquired danger-sensing skills. Doubtless she considers Shaman a friend, but in this instance, he proved not to be a friend."

Julius eyes the ground, and flips his tail in embarrassment. He says nothing, knowing he was amiss in exposing Gretchen to additional trauma. "We protect our felines," Einstein continues. "They perform admirable services for us tomcats, and it's our duty as males to care for them." He turns his attention from Julius and faces the other cats. "Tonight," he informs them. "We have been requested to put in an appearance at the Witches' Coven. I hope you all know how to protect yourselves. It can be dangerous." He glares at Julius as though reinforcing his charge of ineptness, and Gretchen takes pity on him.

"I'm sorry, Julius," Gretchen says. "I didn't mean to get you in trouble. I will learn. I've nearly got that *slick side* down pat, but I didn't think I'd need it with Shaman." She looks at Julius. "Do you think I really was wearing a diamond collar?"

"If it's true, your necklace is probably in some pawn shop by now. What say we check a few before closing time?" Roscoe offers.

"Could we?" asks Gretchen, turning her blue eyes to Roscoe in gratitude.

"Sure," agrees Julius, "But first, let's practice your yowls. You need to have some ammunition to defend yourself. Let me hear you do it."

"M-e-o-o-w," says Gretchen in her loudest voice.

"Not good enough," Julius answers. "Here, watch me." He arches his back, exposes his claws, and bares his sharp fangs. Then he let go with a *y-e-e-o-o-w-w* that rent the air with an ear-splitting crescendo. Julius sits back on his haunches, and purrs his self-satisfaction. "That's how," he says.

"Oh-h-h," says Gretchen, "I can do that." And apes Julius' tenor performance with an equally ferocious performance in a high soprano key.

"Now, you've got it," Julius approves. "You know that, you can go anywhere. Helps, too, if you add a little *spit* to that *y-e-o-w*. Scares the nastiest of felons—cat spit does. It's our poison, you know, and it can kill."

"Why didn't you teach me this before?" Gretchen asks. "I'd still have my necklace."

"We sort'a likes you the way you are—sweet and innocent," Roscoe says.

"Yeah," says Julius, "but in this world, it's not the safest way to be. Come on. Let's go check some pawn shops."

And the three cats sneak around buildings, down back alleys, and over wooden fences—ducking into selected hock-shops, but their trip is futile. They return to the overpass because, as Julius reminds them, "We've a date tonight—at the Witches' Coven."

And Gretchen, feeling brave and invulnerable, trots alongside Julius and Roscoe into the night air ready for an exciting adventure. They head for Cat Monger's Cave—the entrance to a night of terror.

* * *

Shaman sets out for the Coven meeting wearing the clothes of a Seventeenth Century fakir, an ancient pistol tucked in his belt. His silvery hair blows in the wind as he pilots the horse-drawn chariot down the narrow, twisting streets of Dublin. He visits his home once a year on Halloween—the one day he can go back in time—the one night a year he could enjoy the wilds of Ireland and be with his one true love, Elise. The moon darts back and forth among the dark clouds as Shaman heads for the graveyard and his rendezvous with his Elise.

Now, it isn't that Shaman is not a satisfied man—what with his American pub, his wife Gracie, and his wee bairns—but for this one night a year he achieves his Nirvana. Shaman steers the span of black horses through the wide iron gates of the cemetery—opened wide once a year for the annual meeting of little people, the imaginary people of Ireland. Shaman can hardly wait. The horses seem to crawl, although he knows they do their best.

Centuries ago when he first knew Elise, he made a pact with the Devil in exchange for eternal life for himself and Elise, but somewhere among the good intentions and incantations, he'd lost Elise. All his eternal lives since consisted of his efforts to find her again. He never knew what happened—what went wrong—or why the Devil tried to atone his failure by allowing Shaman to visit Elise once a year on Halloween night. Shaman treasured these visits, but had to forfeit his life and the lives of others to the Devil in order to be with her.

As centuries passed, the Devil took over more and more control of the country. Except for Halloween night, when he availed Shaman with his visit to Elise, the Devil pretty much left him to his own devices. He had more important ventures to occupy his time. Evil had become a way of life in the world, and the Devil and his minions worked hard to keep it that way. Tonight, Shaman would discuss with Elise his plans to rid himself of the Devil's curse. He had the equipment he needed to reverse the original pact, but it took two to accomplish this and Elise may not agree.

Then he saw her, perched on her tombstone, as young and beautiful as ever. Her long, tawny hair flowing over a gown of floating chiffon, her blue eyes sparkling under black lashes, and her smile—the smile that lit up his world and caused his heart to beat so rapidly he felt a need to hold it still. He placed his hand on his chest to steady the pounding, fearful of its leaving his body. When Elise catches sight of him, she flies to him, arms outstretched, and the two renew their acquaintance.

* * *

Meanwhile, Professor Ipswitch and Harley also have plans of their own for Halloween. They meet the professor's accomplice in the woods behind the professor's cottage. The gnome-shaped little man pulls back some shrubbery and the three enter what appears to Harley to be an oversized rabbit hole. Inside, a vast cold marsh with coiling weeds greets them. Tough snaky growth holds out splintery arms that attempt to grip and trip him—as though ready to pull him into its depths. The place of darkness reminds Harley of Erebus, he of the Underworld on his way to Hades. Moving down the gloomy trail, the three make slow progress, penetrating deep into the forest, the air becoming more and more suffocating until Harvey feels he could scream. The gnome-like little man leads them into an area where trees grow so thick and undergrowth so dense one can scarcely pass through. But the little man locates a path through the overgrown wood, a deeply scooped hollow place running the entire length of the wood. Moving down the gloomy trail, the three make slow progress, seeming to penetrate deeper into the forest.

"Will we ever get out of here?" Harley wonders. He swears he hears thumping sounds overhead. The little man leading the way stops and mumbles something only the Professor can hear. The two look back at Harley. Harley waits while the two make some sort of decision regarding him.

Finally, Professor Ipswitch says, "We have to chance it. He can't do anything. He's powerless out of his own environment." The little man mumbles again, and they continue toward an opening Harley sees in front of them. The little man exits the opening that appears at the edge of a forest. Harley and the professor follow close behind. Beyond the opening, Harley sees a large expanse ahead that appeared to be a graveyard—a very active graveyard—with little people dancing all around, meeting and greeting each other as though at a festival. Hiding at the edge of the forest, the three observers witness the reunion between Shaman and his Elise, and Harley realizes the thumping sound he hears comes from the stomping of the four-in-hand leading Shaman's ancient chariot.

"Where is this place, Professor Ipswitch?" Harley asks, looking around him in amazement. He feels as though he has dropped into another century. Professor Ipswitch says nothing. He's busy viewing the scene transpiring in the graveyard. Even the gnome-like little man seems entirely too engrossed in watching the reunion between Shaman and Elise.

Harley pulls the professor's sleeve. "What do I call him?" Harley asks of the professor, indicating the gnome-like figure in front of them.

"His name is Morgan," said the professor, "A very great magician in the House of Kahn. You can learn a lot from him tonight. Pay attention."

"Morgan, the magician for the King of Tara? How can that be? He existed centuries ago." Harley looks behind him and sees that the entrance has closed.

The professor ignores his question. When he does finally speak, he tells Harley, "Morgan has an exceptional ability to enter and exit past lives. Not only his own, but all souls. I, myself, am privileged to enter once a year because of my acquaintance with the keeper of lost souls."

"Lost souls? Weird," says Harley. "Where are we? Have we traveled back in time?"

"You do not need to know. Tonight, you are here as my guest, but only because I need your assistance."

"My assistance? What would you have me do?" questions Harley. "You appear to be an expert in the field of *Transmogrification*. What are your plans for me?"

"You want the antidote, do you not?" asks the professor turning to Harley. "Where else do you expect to find the source? If you are unwilling to participate in its creation and brewing of the potion, you may never return the way you came."

"I'm not complaining, merely interested. I will continue," says Harley, remembering the whitewashed skulls he'd seen along their path. *Is this my destiny?* The three continue their surveillance of Shaman. For Harley, at least, they are heading into unknown territory.

"He has the power, " Professor Ipswitch advises Harley. "Do not underestimate him. If anyone can bring Gretchen back, it is he. We follow his lead."

"Lead on, I see no other way," agrees Harley fearful he could not find his way back alone.

* * *

"Elise," Shaman says, after the fury of their reunion subsides. "I have a plan for us to be together for all eternity, but I need your help." He takes her by the hand, and leads her to the chariot.

"But your wife and bairns, how can we be together without causing misery to them?" Elise asks, her blue eyes showing her bewilderment.

"Don't be worryin' about that, Elise. Get in," he instructs her, helping her climb onto the high-seated chariot. "We've only one night—lest we need wait another year. I don't know about ye, my dear, but annual visits be not enough for me."

Shaman climbs up beside Elise, and grabs the reins of the four spirited horses. "I have the evocation we need to get out of my pact with the Devil. Remember Professor Ipswitch? Well, he charges me an arm and a leg for the potion, but I had a bit o' good luck—a diamond necklace that accidentally fell into my possession."

He turns to Elise. "It has to work, Elise, my beloved--our last chance to right a wrong. Evil has spread faster than even the Devil believed possible, and he gets lax as he loses control of his minions." He kisses her, and tells her, "It's now or never, Elise."

"Professor Ipswitch?" asked Elise. "Is he the same Professor Ipswitch who sold you the first incantation so many centuries ago?"

"The one and only," Shaman assures her. "I fair went into shock when he entered my Pub, but he didn't appear to recognize me. I have made good use of him because of that. Nevertheless, his evil cannot be allowed to rule our world. He must go. He has infested my life for the last time."

Elise looks at him, her eyes sparkling in understanding, and kisses him on his ruddy cheek. "My darling, I've waited so long for this time. Of course, I will help you, now that I know your heart is true." She checks the packages in the wagon behind them, and asks, "You have everything?"

"I do," he answers. "I've spent days collectin' the required ingredients. Tonight, we rid the Devil of his Power. Let us go." The chariot and *four-in-hand* tear through the iron gates, Elise clutching her lover's waist to keep from falling, and Shaman's strong hands directing the chariot to a deserted barn outside Dublin, the place where it all began.

Halting his team close to the barn, Shaman stares at the structure, dumbfounded by its prime state of repair after so many centuries. He couldn't believe it still survived, untouched by time and elements. *Well, why not? Is it not himself who is the miracle—transported into the Seventeenth Century by the will of the Devil? The barn remains—as it always has—dark and dreary with an aura of Evil.*

Shaman collects the many mysterious packages he brought from the rear of the chariot, and the two enter the barn. He proceeds to arrange the contents according to the instructions of Professor

Ipswitch, remembering a similar scene many centuries ago. Tonight, he would reverse that procedure. Instead of the Devil, he would call forth an Angel to remove the Devil's incantation. Instead of Darkness there would be Light. Shaman lit a glowing fire in the middle of the room—a fire huge enough to reflect a shimmering Light and fill every corner of the room—from floor to rafters.

The scenery set, he fills a basin with sparkling water secured from a nearby brook. He hangs a lantern from an overhead beam in such a way as to reflect on the surface of the water. From his pocket, he pulls out the professor's potion—the very potion that eluded Gretchen and Einstein—and begins to sprinkle it into the water. He repeats an incantation—not the one Professor Ipswitch gave him—but one he believes will reverse Evil. He instructs Elise to do the same.

Spirit whose breath is in the four winds, breathe, breath on me.

Then, from his pack of supplies, he pulls out a bottle of red wine, adds a healthy dose of potion to the wine, and pours the mixture into two glasses. He sets them by the fireside, as he once again digs into his pack of treasures. This time he pulls out a box, and pours its contents onto the roaring fire. The fire flares up—casting orange flames to the ceiling—illuminating brilliant light into every corner of the room.

Shaman picks up one glass of wine from its place on the hearth, and hands it to Elise. Elise hesitates a moment, then accepts the offering, her soft eyes puzzled. Entranced by the proceedings, Shaman glimpses her moment of uncertainty. He hastens to reassure her.

"If we do this right," he tells her, "We will be able to see an Angel. The Angel will speak to us, and tell us how to right the Devil's wrong." He lifts his glass to hers. "Gaze into the water, my dear, as you drink the wine," he instructs her. The two drink of the bitter wine, all the while gazing deeply into the basin of sparkling water.

Then Shaman pulls out two silk shawls from his pack of goodies. One, he drapes lovingly over Elise's entire being. He refills the glasses with the remaining wine, and lifting her shawl hands Elise one of the glasses. He repeats the procedure for himself, wrapping himself in the remaining silk shawl and partaking of the other glass of wine.

"Drink it all," Shaman advises her. "To the last drop, then we wait." Elise does as she is instructed, and the two quaff their second draught as they sit in silence before the roaring fire awaiting the arrival of their Guardian Angel.

Chapter Eleven

Such as we are made of, such we be.
  --Shakespeare

Gretchen follows Julius through the Cat Monger's Cave into a labyrinth of circuitous routes, any of which could cause Gretchen to lose her way, but she follows Julius, confident he knows the way to wherever it is they are heading.

The route they travel reminds her of a haunted house decorated by the PTA to scare the kids on Halloween night, although the cobwebs and bleached skulls she sees along the way are definitely real. The spidery vegetation gives Gretchen an eerie surreal feeling, and she swears some of the foliage moves in uncanny ways as though it had a life of its own. Gretchen moves in silence along the path to *somewhere* with her newfound friends.

Gretchen, twice rescued by her feline friends, feels a kinship to the cat world she never before appreciated. In fact, as a *humanoid*, Gretchen seldom gave cats a second thought, preferring the friendliness of Amber and the dog world to the haughty cat world. She had definitely developed an understanding of how the feline mind worked, and a much deeper appreciation of the cat world since she'd become a feline. Cunning in the ways of survival and independent of *humanoids*, they accepted few of them into their world.

Lost in thought, Gretchen doesn't notice the other cats are far ahead of her. She hurries to catch up and is suddenly faced with a dilemma. There are too many paths, and she can detect no cat trails. There are two likely pathways. Uncertain which path the others took, she panics and begins to meow in her loudest voice.

"Meow, Meow, where are you?" she calls plaintively, and sits down to wait. But no one comes. "Use logic," she tells herself. "You're not a cat, you know." She eyes the two paths before her.

The path in one direction looks too overgrown, the other path, less so. Thinking logically, she chooses the path of least resistance. Surely, the other cats wouldn't attempt the overgrown path. Gretchen didn't know that whichever direction she chose, the path would open up. That her chosen path appeared more open only because she faced it. Moving as fast as she could down the clearer path, Gretchen tries to catch up with her friends. Too late, she realizes she is lost in a cave that has too many scary paths and no exits.

Sniffing the trail, she senses no feline odors, and fears she has chosen the wrong path. "I should have sniffed first," she tells herself, "before I chose a path." She turns around to retrace her steps, but the path has changed direction, leading her to an opening ahead. A bright light glimmers in the distance, and she moves cautiously towards the light, her cat eyes adjusting to the change. Reaching the opening, she peers around the edge to see if the other cats are waiting there for her. Instead of finding her cat friends, Gretchen sees two shrouded figures seated before a roaring fire in a lighted room. No, not a room, more like a medieval barn—complete with a loft filled to capacity with bales of dry hay.

A lantern hangs from a rusty nail above the rafters, casting a strange light onto a vessel of water placed in front of the fire. Engrossed in a world of their own, the shrouded couple does not notice Gretchen. She creeps in closer keeping a wary eye on the two figures sitting in a trance-like state. She sees the vessel of water Shaman has prepared, and feeling thirsty, stops for a drink—trying not to emit the lapping sound cats are wont to do—alert to any movement around her. She drinks her fill from the vessel until she senses movement from under the shawls. She creeps behind the couple looking for an exit. *I don't need another humanoid confrontation tonight.*

Gretchen starts to feel strange, and realizes her cat persona is disappearing. Her paws are now hands, and her tail—gone. *It's the water! It must contain the antidote. It's changing me!* One of the shrouded figures moves, and Gretchen recognizes the exposed face of Shaman. *What is he doing here?* Shaman, seeing Gretchen in her transformed state reflected in the water, believes her to be the Angel he and Elise await. Not wanting to disturb their Angel, he quietly nudges Elise, shushing her to silence.

Gretchen, remembering her experience in Shaman's truck exhibits surprise when Shaman begins to speak reverently to her image in the water. *Shaman is asking me to grant his wish? Asking me to release him from the Devil's curse so he can be with Elise for all eternity?* Amused, she asks Shaman, "What in Heaven's name do you expect from me? You're the one who stole my necklace, and now you want me to grant you your wish? Why ever should I?"

Shaman, continuing to watch the Angel image in the water, answers. "Professor Ipswitch has your necklace, his fee for the potion. I needed the potion to break the Devil's curse, and free Elise and me from eternal life. I didn't know you were an Angel. Please forgive me."

"Professor Ipswitch has my necklace?" asks Gretchen. "You sold my necklace to him in exchange for a potion?"

"And an ancient pistol," he answers. "Here." He pulls the pistol from his tunic pocket. "It has magic bullets to protect its owner in the *Netherworld.*"

"You fell for that old ploy?" Gretchen asks. "That old relic came out of my strawberry patch. It has no magic, and I have no magic, only a stick I picked up by the fire. I can't destroy your curse, but maybe you can."

"How?" asks Shaman, caressing Elise who has returned from her trance and is watching the Angel's reflection in the vessel of water. "You have a plan?"

"Yes, you must find the Magus and his magic drum. He can lead you out of the Devil's lair and the Evil that surrounds you." She lifts her arm to show him she carries only a stick. "See? No magic wand." But the stick has changed. Instead of a stick, she holds a sparkling scepter.

"Where the Devil did you come from?" she asks the scepter. "Oh well," Gretchen says, accepting it as another unexplainable happening in an unaccountable evening. "If I must, I must!" and she waves the wand over Shaman and Elise, remembering somewhere from her fairy tale days that that's how a magic wand works.

Gretchen waits to see what magic the wand has wrought, watching in wonderment as a dense vapor smoke engulfs the room. Through the smoke she sees a vision of Einstein, Julius, and Roscoe viewing the scene. She waves the scepter at them—they appear unfazed by her new persona. "Follow Einstein," she instructs Shaman. "He will lead you through to the other side."

Shaman rises from the fireside, helping Elise do the same. Drawing her close to his side, he tells her, "Come, my dear. Stay close," and leads her to the shield protecting the cats from the *Netherworld*. Elise disappears into the smoke and vapors, but Shaman hits a hard surface. He can't move beyond the shield.

He panics. "I can't make it," he laments turning to face Gretchen. "What shall I do?"

"Get rid of the pistol," Gretchen answers. "Customs, you know." Shaman drops the pistol into the water. It disintegrates, and Shaman disappears into the void.

"Well, what do you know," Gretchen says, stroking the scepter. "It works. Must be my newly acquired feline abilities." She sits down on the hearth, dips the wand into the water, and asks of the wand, "Harley, I have returned. Where are you?"

The barn door swings opens, and Harley, Professor Ipswitch and Morgan, the gnome-like little man, enter the barn. "Where is he?" demands the Professor. "I know he came in here—he and that witch of his." He stops as he sees Gretchen sitting on the hearth, her white, gossamer gown glowing and a sparkling scepter in her hand, looking every bit the angel Shaman conjured with his incantation.

"Is she for real?" he asks Harley, but Harley sees only the Gretchen he knew, not the angel seen by Morgan and the Professor. He starts toward her, but Gretchen motions him to stay away, and apart from Professor Ipswitch and Morgan.

Morgan, knowing instantly what has happened, attempts to creep behind Gretchen, moving towards her as though to push her into the fire. Professor Ipswitch grabs at Gretchen, causing Morgan to lose balance, and the fire swallows up Morgan instead, pulling him to its bosom. A stunned Harley can only watch as Morgan slowly disintegrates in the blazing fire.

"He's all right," the Professor tells Harley. "Fire is his nourishment. You've detained him for only a moment. He'll be back." He turns to Gretchen. "And you, young lady, your power won't last much longer. It's nearly midnight. You must return from whence you came, or be forever trapped in the *Netherworld.*"

Gretchen watches Harley's reaction. "Can you believe that?" she asks him.

"It's Halloween," he says. "Witching hour is nearly over. We must leave before the witches do otherwise we'll be stuck here." Harley checks his watch. "We have fifteen minutes."

In the distance could be heard the drums of Magus in his annual quest to rid the Four Corners of Heaven from Evil. "Come, Harley," Gretchen says. "I can lead you out, but the Professor has to find his own way out."

"Maybe we can make a deal," the Professor appeals to Harley. "You owe me, you know."

"I owe you nothing. Except for you, we wouldn't be here. Why should we help you?"

"I can't go back without you. Please, Gretchen." The Professor pleads knowing his guide no longer existed—Morgan would not revive until after Midnight—too late for him.

But Gretchen isn't listening. She is drawn to an empty bottle discarded by Shaman when he prepared his ritual potion with Elise—the ashes purchased from the proceeds of her necklace. She knew her power had nothing to do with midnight or the witching hour, but lay in some ingredient in that vessel of water—water in which she dipped the stick—the vessel from which she drank.

Secretly, as Harley and the Professor argue deals and terms, she fills the bottle with water from the basin, and slips it into her tunic pocket. She dips the wand into the water once more, tossing the remaining water onto the fire to put it out. But instead of snuffing out the fire, the fire blazes up anew —reaching and engulfing the dry hay in the loft. Panicking, she screams, and Harley, realizing what has happened, grabs Gretchen and races out of the barn.

They pile into Shaman's chariot—the sound of Magus and his drums growing louder in the distance. The *four-in-hand* stomps their impatience, excited by the sounds around them and eager to distance themselves from the fire. Professor Ipswitch hears the drums, too, but his fear of the fire raging in the ancient barn exceeds his fear of Magus, and he opts to join Gretchen and Harley in the chariot. He pushes them aside and takes up the reins himself. The *four-in-hand* tears down the rutted road heading towards the graveyard and he tries to escape Magus who is rapidly closing in on them.

As the chariot nears the *Netherworld* exit, the professor leaps from the wagon and darts towards the opening, blocking the entrance from Gretchen and Harley. "You can't return," he tells the pair behind him. "You are doomed to eternity." Entering the exit from the *Netherworld*, he seals off their escape route. Gretchen waves her wand, but it doesn't work. She is powerless. The escape area remains sealed. Frantic, she remembers the magic water hidden in her tunic pocket, but as she starts to take a drink of the potion, Magus appears before them in all his power and glory. She returns the bottle to the pocket of her gown.

Magus wears a breastplate and helmet of gold. A mantle of blue satin swings from his massive shoulders, and a wide-grooved, blue-hilt sword hangs from his silver-studded girth. A sash, slung around his massive neck, holds a large, purple drum deeply embossed in silver filigree, and in his strong hands drumsticks—made from the dry white bones of a large animal—beat rhythmically and accompany his songs condemning Evil. He commands a horse-drawn carriage as adorned and ornate as he—a team of chargers who barely touched the ground beneath their thundering hooves.

"Magus," Gretchen calls out to him. "Help us. We must return to our world before Midnight. Only you can help us. Professor Ipswitch has deserted us."

"Wave your wand, Gretchen," Magus commands. "Wave your wand."

Gretchen does, and magically the seal breaks open. Magus enters the exit and his long tentacles reach in far enough to reel in Professor Ipswitch. He deposits him in Shaman's chariot, and the *four-in-hand*, eager to do Magus' bidding, charge out of the graveyard—manes and tails flying over galloping hooves—back to the *Netherworld* with their cargo—back to the tomb of all Evil doers.

The Professor, shocked at the sudden turn of events, waves and calls to Harley and Gretchen from the rear of the chariot. "I didn't mean it, Harley. I didn't mean it. We can make a deal—we can make a deal," as the *four-in-hand* races to the ends of the earth.

* * *

Gretchen awakens up the next morning in her own room, Harley sleeping soundly beside her. She looks at her hands, no longer paws, and feels around her neck for her necklace. It's gone. "Did I lose it last night? I know I wore it."

She lies back down on her bed trying to piece together scraps of memory. "I sure don't remember coming home last night. How did I get here?" She thinks about the funny-looking man at Shaman's—Professor Ipswitch he called himself. We talked about a love potion Kristin sells in her shop, and he told me about his newest invention, *Resurrection*.

"Did Harley bring me home? She nudges him, and he arouses sleepily.

"Harley," she says. "I had the strangest dream last night."

* * *

PART 11

THE CAT MONGERS CAVE

TRILOGY TWO

THE CAT MONGER'S CAVE

Chapter One

Let the past be content with itself for man needs forgetfulness as well as memory.

Shaman's Pub crackled with vitality that cold November morning as **Gretchen Dandrich** hurries to meet **Kristin Sanders** at **The Brass Rail,** Kristin's antique shop, for their weekly lunch date at **Shaman's Pub.**

Gretchen had just put the final touches on her new mystery novel that morning. **Harley**, her husband, never bothered to read her stories, using the excuse that he had enough reading to do what with law books, writs, depositions, etc., and didn't have time to wander into realm of fiction. Today, he surprised her by asking to read this one. *Maybe Harley half-believed her strange stories.*

The morning after her dream, Harley had listened—then told her she attached entirely too much significance to a dream. "Forget it," he'd said, dropping the newspaper in his briefcase. "Aren't you meeting Kristin for lunch today?"

"That's Friday," she'd reminded him. Today's Sunday," then noticed he'd dressed for the office. "Isn't it?"

"Hey, I'm the one who was out-of-town all week—working on a case for Dr. Morgan. You were asleep when I came in last night."

Gretchen remembered the look he gave her as she struggled to remember. "Are you all right?" he'd asked.

Now, heading for **The Brass Rail,** that feeling of apprehension returned. *If today is Friday, where have I been all week?* Harley says, *"Forget it, but I can't."* She shook off the feeling. *I'm going to have to spend more time in the real world instead of delving into the supernatural for my book.* She thought about Kristin and their luncheon date, a ritual since their college days and a way to keep up with their varied world. At that time, there'd been three of them—she, Kristin, and Lauren Calloway—rendezvousing at **Shaman's Pub** every Friday. Then, Lauren had taken a job with the FBI and spent most of her time in Washington, DC, seldom returning to Ridgecrest after her parents had died and the old homestead sold. Gretchen missed her.

Shaman held court at his Pub for his many customers in the small village of Ridgecrest, Connecticut, and rumors abounded of his having wandered the world for centuries. Shaman didn't mind the rumors, and neither accepted nor rejected the fantasies that followed in his wake.

"Great for business," he would say, the sum total of his comments.

Ming, his Siamese cat, and Einstein, her newly acquired mate, seemed part of the mystic his Pub attracted. Shaman left it to the imagination of his customers to determine the authentic from the fantasy, but everyone agreed his two Siamese cats knew more than anyone suspected of his past lives. Harley and Shaman—a odd combination of personalities—developed a strange sort of rapport. Gretchen wrote them both into her mysteries—about Shaman and his Irish folk tales—recreating his stories and intertwining them with weird memories of her subconscious dreams.

Gretchen sees Kristin entering the Pub as she rounds the last corner, and calls to her, but Kristin doesn't hear and continues into the Pub. As Gretchen enters, she finds her engrossed in reading the headlines of the *Hartford Courier,* a courtesy copy Shaman keeps on the counter for his customers. Gretchen stares at the headlines over her shoulder, and her blood chills as she sees the picture and caption:

Who Is He? Her hair crawls up her scalp as she recognizes **Morgan,** the fantasy creature of her dreams. It *can't be.*

"What's wrong, Gretchen," asks Kristin, observing her friend's ashen face. "You look as though you've seen a ghost."

"I think I have—that man—I dreamed about him."

"Sure you did, Gretchen." Kristin laughs. "Come back to reality, you're still in your fantasy world."

"You're probably right," Gretchen says. *I feel as though I've been on a weird LSD trip—completely detached from this world.* She shakes off the weird feeling. As she glances around Shaman's totally Irish Pub, a replica of Seventeenth Century Ireland, reality begins to take shape. *I'm in* **Shaman's Pub.** *Shaman tends bar—his customers clamor to hear his wild Irish tales of sorcery and witchcraft—I've got to stop this nonsense.* As the reality of the Pub takes over, she relaxes.

The two select a booth, and Kristin puts aside the newspaper, changing the subject. "Did you try the potion I gave you?" she asks after Shaman takes their order and brings them their wine.

"Not yet. Harley's having it analyzed. He's as curious as I am about that secret ingredient. Professor Ipswitch refuses to tell him what it is—*his own secret recipe, he says.*"

"Can't blame the Professor," Kristin says. "That recipe might be worth its weight in gold—if it does what he claims it does."

"No doubt." Gretchen sips her wine, drifting away from the subject at hand, and wondering how much of her crazy dream to tell Kristin.

"Something's on your mind." Kristin says. "What is it?"

Gretchen pulls herself out of her daydream and grins. "Do you read minds?" she asks.

"I know you. Remember?"

"I worry about me sometimes," Gretchen says. "I woke up this morning and swore it was Sunday. What happened to my week? Scares me."

"I know," Kristin says. "Sometimes, I have days like that, too."

She takes a sip of her wine before she says, "I dreamed about Magus last night."

"The power of suggestion?" Kristin amuses, wondering where Gretchen drifts off to in her reveries. "How do you do that?"

"Do what?"

"Disappear—into a world of your own, I suppose. Maybe that's how your week disappeared. You do it quite often, you know. Is it because you're a writer?"

"Maybe. I don't know. Tell me about Magus. I think I met him last night, too."

"Wow, you do lead a fantastic life."

They dig into Shaman's special Irish soup and order another glass of wine while Kristin begins her story of Magus. "It's an ancient Irish fairy tale. You've probably already heard it since Shaman has told the story many times. According to legend, Magus had enormous powers. Some folks swear he really exists. It all started in Central Asia—back in the days when old hags performed horrible witchcraft practices—like loitering around graveyards and hanging trees, and gathering up body fragments and rotting limbs of the dead. They would burn the pieces of flesh and use the ashes in their rituals. Some of the potions they used as punishment for the damned—with weird consequences—such as turning people into some form of animal."

"Animals?" Gretchen's eyes widen. "Ashes of dead people?" She glances at Einstein, suddenly aware of his intense interest in the story and recognizing his stance from her dream—ears in alert mode while appearing disinterested. He turns away—an abrupt snub. Kristin stops talking, surprised at the interruption and byplay.

"You okay," she asks. Gretchen nods and turns her attention back to Kristin who continues, "The witches use the ashes of the dead to create mysterious potions and use them to attract the Devil."

"Why attract the Devil? Didn't they have enough troubles?"

"Because, as the legend goes, the Devil appears to anyone who knows how to create the special ashes and chant his specific incantation. When the ashes are scattered on water, it attracts the Devil. He's the only one with the power to grant wishes for eternal physical existence. In those days, people liked the idea of living forever, and kept the

Devil busy performing his rituals and muttering his incantations. Sort of like our modern day shrink except Magus also had the power to perform sacrifices and exorcise evil. He'd alert people of his presence by beating a magic drum and singing his magic songs —chasing the Devil out of the four corners of Heaven. Can't you just envision it?"

Aloud, Gretchen comments, remembering the Magus of her dream. "I'm sure he had his hands full." *I've got to get over feeling that my dream wasn't a dream.*

"Be that as it may, Magus held sway over his own legions of guardians—both good and bad. They assisted him in his quest to dispel Evil, and he spent his days crying out against the Devil and chanting his incantation, *Spirit whose breath is in the four winds, breathe, breathe on me.*

Gretchen shudders. "The incantation on the love potion you gave me."

"The very one. Good and evil never changes, does it? I hope Harley gets the potion analyzed. I'd love to know what's in it."

"I think I drank some of that water, Kristin. Maybe that's why I lost a week of my life."

Kristin laughs aloud, startling the two cats on the hearth. "You really take these legends seriously, don't you?"

Gretchen is not amused. "You don't understand. I've been there."

"Sure you have," Kristin hastens to assure her. She reaches across the table, and pats her hand. "We'll figure it out. I doubt you've lost track of time—probably had one of your out-of-body experiences." She smiles. "You know what I mean—one of your subconscious nighttime wanderings."

"You're teasing me."

"Maybe. I'm more inclined to believe someone slipped you a Mickey last Saturday night."

"Or, maybe I really did *morph* into a cat," Gretchen laughs, then becomes serious. "You're right, Kristin, there's usually a logical answer."

"Sure there is. But enough of Magus, I want to hear about this mysterious dream of yours."

Gretchen relates the highlights of her dream—from the time she met Harley at Shaman's 'til she woke up in her own bed. As she talks, she notices Einstein paying particular heed to her words, listening intently. As she ends her story, Kristin sits back and looks at her friend in disbelief.

Kristin grins. "You witnessed a murder?" Her grin widens. "As a cat?"

"You're laughing. You don't believe me." she draws back.

"I didn't say that." She picks up the newspaper she'd tossed aside earlier. "You didn't read this?" she asks. "Your dream made page one."

"You mean that picture?"

"The article." Kristin reads the article accompanying the picture that had startled Gretchen when she first entered the Pub.

> Police are trying to solve a mystery surrounding the death of an unidentified body found under the old highway overpass entering the town. A search for the murder weapon is being conducted. Anyone knowing the identity of the victim is asked to contact the local police department.
>
> Police believe the murder occurred sometime during the night of October 31, and may have been a prank that went awry. The victim is male Caucasian, about five feet, two inches, and has a noticeable humpback.

"No wonder Harvey warned me not to get involved," Gretchen says.

"But if you know where the murder weapon is, Gretchen, you need to tell the police."

"How can I? Harley calls it my *loony-tunes* defense, and says if I say anything, I may wind up being the accused."

"He's probably right." Kristin laughs. "*Loony-tunes*, that's funny."

"I'm glad you're amused. Harley thinks I should see a shrink."

"Really? Now, that's serious." Kristin looks at her empty glass, signals to Shaman, and requests a refill. Shaman brings the wine, and clears away the empty dishes.

Gretchen looks puzzled. "You think it's amusing and Harley thinks I've flipped."

Kristin concentrates on the wine in her glass. She takes a sip, looks at Gretchen, and turns serious. "You know, before we get too caught up in this, we might do a little advance sleuthing on our own. Then, if we turn up anything worth reporting—that is, if we locate the weapon—we can bring Roscoe in on it."

Gretchen perks up. "Hmm-m-m, that sounds logical. Not even Harley could object."

Kristin laughs. "Does he need to know?" The two chuckle as Gretchen gets into the mood.

"Do you think we can swing it?"

"Why not? There are people with psychic powers—those who see things others can't. We could tell the police you're a psychic. She grins. "Maybe you could become a phantom sleuth."

"Phantom sleuth," Gretchen muses. "I like that."

The two silently sip their wine, deep in thought. Kristin toys with her glass. "They don't have to know the particulars," she says suddenly turning serious.

"You mean, if my dream has any validity."

"You don't want me to come across as a *loony-tunes*, too, do you?"

Gretchen laughs. "Would it bother you?"

"Of course not. I've been accused of worse." Choosing her words carefully, Kristin says, "Look, I will talk to Roscoe. He could use a good lead. As far as the police know, the guy's a transient."

Gretchen glances up as Professor Ipswitch enters the Pub, taking his usual position at the end of the bar. She stares at him as though seeing him for the first time. Kristin turns to see what caught her interest.

"Why do I feel there's something evil about that man?" Gretchen asks.

"You're letting your dream influence you—Professor Ipswitch is Magus' bad guy," Kristin reminds her.

"You're right. Shaman's the one who stole my necklace and traded it for a gun—and a potion to use on Elise."

Kristin laughs. "Why not check with Shaman? Maybe he found your necklace."

"It's a dream, Kristin."

"But you did lose it, didn't you? She catches Shaman's eye as he approaches their table. "Shaman," she asks. "Gretchen seems to have misplaced her necklace. She didn't leave it here, did she?"

"Well, you know, come to think o' it, some gent did bring in a bauble he found in the parking lot. I'll get it for you. Might be the one."

Trudging back to the bar, he returns carrying a necklace. "The clasp's broken, but with a little fixin' and cleanin' it'll be good as new."

Gretchen thanks him, and vows to take it in for repair before she loses it again.

"So much for my dream," she tells Kristin. "We probably won't find the murder weapon, either. Time to get back to reality."

Kristin agrees. "The legend of Magus hardly belongs in the Twenty-first Century."

"I agree, but you know—it was rather fun being a cat," says Gretchen as she pockets the necklace.

"Who knows, maybe you were, Gretchen. Maybe you were."

* * *

Chapter Two

There are none so deaf as those who won't hear.

Kristin did call Sergeant Baguette as promised. When she tells him about Gretchen and her psychic experience, without divulging her psychic's name, he laughs. Then explains, "You know, Kristin, police attempt to use psychics in many of their cases. Some prove to be valid, but most of them have no basis in fact because they're too vague. Psychics see symbols, but usually have no earthly idea how to read the symbols they profess to see—and location is usually nebulous. It's a miracle if psychics and police actually team up and create useable evidence."

"But it does happen, doesn't it?" Kristin argues. "Maybe this is one of those times."

"I doubt it. Whoever your psychic friend is, humor her, but don't involve the police. We tend to be leery of psychics."

"Not the police—you." Kristin says. "If we locate anything, will you help us?"

"That depends on what you find. So far, you've given me nothing solid to work on, and I have no intention of following up on some psychic's meandering into an ethereal world."

"Maybe it does sound like a chase down the *yellow brick road*, Roscoe, but I really think you should check this one out."

"What makes this psychic so special?" he asks. "Give me a good reason for going along with your crazy scheme."

"Because I'm asking—you don't have to tell anyone. 'Course if you're afraid of being teased by the boys at the station…" Kristin teases.

"That's enough. What do you have in mind?" Roscoe asks.

"I've a plan."

"Why doesn't that surprise me? Okay, what is it?"

"I thought we could plan a picnic by the scene of the crime, and sort of casual-like check out that cache Gretchen dreamed up?"

"Gretchen? You mean she's your psychic—the one married to that attorney fellow? My God! Don't get me involved with any attorneys."

Realizing her mistake, Kristin panics. "Don't hang up, Roscoe. I'm sorry. I guess I blew it, but it's not what you think. Harley isn't in on this, just Gretchen. All I ask is that you listen to her story. Please, Roscoe, give her a chance. I'm convinced she really did witness your murder, and you don't have any other leads."

Roscoe relents, a sucker for anything Kristin wants, "Okay, Kristin, set it up, but no attorney."

Kristin grins. *All right!*

* * *

Later that day, at Kristin's bidding, Gretchen retells her dream sequence to Sergeant Baguette. Feigning contempt for venturing into someone else's dream world—although in some deep recess of his mind he deemed his *sixth sense*—Sergeant Baguette convinces himself that this clandestine rendezvous might uncover something of value. In his world, stranger things happen. If nothing else, his uncertainty did need satisfying. Roscoe consoled himself into believing that this little venture might even be therapeutic for Gretchen. She seemed in an absolute state of confusion, according to Kristin, in trying to decide if her dream is prophetic or mere wishful thinking. Regardless of the ribbing he might expect from his fellow cops, he decides to satisfy his curiosity.

Later, as Gretchen talks to Roscoe, she deliberately withholds information about her journey into the *Netherworld* as a cat and her conversion to angel status. Kristin nixed that part of the dream—concerned Roscoe might pull out. Besides, after that incident yesterday she doubted her own sanity. When Gretchen returned home after telling her tale to Roscoe she tried to discuss her visit with Harley, but he *didn't want to hear about it.*

Amber enters her doggie door and places her head on her lap, looking up at her with sympathetic brown eyes. Gretchen ruffles her shaggy fur. "You understand don't you, Amber? You were there." Giving Amber a final pat, she heads upstairs. *Maybe a shower will clear my head.* Under the relaxing spray of the shower, she reviews the past week. *Harley says, "Forget it," but I can't. I've got to find out.*

That's when Gretchen decides to return to the scene of the crime. *I don't know what I expect to find.* She finishes dressing, grabs her car keys, and heads for the overpass. Leaving her car in the parking lot by the bridge, she walks towards the overpass—reminiscing how Roscoe and Einstein tossed the knife in the Cat Monger's Cave. She sees Julius sunning himself on the grass. She walks towards him, and he raises his head and watches her approach. She sits beside him on the grass.

"I lost you the other night, Julius, you and the other cats. I must have taken the wrong path. It led me *somewhere* into a barn. Did you know where the cave would lead us?" she asks the black cat, wondering if he understood.

"You took the path to the *Netherworld*," Julius transmits to her in cat language. "We do not go there." Gretchen is surprised that she understood him. She continues her questioning.

"Did you let me lose my way deliberately?" she asks.

"You needed to go there to get the antidote."

"Did you know Shaman would be there?"

"Yes, Shaman isn't a bad guy. He explained his activities to us when he came through the shield, but we couldn't reach you. We had to find you another way out. I see you made it. Are you all right?"

"Yes, but I'm having difficulty understanding the time lapse." Gretchen looks around hoping no one sees her talking to a cat. "I'm beginning to feel foolish," she tells Julius. "Not knowing how to explain my actions for a week. What shall I do?"

"You'll think of something. We'll help if we can."

"I'm not so sure of that. Einstein ignored me at the Pub yesterday."

"That's because you were with one of them," he explains.

"Would you get the knife for me?" Gretchen asks.

"The knife? What knife?"

"The one in the Cat Monger's Cave—the murder weapon. You do remember, don't you?"

Julius places his paw on her hand, reminiscent of her days as a cat, and ignores her question. "Maybe we could meet on the chaise tonight and discuss old times?"

"Why you old fox!" she accuses him, cuffing his head with her hands and placing a kiss between his ears. "The knife? You'll get it for me?"

Julius turns serious. "What did you do with the antidote, Gretchen?"

"I don't know. I must have lost it on the way home, but that's all right. I don't need it any more. I'm my old self," she assures him. " Will you help me get the knife, Julius?"

"I don't believe that is wise," Julius transmits. "All is not as it appears," he warns.

Gretchen gives up, and returns to her car. *I wonder what he means—all is not as it appears.* She shakes off the intangible feeling of having reentered the *Netherworld,* and scolds herself. *What does he know? He's only a cat. I'm probably dreaming again.*

Saturday morning in the light of day, she'd nearly forgotten her visit with Julius. Harley had gone to the office before Kristin and Roscoe arrived —dressed in their oldest digs. Gretchen doubted he'd be back before they left on their excursion. She decided not to tell them of her recent visit to the overpass. *They'll think I really do need a shrink. Even I can't believe I actually talked 'cat talk' with Julius.*

Armed with a variety of tools and a hamper of goodies, they pack the trunk of Roscoe's beat-up Chevy Blazer. As luck would have it, Harley unexpectedly returns from his office as they were loading the car. Unable to get into his driveway, and curious about the strange-looking automobile blocking his entry to the garage, he calls to Gretchen, "What's going on? You heading somewhere?"

"We're going on a picnic," she tells him with her usual candor. "They're going to help me find the murder weapon. You're welcome to come along, but please don't try to stop me."

"Oh, no, not now," she hears Roscoe and Kristin groan.

"Hi, Kristin," Harley says. "Sergeant Baguette. What's up?"

Roscoe shrugs, and before he can speak, Gretchen interrupts.

"They're helping me recreate my dream," she tells Harley.

Harley looks concerned. "Are you sure you're up to this?" he asks Gretchen.

"I'm all right." Gretchen looks to Kristin and Roscoe for confirmation.

"Wouldn't it be better if you talked to Dr. Morgan?" Harley continues to press her.

"No, " she says. "We're making an outing out of it—a picnic—you don't have to go, you know. It's your choice, but please don't try to stop me."

"I understand—I think," he reassures her as he folds his lanky frame into the back seat of the Blazer next to Gretchen. He looks at Roscoe, and shrugs. "I won't say anything to your cop friends, Roscoe, if you don't spread this around my office."

"It's a deal," Roscoe agrees, breathing easier and thinking Harley a real good sport about the whole venture. "At least," Roscoe tells Harley, "The food will be great, whether we find anything or not."

"Do you expect to?" asks Harley of Roscoe.

"Not really," Roscoe grins. "It's a long shot, but I'm stalled in my investigation. Sort of hope we do find something. I need answers. So far, I've only got questions."

The ride was short—the town wasn't that big—and arriving at the crime scene, the four find a grassy knoll near the overpass. Gretchen and Kristin spread out the picnic lunch. Harley and Roscoe watch a soft ball game going on in the open field. Then, amidst small talk and banter, they eat their fill of Boston Fried Chicken and Kristin's crunchy potato salad. They finish off with ice-cold lemonade from the cooler, and the two men discuss how best to play out the next scene. Gretchen and Kristin offer intermittent suggestions making the occasion appear both festive and intriguing. The game over, the boys and cars disappear and Gretchen leads them to the entrance of the Cat Monger's Cave.

"You do the honors, Roscoe," Harley suggests as Gretchen points out the cache where the cats keep their trophies. "I'm not dressed for digging, but I'll supervise."

"Spoken like a true attorney," Roscoe comments, checking out Harley's expensive cord slacks and cashmere sweater in sharp contrast to denim jeans worn by the others. He gathers up his equipment—a long pole with a hook on one end—and follows Gretchen to the cache under the overpass. Harley and Kristin follow, quietly watching the proceedings.

"Don't disturb anything else, Roscoe," Gretchen says. "I don't want Einstein mad at me. We only want the knife. It's in a plastic grocery bag."

Roscoe glances at her, and shakes his head. Then, crawling on his belly to the spot Gretchen indicates—the exact spot she entered as a cat for her Halloween trip—Roscoe angles the pole into the opening, pushing weeds away from his face. He tries to ignore the flying insects looping around his head as though buzzing their resentment to the invasion of their territory.

"What I don't do for money," he says, and despite his discomfort, begins bringing various objects to the surface.

"I'm almost afraid to look," Gretchen says to Kristin and Harley as she recognizes bits and pieces of cat memorabilia falling around Roscoe as he brings them out one by one to the surface.

"A plastic bag, you say?" Roscoe asks, rummaging through the collection of items around him. "Well, I'll be damned," she hears him say, "I can't believe this—it is here."

Roscoe drags out a plastic sack from his collection and it contains a knife. Separating it from the other trophies, he returns the rest of the cat collection to the cave. Then, sliding backwards, he crawls out from under the overpass, clutching the evidence in one hand and his pole in the other hand.

"If this isn't the craziest thing I've ever seen!" He looks at Gretchen with renewed respect. "A dream, h-m-m?"

"Will she need an attorney, Roscoe?" Kristin asks.

Startled, Gretchen turns to Harley, "Oh, no, Harley. You told me to let it go, but I was so sure—like the necklace—there'd be a logical explanation."

Sergeant Baguette smiles. "Don't worry, Gretchen. This knife may have been here for years—another time, another murder—that your dream keyed in on. Let's get it to ballistics first to check for identifiable prints. You didn't touch it, did you?"

Gretchen shakes her head. "No, Roscoe nosed it," she tells him.

"Roscoe?" Sergeant Baguette asks.

"A cat—Kristin's—oh, no!" Gretchen says, making the connection. "I didn't think... You were all in my dream—you, Kristin, Professor Ipswitch, Shaman, Harley.... Oh dear, it *is* a dream"

Sergeant Baguette shakes his head. "That's enough—I don't want to know any more." Then, catching her apprehensive mood, he quickly reassures her. "It's way too early to jump to conclusions. There may be no fingerprints—or the bloodstains won't match the victim...."

"But what if it does check out?" asks Gretchen.

Harley laughs. "You'd be a phantom sleuth, my dear--famous the world over—television shows—talk shows—maybe asked to write a book about your adventures—all the notoriety accorded a celebrity. Think you could handle it?"

"I'm glad this amuses you, Harley, but it's my head on the chopping block."

She watches Roscoe transfer the knife in a clean police bag, taking care not to touch it. "Come on, we're through here. Let's roll. I'm anxious to see what we have." He directed his part in the job over. Anxious to leave, he drops a puzzled Harley and a perplexed Gretchen off at their home.

Monday morning, Sergeant Baguette arrives early at the station house, registering the knife in as police evidence. He asks the police lab to dust the knife for prints, and requests that the medical examiner to analyze the stains on the knife. Then he returns to the station house—to the ribbing of his buddies.

"A psychic, h-m-m? Where'd you dig up a psychic in this neck of the woods?" his buddies tease. "You been nippin' a few too many at Shaman's?" Roscoe takes his teasing with jolly good English humor. While he waits for results, he decides to question a few of the people Gretchen targeted in her tale to Kristin. He decides to start with Shaman.

Entering the Pub, he settles himself at the end of the bar, appraising the Irish décor of the famed establishment. Shaman reigned supreme behind the solid mahogany counter, with an array of unusual bottles lining the wall on the rear. Some of the names on the bottles, Roscoe had never heard—not even from his many visits to English Pubs in the old country, but they seemed at place in Shaman's Irish Pub.

"What can you tell me anything about the night of October 31st?" he asks the gregarious bartender. "Where were you between the hours of six and nine?"

"Huh?" Shaman stammers, eyeing Roscoe in awe. "Me? Why, I suppose I be right here, tendin' my customers. Why?"

"Anything unusual happen that night?"

"No, don't know as it did. What's this all about?"

"I'm investigating a murder that occurred that night," Roscoe tells him. "And I'm talking to anyone who might know anything. Your Pub seems like a good place to start."

"Ya' don't say. Why's that?" Shaman continued to clean the spotless counter.

"Bartenders tend to hear things…"

"Oh? Is that so? And you want to know what I hear, eh?"

"Yeah, something like that. Can you tell me if anything out of the ordinary happened that night?"

"No, don't recollect nothin'—a few strange customers, maybe—that's to be expected on Halloween, I guess."

"How strange?" Roscoe asks.

Shaman shakes his head, "They be comin' in from all over—lookin' for treats—bar treats."

"You heard nothing unusual?" Roscoe presses for more.

"No-o-o," Shaman drawls. "Had one strange episode, but it had nothin' to do with my customers…"

"What's that?"

"A fight in the parking lot."

"A fight? What time?"

"Early—couple a' guys trying to catch a cat out in the alley. Weirdest thing—fightin' over a cat."

"The cat worth anything? A reward or something?"

"Not in my book, but the Professor seemed pretty interested in this particular white cat. 'Had a diamond-studded collar,' someone said. Could be the collar they were fighting over. Never knew cats to wear diamonds, but ya' never know—not in this day."

"A diamond collar, eh? That's what the fight was about? Who wound up with the cat?" Roscoe asks, writing a notation in his book.

"I've no idea." Shaman turns back to washing glasses behind the bar.

"Did you know them?"

"No, didn't see 'em. Just heard the talk," Shaman says, stacking clean glasses on the shelf behind him.

"The Professor? Ever ask him about his interest in that particular cat?"

"Nope. I mind my own business." He turns around. Roscoe looks at the man's back and knows the conversation is over. He leaves the Pub.

A cat with a diamond collar—wonder if anyone caught the cat. He heads for the university chemistry lab to check the next man on his list, Professor Ipswitch, the man Shaman said expressed an interest in a particular white cat. Roscoe remembers Kristin mentioning a professor who created some ancient concoction that she sells in her gift shop. Maybe it's the same one.

He heads for the university and learns that the laboratory is on the top floor of the main building. *Why are laboratories always on the top floor?* Reaching his destination after the long climb up steep steps, he parks himself at the top to catch his breath. *I'm getting out of shape. It's no wonder college kids stay so damned skinny—climbing stairs like these all day long.* He sniffs the air. *Damned stinky up here.*

He enters the laboratory, and sees one lone, white-coated individual bent over a beaker, eyedropper in hand, dripping a solution into a beaker a drop at a time. Occasionally, the man stopped long enough to make a notation in a notebook next to him, then continued watching the beaker.

Roscoe watches the man until he puts down the eyedropper, and places his hands on the edge of the counter, staring down into the beaker. He takes off his glasses, rubs his eyes, and returns the glasses to his angular-shaped nose, continuing to stare at the bubbling beaker as though expecting it to do something unusual. Roscoe approaches, waiting patiently until the man noticed him and turned around.

"Can I help you?" the man in the white coat asks Roscoe.

"I hope so. What is that you're mixing?"

"Something someone asked me to analyze. There's supposed to be some secret ingredient in it—so the guy says—and I'm trying to figure out what it is."

"Have you?" Roscoe asks.

"Yes, and no. I've isolated something, but can't categorize it. Seems to be some strange form of LSD, but what type is still a mystery." Frustrated, he turns to Roscoe. "What can I do for you?"

"LSD on a college campus. That is news," Roscoe says.

"Yeah, I know," says the lab assistant. "This one's a different strain, though. Nothing I've seen here before." He looks at Roscoe. "You're not here because of this, are you?"

"No, I'm looking for a Professor Ipswitch. I'll settle for anyone who can tell me something about him. Do you know him?"

"Sure, who wants to know?" the technician asks.

"Sergeant Baguette from the Ridgecrest Police Department," Roscoe says to the man, flashing his badge. "We're conducting an investigation into a recent murder. You've probably heard about it."

"Yeah, I have. The professor mixed up in it?"

"Not that I know of—just need to ask him a few questions."

The lab technician turns from his beaker and faces Roscoe. "Professor Ipswitch does some research work for the government—disease control, I believe. Don't know what he's working on right now. His partner tells me he's discovered some kind of youth potion."

"That's interesting. The partner or the professor?"

"The partner, I presume. Says he has proof positive it works. The professor plans on writing it up for the next Medical Review Journal. That who you're looking for?"

Roscoe ignores his question, and asks, "Where can I find this partner?"

"Check with Professor Ipswitch. You passed his cottage down by the gate," the technician says. "He's probably there. Let him tell you about his partner. I've never seen him—just talked to him on the phone."

The lab technician turns back to his beaker. "If you don't find him there, you might check Shaman's Pub. Professor hangs around there a lot."

"Thanks," says Roscoe. "Hope you isolate the magic ingredient and make a million."

The technician laughs. "Don't I wish," he says, and continues staring in the beaker.

Roscoe wanders back down the path toward the cottage, passing the forest where the professor, Harley, and Morgan entered. He feels a cold dampness as he passes and shivers. Reaching the cottage, he locates the professor out back—engrossed in stirring some mixture in a black kiln with a fireplace poker. An odor of singed wet feathers fills the air.

"Weird," Roscoe thinks, approaching the little man with the spiked hair and octagon-shaped glasses. "What are you making?" he asks.

"Ashes," the professor answers continuing to stir the foul smelling contents of the kiln. *Ask a stupid question . . .*

"My fortune is in these ashes," the professor says, and turns to look at Roscoe. "Do I know you?" he asks.

"Sergeant Baguette with the Ridgecrest police. I need to ask you a few questions."

"Shoot," says Professor Ipswitch.

"I'm investigating a murder that occurred this past week. Know anything about it?" Roscoe asks.

"Nope. Should I?" The professor returned to stirring the burning embers.

"I'll ask the questions, sir," Roscoe says. "That's the way it's done. Where were you between the hours of six and nine, the night of October 31st?"

"Right here. Oh, I did go by the Pub earlier, but I was back by six," he answers quickly, his eyes darting up the path toward the forest.

"Anyone verify that for you?"

"No, I work alone."

"You have an associate, do you not?"

"No, I work alone," he repeats. "My inventions are my own. I share them with no one."

"Then it's not true you have a partner?"

The professor faces Roscoe, poker in hand. "When you find proof of that, let me know." He shakes the poker in his face, and Roscoe backs up.

"Careful," he says. "Maybe you'd like to come down to the station and take a polygraph test?"

"Why should I?" the professor asks.

"So we can remove you from our suspect list, and get on with the investigation," Roscoe says, eyeing the poker in front of him.

"You put it that way, I'll be glad to," says the Professor, turning back to his ashes. "How's ten in the morning?" he offers.

"Suits me," Roscoe says. He leaves the professor stirring his ashes.

When Roscoe returns to his office, he's greeted with smirks and snide looks of amusement from his fellow cops. When he sits down at his desk, he understands. His entry into the evidence room has been returned with a note attached: "The evidence contained herein does not add anything of value to the case in question. Not only is it devoid of any blood stains, but stab wounds in the victim do not match. Conclusion, Sergeant Baguette, you've been had." And signed by the medical examiner.

"So much for psychics," Roscoe says, under his breath, reaching for the telephone to call Gretchen.

Chapter Three

"Quit worrying about the knife, Gretchen," Roscoe tells her when he calls. "It isn't the murder weapon. Evidently it's been under that bridge for years." Gretchen took the news calmly, and decides to take Julius up on his offer to meet on the chaise lounge behind her house. She keeps a sharp eye out for him all that day and about eight o'clock that evening sees him skulking long the garden fence watching the house. She puts on her coat and goes outside to join him.

"What did you do with the knife, Julius?" she asks. "Did you switch it?"

"You didn't do as I asked," Julius replies. "I told you things are not as they seem. You know who the suspects are. They've made a mistake."

"I can't do this alone, Julius," Gretchen pleads. "I trust my friends. They help me."

Julius flips his tail at Gretchen, and jumps onto the fence. He turns to look at her, his tail up and rigid, a stance that Gretchen knew meant *Get moving*.

"Get moving on what?" she asks, but Julius is already gone, disappearing over the back fence, leaving Gretchen to figure out what he meant. She lies back onto the chaise. "Does that mean Kristin and Harley are suspects?"

Later that day at Shaman's, Roscoe tosses his notepad onto the table in front of Kristin. "You're not telling me everything," he accuses her. "It all points to you—*Heaven-Scent,* Professor Ipswitch, Gretchen,

Harley—you were even the instigator of that wild goose chase we went on last Saturday."

"Whatever do you mean? Kristin hedges. "There's nothing else."

"Why don't I believe you?"

"Because you're a cop. You suspect everyone," she says. "I can't imagine how I can help you without having my own psychic visions," she teased.

"Don't be facetious. What do you know about a partner—an associate—or whatever he's called," Roscoe probes. "Have you ever seen the professor's partner?"

"No, I haven't." Kristin glares at Roscoe. "Professor Ipswitch only talks of his own inventions. He has someone to help with research. He never mentions a partner."

"Did Gretchen ever meet him?"

"The partner? I don't know—maybe in her dreams. Not for real. Why?"

"As long as I'm knee deep in the occult, I may as well dive in headfirst. Tell me the rest of the dream."

"No, you'll have to ask Gretchen for that, Roscoe. I won't tell you." Her voice changes as she notices his defeat. "Look, she's trying to get her life back on an even keel. Harley watches her like a hawk—afraid she'll go off the deep end. If you talk to her, be careful."

"I know. That's why I'm asking you, Kristin. As a friend, she talks to you."

"I can't do that. I promised."

"You'd rather see a murderer go free?"

"You got his fingerprints, didn't you?"

"That's what I mean by *wild goose chase*, Kristin. The knife we found has never been near a murder scene. It's an everyday, ordinary knife—used by movers to open packing crates."

"The stains?"

"Paint. Kristin, if you won't tell me, I'll have to ask Gretchen and I don't want to do that. What can you tell me about the missing associate?"

Kristin looks down at her coffee cup, and shakes her head. "Nothing."

"Look, Kristin," Roscoe continues, "I went back up the hill again to talk to the lab assistant and he couldn't even give me a name. He's never seen the guy."

"A silent partner? Is he the dead man, do you think?"

"That's how I figure it. No one knows him. No one's seen him, and no one can identify him."

"The perfect murder," laughs Kristin. "What a kick."

"You laugh, but that's how it looks. Unless I learn more, someone committed the perfect murder." Roscoe looks dejected, and Kristin takes pity on him.

"Gretchen saw the dead man, but didn't recognize him—only seemed relieved it wasn't Harley. Then she hid the knife—afraid Harley did it. That's crazy though, isn't it?"

"So it seems. You say Gretchen was missing a week, then turns up at home unable to remember anything except that she witnessed a murder. She professes to know where the murder weapon is, but can't identify the killer. And the knife we find turns out not to be the murder weapon." Kristin looks sympathetic. "That's all there is?" asks Roscoe.

"No, she remembers being a cat, and seeing all kinds of things—but as a cat, Roscoe. She refuses to believe her dream and the murder are connected. You jumped to that conclusion."

"But you know they are, don't you?" Roscoe continues to dig.

Kristin grins, amused. "This case is really getting to you, isn't it?"

"Yes, maybe there's something she's forgetting. I need to find out what it is. Can you set up a sort of casual meeting, Kristin?"

"Okay, that I can do," she agrees, adding facetiously, "but it will cost you."

He grins. "That I can handle. Whatever you ask—consider it done."

"We're having lunch Friday at Shaman's. Care to join us?" Kristin invites.

"I'll be there."

"Better keep an open mind. Gretchen is like no other. You might even begin to agree with Harley."

Roscoe leaves, and Kristin plots. *Won't do for Gretchen to tell Roscoe too much—he's too sharp—and I'm not too certain about her state of mind, either.*

* * *

"Roscoe thinks there's something you're not telling him. He's fit to be tied," Kristin accuses Gretchen. "And I'm beginning to think you made it up, too."

"You give me too much credit. I don't have *that* much imagination. And you *know* I can't tell him *all* my dream," Gretchen argues.

"We have to give him something to go on—something that won't implement Harley or make him suspect you."

"Kristin, you're smarter than me. What do you suggest?"

And Kristin has it figured all out. "If we play the game right, Gretchen, we could make a fortune."

"How do you mean?"

"If there's some way we could get hold of the secret recipe, we could mix it." Kristin looks absolutely elated. "That's a motive for murder, you know—that recipe. And if Professor Ipswitch gets nailed for the murder… Gretchen, can you imagine how much we could rake in if we had control of that recipe?"

And Gretchen, suspicious of Kristin's motives for the first time, remembers Julius' warning. *Maybe Julius is right. She is involved.* "Tell me you're not serious, Kristin. You wouldn't try to capitalize on this, would you?"

"Of course not," Kristin sighs, noticing her concern. She hastens to reassure her, "I'm only trying to help Roscoe solve his case without throwing suspicion on the rest of us."

"You're sure that's all it is?"

"Oh, come on, Gretchen, don't be so serious. Where's your old spirit? You used to love doing crazy things in college."

"We're not in college, Kristin. We're in the real world. You don't play with people's lives like that."

"Oh, well, Roscoe is so paranoid—he's a challenge at times. Anyway, it would break up the monotony. Are you with me?"

"I'll help you solve the case," Gretchen concedes. "But no profiteering."

"Agreed, spoilsport," Kristin accuses.

"What do you suggest?"

"Tell Roscoe the entire story—the way you told me—about what happened to Morgan."

"But it's only a dream, Kristin. You said so yourself."

"Then how do you account for the lapse in time? Alien invasion? You were gone for a week," Kristin persuades her. "I'm surprised Harley didn't tear the town apart looking for you. Did he ever file a missing person's request?"

"I don't know," Gretchen looks off in the distance. "I didn't ask."

"Well, you don't have to tell Roscoe everything—that bit about old Ireland and time travel is a bit much—but your adventures as a cat can't do any harm. Roscoe needs to solve the case, and I'm willing to pull a few strings to help him."

"Let me think about it," Gretchen promises. "One thing about dreams, they usually mean the opposite of real life."

"I'm banking my future on your dream version," Kristin says.

"After my track record, I don't see how it contributes anything, but confusion."

Having won round one, Kristin returns to her antique shop, and Gretchen heads home to dwell on the next step. Relaxing on the chaise lounge on her deck, Gretchen reviews her rapidly disappearing dream.

Odd, Kristin's using that phrase: 'Banking her future on my dream.' What did she mean, and what do she and Roscoe want from me? Is there something I'm forgetting—something that happened and I can't remember?

The bottle of *Heaven-Scent* had disappeared from her dresser, but she understood that. Harley planned to have the secret ingredient analyzed. Did he? *I'll ask him. What else must I remember?* She looks around the garden—so peaceful and quiet. Her strawberries, huge and succulent—even in November—odors and sound are so much keener since my dream. *Am I still part cat?*

Peeking through semi-closed lids, she observes Julius walking the white picket fence towards her and smiles as he jumps down into her garden. Glancing at Gretchen lying motionless on the chaise, he heads for her strawberry patch and begins to dig. Then, with his front paw poised in midair as though pointing, he leaps back to his spot on the fence, and watches her pretense at sleep.

The strawberry patch! Why didn't I think of that? I'll bet that's where Julius hid the knife. She moves to the spot where Julius dug—aware that he's watching her movements. Seizing a trowel Harley had left in the garden, she digs deep into the selected spot until her trowel hits a solid object. *The gun? No, Shaman has the gun.* She pulls out a plastic sack—the very one she thought Roscoe found on Saturday. Thinking *evidence,* she doesn't touch the knife inside. She tosses the sack in her car and heads for the police station determined to unload her problems on Roscoe's broad shoulders.

"I don't care what Kristin says, I'm taking this to Sergeant Baguette before I change my mind."

Later, walking into Sergeant Baguette's office, she begins to waiver. *How can I explain to Kristin's boyfriend how I got this package—after what happened Saturday? I'll be an idiot for the second time. Maybe I should tell Kristin first.* She turns and is heading for the exit when Roscoe enters.

"Hi, Gretchen, looking for me?" He detains her exit, motioning to the package in her hand. "What do you have there?"

She hedges, backing toward the door. "Oh, Roscoe, after Saturday, you'll think I'm crazy...I can't explain..."

"Is that another knife you have there?" He stares at the package Gretchen is trying to hide behind her. Gretchen nods and hands him the plastic sack.

"I think this is the evidence we should have found Saturday. I won't bother to tell you how I got it. If it's what you're looking for—I'll try to explain…otherwise…."

"Let's see that." The grinning Sergeant Baguette takes the package from her and motions for her to follow him. He heads for the interrogation room, and once there, he peeks into the bag. Then, pulling on a sterile glove, he removes the knife and places it in a plastic police bag.

"Now," he tells here. "I need the whole story. "I've been inheriting bits and pieces of senseless information for weeks. It's time to pull it all together." He motions her to a chair across the table. "Sit, please."

"Do I need a lawyer?" she asks.

Sergeant Baguette looks at her. "If you're thinking Harley, I don't advise it. He's a suspect, too. Anyone else you want to call?"

"No. I know it looks bad for Harley, but he's a casualty, too." She bites her upper lip, looks up at Sergeant Baguette, and asks, "Do you know if Harley ever filed a *Missing Persons* report?"

His eyebrows lifted. "Yeah, I found one in the files. We give everyone 48 hours to turn up. No one reinitiated the request. Why?"

"I lose a week of my life, and no one cares? It's as if Harley and Kristin knew, and won't tell me. Too many things…don't make sense…I don't know…."

Sergeant Baguette sympathizes. *I want to believe her.* "I suppose Kristin dreamed up that bit about you being a psychic—in case we found the knife."

Gretchen nods. "I can't keep up the deception, Roscoe. I'm basically honest, but Kristin does have a tendency to sway me at times. I don't know why I go along with her." She pauses as though recalling some fun incident and smiles. "For the rush I get, I suppose. She's not entirely to blame."

Roscoe nods at the package on the table between them. "Without giving me a replay of Saturday's fiasco, how did this come into your possession?"

"I'm sorry, Sergeant Roscoe. I know I haven't been completely open with you, but I need someone who'll listen to me—someone who doesn't think I'm making everything up, or that I've flipped. Harley's at wit's end—afraid he'll lose credibility—and after what I'm about to tell you, you'll probably agree with him."

Her remarks surprise Roscoe. "Do you have anything—anything at all—that will convince me I should listen to you?" he asks. When she hesitates, he prods her. "Go on. You want someone to listen. I'm listening." He leans back in his chair, puts his feet on the desk, and closes his eyes. "Talk," he says.

And Gretchen does. She tells Roscoe about Julius. How Julius indicated to her where he hid the knife, saying, "Julius replaced the knife because I brought in too many people. He warned me not to talk to anyone, but you. Maybe because of Kristin's business dealings with Professor Ipswitch."

"Who is Julius?" Roscoe asks. "And how does this Julius fit into the scene? Is he our illusive partner?"

"No." Gretchen says, looking away and wishing she could disappear. "Not exactly." Collecting her courage, she turns and faces the police sergeant. "Julius is a cat."

Roscoe's feet came off the desk and he stares at her. "Sure he is," he says facetiously. "And I'm supposed to believe that you talk to cats?"

"Think what you like, you can't know for sure." She turns a smug look in his direction. "Think of the convenience, Roscoe. Cats can get into places you and I can't—without raising suspicion." Suddenly, aware she's losing him, she adds quickly, "Check out the knife, Roscoe. It's for real."

"Well, why not. Makes as much sense as anything else." He picks up the evidence bag, and pockets the knife.

"Trust me, Roscoe. "It's for real."

He stares at her. "Trust, huh? I'm supposed to trust someone who thinks it's normal to talk to cats?"

"What choice do you have?"

"Oh, what the Hell. You're right. I'll check out the knife."

As he turns to leave, he looks back as though remembering something. "By the way, Gretchen," he says. "You mentioned a business deal between the professor and Kristin. Is she the partner in this deal?"

"I don't know. In my dream, Professor Ipswitch had a partner. That partner was a dead- ringer for the victim. I can't be sure. Maybe Julius can lead us though the maze."

Roscoe shakes his head, wondering if he's being led down a garden path for a second time in a week. He motions to his coat pocket. "I'll check this out. We'll talk later."

* * *

Chapter Four

Conscience is the traitor that fights the battle of society.

It's a week later before Roscoe calls Gretchen. "It's the murder weapon," he tells her. "It fits the stab wounds and the blood matches that of the victim. Can you come in? I'm ready to hear it all, and promise to keep an open mind on whatever you tell me."

Gretchen agrees. As soon as she arrives, Roscoe jumps in with his inquiries. "Since you and Julius seem to be my only lead, I need your input, Gretchen. You say the professor has a partner, and the partner looks a lot like the victim. Did you ever meet this partner?"

"No, but I've seen him. He fits the description of the man you found under the overpass, although I didn't know at the time."

"When did you recognize him as the professor's partner?"

"Halloween night, but you see, in my dream he wasn't dead. He led Harley and the professor to Dublin." She hesitates, seeing the officer's pen stop. "Oh, I'm sorry," she says.

"Dublin? You mean, as in Ireland?" Roscoe asks. "First, you talk with cats, then you travel back in time. Explain, please." He stops writing as he listens to Gretchen and her journey into the *Netherworld*.

"I know it sound crazy—sort of like Alice walking through the looking glass into another world, but it did happen. I walk through a cave into the seventeenth century—and meet Magus and the Devil. What can I say?"

"Look, Gretchen," says a skeptical Sergeant. "I'm a policeman, and not into fairy tales. You'll have to do better than that."

"Forget it," Gretchen says, and gets up to leave.

"Sit down," he orders. "You started this. You'll stay until your story makes sense to me." He shakes his carrot top hair. "No wonder Kristin was so evasive."

"She told me to tell you everything except about Ireland. She thought that a bit much," Gretchen said. "I made a mistake. I should have skirted around that."

"That I understand," Roscoe agrees. "Go on. What else did you learn that might help me in *this* century?"

"Isn't there something about dreams—even in *this* century—that are sort of symbolic. You know—like things aren't always what they seem. Shaman and his wild tales of old Ireland, Harley and his over-protection of me, my need for my own identity, and Kristin's desire to control?"

"The power of suggestion, you mean?"

"Something like that—unfulfilled desires. I can't prove we were in Ireland. It may have happened right here in Ridgecrest. Graveyard scenes are pretty much alike, and there are many ancient barns in Connecticut—like Professor Ipswitch and *Resurrection*—his magic potion. Maybe I've always had a secret desire to be a cat."

Sergeant Baguette watches her, surprised by the sudden outburst in her own defense. "Stop," he says, running his fingers through his rumpled hair. "I might start to believe you."

"Maybe I should leave before I really confuse you."

""No, stay where you are," he orders. "I plan to get to the bottom of this. There's been a murder—and you've literally plucked the murder weapon out of thin air. That, at least, makes this conversation a reality."

Gretchen takes a deep breath. "Regardless of where it takes you?" she asks.

"Regardless—I'm steeled for anything at the moment—tomorrow, I may not be in any mood to listen. What did happen the night of October 31st?"

Gretchen dives in. "All the cats meet at the Witches' Coven on Halloween night. I followed them, being a novice in the group—not knowing where they were heading. Evidently, I daydreamed along the way and didn't realize they were far ahead of me. I try to catch up, but I can't find the other cats. Then, I take a wrong path and lose my way. I keep on walking trying to guess which path they took—when I see a light ahead. Believing I've caught up with the other cats, I run faster—but instead of finding my friends, I wind up in an ancient barn."

"In Ireland." Roscoe interrupts.

"I didn't know that."

"What did you find in the barn?" he prompts.

"Two figures sitting before a roaring fire, wrapped in shawls. They don't see me, but there's a bowl of water in front of the fire. Feeling thirsty after my long walk, I take a drink from the bowl. That's when everything turns topsy-turvy."

"You could have fooled me," Roscoe says.

Gretchen ignored his comment. "I recognize one of the figures when he looks out from under the shawl. It's Shaman…"

Roscoe stops her. "Shaman? The bartender at the Pub?" Gretchen nods. "The other figure is Elise."

"Who is Elise?"

"Shaman's love from another lifetime. He meets with her once a year."

Roscoe blinks. "Did he tell you this?"

"He told me he'd cut a deal with the Devil to bring her back with him."

"Did he?"

"I don't know. They did leave together."

"Let's get back to the barn. What else happened?"

Gretchen continues her story despite her skeptical listener. When she reaches the part where she wakes up in her own bedroom, he stops her. "I've got the picture—now for the big question. How did

Harley get to Dublin? And, don't tell me he went by time machine, I don't buy that."

"I don't know, but he and Professor Ipswitch—and the professor's partner—all show up at the barn after Shaman and Elise leave."

"Through the shield?"

"Yes. Morgan tries to push me into the fire, but he stumbles and falls. The fire swallows him up." She stops to see how he's taking this part of her story. He seems resigned, so she continues. "Then, the hay in the loft catches fire, and the entire barn burns to the ground."

"Who's Morgan?"

"The professor's partner—your murdered victim—the hunchback," she explains.

"He's alive?"

"Yes, when I saw him."

Roscoe stops taking notes, "First, you tell me you saw Morgan killed that afternoon. Then you tell me he's alive and well nearly six hours later. How do you account for the time lapse?"

Gretchen frowns. "You asked me...."

"I know I did. Go on."

"By this time it's nearly midnight, and we head back to the graveyard."

"You, Harley, and the Professor?"

"Yes. That's when Magus shows up in his magic chariot—and leads us home."

"Of course. Why not?" Sergeant Baguette sits quietly, and doesn't move. He stares at the woman sitting across the table.

"Please, it's a dream." She gives him time to absorb this latest revelation.

"I know I'm going to regret this next question," Roscoe says, running his fingers through his already rumpled mop of red hair, and wishing he were anywhere but here. "How did you get back?"

Gretchen hesitates before taking the plunge. "Magus opens the magic door, and Harley and I leave, but he keeps the professor with him in the *Netherworld*. I don't know how he got back." She looks down at her hands, moving nervously in her lap.

"Don't ask me anything else, Sergeant Baguette. I don't remember coming home." She lays her head on the table, her eyes close to tears. "I can't explain it. I only know it happened." She looks up at the cop. "I'm sorry, Sergeant Baguette. "I don't blame you for not believing me. It's hard for me to believe."

"I'm trying, Gretchen. I'm really trying," Roscoe sympathizes. "You understand my position. I've got to make logical connections between your dream and reality. It leaves me with a lot of question, such as: Why did Harley do nothing while you were gone? Why would he call your defense a *loony tunes'* defense? Why did the professor deny he had a partner? What part did the gun play in this scenario? It wasn't the murder weapon. What happened to it?"

"The gun was ancient. When I threw it in the water, it disintegrated."

"Disintegrated?"

"Yes. Shaman couldn't get through the shield until he got rid of the gun. When he drops it, it falls in the water, and disintegrates. It doesn't exist any more—not in this world." She notes his puzzled expression, and feels empathy. "I don't know the answers to your questions, Roscoe. Maybe Harley didn't want to involve me. Maybe the professor killed his partner. Maybe Kristin knows more than she's telling us. Maybe it is only a dream. See? I've got more questions than answers, too."

"Why did Harley have a gun in the first place?" ignoring her questions with another of his own.

"To protect me. He had a client who threatened him, and he got me the gun—in case I needed it. I thought he'd sold it, 'til I saw him dig it up from my garden."

"Your garden? The same place you found the knife?" Gretchen nods. "Do you know the name of his dangerous client?"

"No, some guy Harley defended in court. He lost the case. After the defendant was sentenced to a prison term, I gave the gun back to Harley and forgot all about it"

"I need to know the name of the fellow Harley sent to prison. It's possible he's been released, and renewed his threat. I'll check that out."

"Will you need me again?" Gretchen asks.

"Not right away, but quit plotting with Kristin. She loves to play pranks."

"And you fall for them."

He grins. "She does have a way with her, doesn't she?"

* * *

Chapter Five

Power is a measure of man's morality.
There is no such thing as truth.

Sergeant Baguette walks into the attorney's office determined to confront Harley with his latest discoveries. His desk is piled high with case files and law books, as are the chairs and table, with files sliding off onto the floor. Harley dumps a stack of folders from a chair to give Roscoe a place to sit.

"We usually meet clients in the conference room," Harley says. "Image, you know. Don't want them to think we actually work. What's on your mind, Roscoe? Have you been talking with Gretchen?"

"Yes, and she fed me quite a story. I'm not into checking out ghosts and goblins to verify an investigation, but I do need your confirmation on some of what I've heard."

"Shoot," answers Harley. "How can I add to your confusion?"

Roscoe takes a deep breath, and begins. "First, there's the gun—the one you got for Gretchen. Where did you get it, who did you give it to, and why?"

"And where is it now? That your next question?" asks Harley.

"No, but I've a theory. Gretchen says you got the gun to protect her because someone threatened her—someone you defended in court. Tell me about him. Who is the guy, and where is he now?"

"Jake Dunbar—a petty thief who got in over his head. Thought he could join the big leagues and pull off a bank robbery. He went up the river. I've no idea where he is now."

"You remember the case?"

"Sure, I defended the guy," Harley tells Roscoe. "Never did believe him guilty, and surprised at his conviction—but the threats I received during and after the trial—they were real. Didn't make sense. Why the sudden interest?"

"Is he still *up the river,* as you say?"

"Someone told Shaman recently that he'd been released, and knowing of the threats on my life, he called to warn me—promised to keep an eye out for him at the Pub. Shaman tell you about the gun?" Harley asks.

"No, the gun doesn't interest me," Roscoe assures him, "Except that it keeps popping up in my investigation. No, I'm more interested in Dunbar."

"Really? After Shaman called, I checked with the prison. The guy's still there. Don't know how the rumor of his escape started. Did you ask him?"

"No, not about this. Last time I talked with Shaman, he gave me some *gobble-de-gook* about a partner of the professor that no one's seen—and whom the professor says doesn't exist."

"So? What's the problem?" Harley asks.

"Time element. The victim dies early in the evening, yet he appears to be in perfect health well close to midnight. How do you explain it?"

"I can't—unless . . ."

"Unless what?"

"Time zones. Have you accounted for time zones?" Harley asks.

"Why would I do that?"

"I know it sounds crazy, but what part of your story isn't?"

"I expected a sane answer from an attorney. Is that the best you can do?" Roscoe needled.

"Outside of declaring a perfect murder and accepting the impossible, what choice do you have?" Harley hesitated. "At least, that's what my logical mind tell me."

"Logic, huh?" Roscoe falls silent. He stares at the attorney intently. Then he laughs. "By Jove, Harley, I believe you've hit on it. Thanks." Then, his energy renewed, Roscoe rushes from the attorney's office.

"What did I say?" Harley asks the officer's disappearing back. But Roscoe doesn't answer. He's half way back to the station.

Once there, he garners together his bits and pieces of information. His main concern, *How did Kristin get involved, and why?* He remembers their good times as kids in Yorkshire—her love of a good time—her love of adventure—and his sharing in those adventures. She had a rare talent for making life come alive. At times, he'd find himself drawn into a number of her escapades—much to his regret on occasion. He pushes his chair back against the wall, puts his feet up on the desk, and reminisces. He hadn't seen Kristin for years, until their paths crossed recently.

Outwardly, he found her unchanged—the same mischievous glint in her eyes he remembered from his youth—now a more serious, intense Kristin. The same devil-may-care attitude, but now she seems too use it more as a shield. *Why? What changed her? What made her plot against her best friend? The entire episode smacked of Kristin's technique—time travel, ancient rituals, secret ingredients—and the final coup d'etat—introducing him, a cop, into the mix.*

Why would she take the chance? She and the professor had a good thing going—he creating and she selling—unless . . . Roscoe pushed the chair back against the wall as his feet crashed to the floor. A sudden thought hit the gregarious lawman as he recreated the scenario. *Aha, that's it! It isn't the professor's invention—it's his partner's—grounds for murder!* Roscoe grabs his coat off the rack, and heads for the door. *That guy at the university lab—he holds the key.*

Heading his police car towards the university, he finds the lab assistant getting ready to leave. Roscoe stops him. "You're the only person I've interviewed so far who makes sense," he tells the startled assistant."

"Well, thanks, I guess. What's up?"

"Remember on my last visit—you were analyzing some potion? Did you ever discover the secret ingredient?" His enthusiasm bubbles over in his excitement.

The lab assistant smiled. "Sure. Didn't I mail you a copy? Come on in, and let me check. I can run you off another copy, if you like."

Roscoe follows him into the lab. "If it isn't too much trouble, I'd appreciate it—and I'll wait for this one. You'll probably need to explain it to me anyway." He had no intention of returning to the station empty-handed.

"That illusive ingredient quite surprised me," he tells Roscoe. "Although, I don't know why it should. You hear about drugs on campus all the time, but you seldom get involved in the business end of it." He pulls a file from his desk drawer. "Here it is. I ran this for an attorney here in town, Harley Dandrich. He has the original—I sent you a copy." He grins up at Roscoe. "You should check your mail oftener."

Roscoe ignores him. "What does it say?"

"It's relatively harmless, but it's a derivative of LSD and shouldn't be sold over the counter," he tells Roscoe. "There's always someone who overdoes a good thing. When I didn't hear from anyone, I considered the matter closed."

"You didn't question the attorney?"

"No, why should I? I did contact the marketer and advise her of its potential danger."

"The marketer?" Roscoe asks.

"Yes, an antique shop—**The Brass Ring**—markets the potion under the pseudonym, *Heaven Scent*. The owner is one of the partners as is the attorney. He's the one who requested I analyze its so-called *secret* ingredient."

"Thanks. You've been a big help." Roscoe put the copy of the report in his pocket, and returned to the station, his mind reeling with facts instead of suppositions. He knew how close he'd come to ignoring Gretchen and her input, but things were beginning to fall into place. *If that lab technician hadn't discovered the secret ingredient, I'd have absolutely nothing to base my suspicions on. And if Gretchen hadn't been so susceptible to suggestion, I'd probably still believe in phantom sleuths and psychics.*

He checks his watch. *Time to confront Kristin.*

* * *

Kristin nibbled on her BuffaloWings as she occasionally dipped celery sticks into Shaman's special dressing. She looked from Roscoe to Gretchen seated across from her. They'd met as she'd prearranged—at their weekly Friday luncheon—but things weren't right. Roscoe didn't look happy, and Gretchen looked strained. *What's going on?* She begins to worry. She catches Gretchen's puzzled expression, and redirects her attention to Roscoe.

"When did you figure it out?" she asks in a low voice.

"Did you really think you'd get away with it?"

"Get away with what?" Gretchen asks, looking from one to the other. "What are you talking about?"

Roscoe ignored her, and waited for Kristin to answer.

"Yeah, I guess I did. What tipped you off?"

"*Heaven-Scent.* If you and Professor Ipswitch want fame and fortune that's fine, but you enlisted the innocent participation of Gretchen and Harley in your scheme."

"That's preposterous. I don't even know Professor...." She stops at Gretchen's expression. "Well, we did have a business relationship," she admits. "That doesn't mean anything."

"Not in itself, it doesn't. You had me fooled. That is, 'til Gretchen tells me the rest of the story. My suspicions started when Harley unwittingly made a comment that didn't make sense—unless he knew something I didn't," Sergeant Baguette tells her.

"What did he say?"

"He asked me if I'd checked time zones. He meant it to be facetious, I'm sure. Time travel didn't make much sense to me. The disappearance of Gretchen for a week, however, did make sense."

Kristin shrugs. "Doesn't prove anything."

"No, until I talked to the lab technician who isolated the secret ingredient. He warned both you and Harley of its potential danger—warnings you both ignored."

"Harley?" Gretchen interrupts.

Sergeant Baguette ignores her, his attention focusing on Kristin. "My bits and pieces began to make sense when he tells me the secret ingredient is *psilocybin,* a hallucinogenic drug originating from a mushroom known to grow only in Mexico."

"What does that have to do with me?" Kristin asks.

"You wrote me you vacationed there last summer. Did you bring anything back for the professor?"

"Kristin, you didn't!" Gretchen stares at her friend in disbelief.

Kristin concentrates on the wine in her glass.

"He asked me to bring him back a particular kind of Mexican mushroom. I didn't know why he wanted it, and I certainly didn't know his plans for *Heaven Scent* at the time. I figured it a *pie in the sky* fantasy, and indulged him. That's all."

"What did he promise you, Kristin?" Gretchen prods. "Marketing rights to *Heaven Scent*—a percentage of the gross."

"Then things got out of control, all Hell broke loose, and you had to regroup. I understand, Kristin," he says softly. "Now I need you to fill me in on the details. What happened to your big plans?"

"I'm not involved in any murder, Roscoe," Kristin answers. "You can't pin that on me."

"No, I don't believe you are. What happened was unintentional—a string of unexpected circumstances. My guess is the partner created the potion, but the Professor laid claim to it—that is—until the partner complained. Am I right?"

Gretchen looks at Kristin accusingly. "Kristin how could you?"

"I'm sorry, Gretchen. I didn't know anything about a partner—and didn't know of any murder until I read it in the newspaper. Even then, I didn't tie the two together."

Gretchen turns to Roscoe. "I'm inclined to believe her, Roscoe. Who did kill the professor's partner?"

"I've no idea. We've not positive I.D. He may or may not be the partner. That's why I need Kristin's input. I think she knows more than she's admitting."

Kristin is silent.

"Maybe she'll remember at the station," Roscoe threatens, glaring at her. "Shall we go, my dear?"

"You're going to arrest me?" Roscoe shows her a pair of handcuffs. "Don't cuff me. I'll go with you."

"Wouldn't think of it," he says, pocketing the cuffs and preparing to leave. "Coming, Gretchen?"

* * *

Later, at the station house, Sergeant Baguette guides them to an interrogation room equipped with a recorder. "Okay, Kristin," he says. "Let's have it from the beginning. Why?"

Kristin shrugs. "Why not? The professor had a product. I had a gift shop and clientele. It sounded like a marriage made in Heaven. When he offered me a partnership in exchange for a few mushrooms from Mexico, it didn't sound like any big deal. I already had plans to vacation there. How could I refuse?"

"Knowing you, I don't suppose you couldn't.

Gretchen sits listening at a comfortable distance as Kristin tells Sergeant Baguette about the professor's intention to try out his new creation at **Shaman's Pub** that evening, and how she'd advised against it. "I suggested he experiment on an animal first, but he ignored me. I didn't know he'd given some to Gretchen until too late."

"His new creation—not the one Harley had analyzed?"

"Yes, *Resurrection,* his latest experiment—an age-controlling potion.

That's the one he gave Gretchen at the Pub," Kristin tells him.

"Is there a difference?"

"I don't know. He didn't confide in me. I gather it's the same, but stronger."

"Did Shaman know what he'd done that night?"

"No, not until later."

"How much later?"

"When Gretchen disappears, Shaman starts questioning Harley, and the professor gets nervous. He had plans to keep Gretchen at the cottage, and observe her reactions to his potion, but he lost track of her. He got pretty scared at that." She looks at Roscoe before continuing. "I didn't know anything about Gretchen until Harley came by Monday morning. You've got to believe me."

Gretchen drifts back to her dream experience. *That's how I became a cat.* Vaguely, she listens as Roscoe continued to question Kristin. "The professor's partner—no one except Gretchen and her cat friends seem to have met him. Who is he?"

"I've no idea. The professor claims they were his inventions—that *he* creates them in his laboratory. They were his inventions. I never saw a partner. I did business with the professor."

"The dead man—ever see him before?" "No."

"Can you add anything, Gretchen?" Roscoe interrupts her daydreaming.

"What?"

"Can you add anything further to Kristin's version of events?"

Gretchen searches her conscience. *Would anything I say now help the situation?* "Professor Ipswitch isn't the murderer, Roscoe. Morgan killed his partner for the potion, and he's already paid. He burned up in the fire."

"There you go again, Gretchen—disassociating yourself from reality," Sergeant Baguette accuses her. "Who is the partner? Where did he come from? I have to deal with facts, not illusions. I live in this world, not your *Neverworld.*"

"*Netherworld*, Roscoe. Don't convict the wrong man."

"I don't intend to." He prepares to go and gathers up his papers. *Maybe they'll talk if I'm not in the room.* "I'll leave you two to settle your differences," he tells them and leaves the two friends alone.

As soon as Roscoe leaves the room and the recorder is off, Kristin turns to Gretchen. "You have to believe me, Gretchen. I never met a partner. The professor told me he met this weird chap in trouble with the law and befriended him. The fellow went to prison, and did some research in the prison library. There, he discovered an ancient recipe, and for the fun of it, he mails it the professor. The professor creates *Heaven-Scent* from the recipe. I didn't know he added those Mexican mushrooms to the mix."

"Is he still in prison?" asks Gretchen.

"I don't know," Kristin answers. "And that's the truth. If he isn't, maybe he and the professor fought over who would get the lion's share of the profits, but the Professor didn't kill him."

"How do you know, Kristin? He could very well be the killer—if what you say is true."

"He had nothing to gain by killing the goose that laid the golden egg," says Kristin. "Could just as easily have been Harley—or Shaman. They both have reasons for wanting the professor out of the way."

"Harley? Why would you say that?" she asks. *She's changing her story.*

"Harley's on the board of directors, too."

"As an attorney for a corporation the professor set up. That's not a motive for murder. Who else is on the board?"

"That's it. Me, the professor, and Harley—it takes three to form a corporation."

And Roscoe has three suspects. "Go on. Where does Morgan fit in?"

"I've no idea. I told you, I never saw a partner."

"My guess is that Morgan and the partner are one and the same."

"That's the way I figured it," agrees Kristin.

"Are you saying that the professor's partner broke out of prison, and Professor Ipswitch hid him out at the university? That's why no one has seen him? Why would he do that?"

"To keep him from gaining control of the potion."

"Did the potion belong to Morgan?"

"No, that's why they fought. The professor tried to reason with him—to tell him there's enough for everyone, but Morgan wouldn't listen."

"So the professor kills him?"

"The professor had all the necessary credentials to create and patent the potion. He didn't need Morgan, and hires Shaman to do the honors. Harley provided the gun."

Gretchen interrupts her. "I don't believe you," she says. "Shaman has absolutely no interest in the professor's creations. Nor does Harley."

"Shaman is the assassin," she says.

Gretchen looks at her long-time friend in disbelief. "Why didn't you tell Roscoe?"

Kristin is silent, her mind traveling in high gear. Then it clicks.

Gretchen isn't going to help me.

"It won't work, Kristin. Roscoe will identify the fingerprints on the knife, and prove that neither Harley nor Shaman were involved. That ruse won't work."

Kristin voices her thoughts. "You're not going to help."

"Not so," Gretchen assured her. "But I find it difficult to forgive you and Harley for leading me on, when you suspected something all along."

"I'm sorry, Gretchen, we didn't expect *you* to get involved in a murder —talk about dumb luck…"

"That isn't luck, that's reality. Murphy's Law—whatever can go wrong will go wrong—you know that, Kristin." As Gretchen digests what Kristin has told her, she adds, "I don't believe you're responsible for the murder, Kristin, but you did allow money to influence your decisions. And you did attempt a cover up in league with the professor."

"What do you intend to do?" a penitent Kristin asks.

Gretchen sits quietly before she voices a suggestion. "If you tell Roscoe what you've told me, I'll help you in any way I can, but you have to level with him, otherwise the deal's off."

When Sergeant Baguette returns, Kristin relates the entirely different story to him. He reschedules an interrogation with Harley and Shaman, and allows Kristin to return to her antique shop. He incarcerates Professor Ipswitch—-pending further investigation.

Chapter Six

Whatever can go wrong, will go wrong.
—Murphy's Law

Once again, Sergeant Baguette visits Harley Dandrich in his office. This time, he intends to compare Harley's version of what happened to the story Gretchen elicited from Kristin. *I wonder if Harley knows Kristin accuses him and Shaman of the murder.* He finds Harley deeply involved in reviewing the Jake Dunbar case file, his coat tossed on a table, his shirt open at the collar, and his tie askew.

"I thought we verified that Dunbar is still serving his sentence," Roscoe says.

"I know, but there's something odd about that old case of mine."

"Oh? How come?"

"Well, I never could understand why the threats continued *after* Dunbar's sentencing. I've been checking his history and guess what I've discovered?" He turns and grins at Roscoe. "Sit down, I'll fill you in."

"I'm listening." Harley clears a space on a chair, and Roscoe fills it, waiting expectantly. "What's the big news?"

"Jake Dunbar had a twin—an identical twin brother. I'm thinking we sent the wrong man to prison."

"You think the victim is the one who should have been jailed?" Roscoe asks.

"According to what I've been able to find out, they were separated at birth and adopted by different families. Neither one ever met the other."

"You understand what that does to my case, don't you?"

"Yeah, but if there are two of them, it answers a lot of questions." Harley squints at Roscoe over his wire frame glasses. "We'd need birth records to prove there's more than one person in the mix."

"Seems the professor knows more than he's telling," Roscoe says.

"Yeah, think you can squeeze the professor enough to make him talk?"

"It's what I do best, " Roscoe assures him.

"Now, what's on your mind?" Harley queried. "You didn't come by for a friendly visit, did you?"

"No, I need to know how involved are you with the professor and Kristin. Is there some diversionary tactic you two have cooked up to keep me off guard?"

"Not at all. I'm trying to clear Kristin. Granted, she's a little *harum-scarum* at times and thrives on suspense, but she's basically honest. I'd hate to see her railroaded—like Dunbar."

"You'd better convince me," Roscoe says. "I've known her for years, too, and I believe she's stepped too close to the edge this time."

"That doesn't make her a criminal, or even a worthy accomplice. She wants success—there's no crime in that. She saw her chance and took it. If that's guilt, we're all guilty." He peers at Roscoe. "Let me show you what I've found."

"I hope you're not trying to head me off in another direction. I'm confused enough."

Harley grins, and begins his tale of suppositions. "What if I'm right? And there are identical twin babies—Jake and Morgan—adopted at birth by different parents? They could live their entire lives and never know they have a twin."

"That's your theory?" Roscoe asks. "Then they meet accidentally and figure it out?"

"Something like that—or maybe one knows and the other doesn't. I'm more inclined to think that's what happened. Dunbar spent a lot of time digging through the prison library. Maybe he found out more than that controversial recipe."

"I see where you're going," Roscoe agrees. "Morgan discovers he has a twin brother when Jake's picture—as the accused—is in all the newspapers. He lets his twin take the rap. Meanwhile, Morgan has his own reasons for keeping his silence, and uses the knowledge to his own advantage. That about it?"

"That's one theory," Harley agrees. "Or maybe our illustrious Professor Ipswitch, who knows Morgan, recognizes the startling resemblance to his partner, a known criminal, and takes advantage of the situation. He hides the real criminal from public view, and takes advantage of Morgan's expertise."

"You think the professor knew Jake was innocent, but pulled the switch and allowed the wrong twin to go to prison?" Roscoe asks. "Kind'a far fetched, isn't it?"

"I'm trying to prove a theory, Roscoe. What if Morgan knows he has a twin, but the professor doesn't?"

"And he sat back and watched while his innocent twin went to prison? As long as you're only supposing, I might go along with that," Roscoe agrees.

"Answer me one question, Roscoe. Why did threatening letters continue *after* the trial?"

"Without the letters, we may never know." He gets up to leave. "It's been an interesting meeting, Harley. You think the professor's involved in the scheme, and you may be right." *If you are, I may wrap up my case.* "I've arrested the professor on the information I have. It's circumstantial—maybe this information will help squeeze him."

"How about Kristin?" Harley asks. "What are your plans for her?"

Roscoe hesitated. "Kristin?" he asks. "I don't know. You may be right about her. Maybe I'm too moral to believe she's completely innocent. That's a stretch."

* * *

Professor Ipswitch went on trial for murder later that spring. Harley testified that the victim's twin brother—the man he sent to prison five years ago due to mistaken identity—was innocent of the charges brought against him at that time. He requested a review of the charges based on new information. The court agreed.

Gretchen testified on the professor's behalf—believing that Morgan killed his twin to keep the recipe from being exposed to a profit-seeking world—then escaped into the *Netherworld*. She knew Morgan would never be found to prove or disprove her theory, but her testimony did help Kristin. The court exonerated her from any liability after she confessed her part in the scheme.

Facts brought out during the trial failed to prove Roscoe's theory—that the professor murdered his partner in order to gain full control of a very lucrative product. The court refused to accept Harley's theory that Morgan, the supposed twin brother of Jake Dunbar, robbed the bank and disappeared leaving Jake to take the rap for his criminal twin as the existence of Morgan, as the professor's partner, could never be verified. The lab assistant had never seen him, nor had anyone else. Shaman denied all knowledge of his ever being in his Pub, and Harley could not positively prove that Dunbar ever had a twin, although new evidence garnered from Professor Ipswitch did clear Jake with the court.

The victim's body was never positively identified, and town officials buried him in a pauper's grave outside town. The jury acquitted the Professor for lack of evidence since none of the story Gretchen told Roscoe could be admitted as evidence. No one except Kristin and Roscoe believed her fantasy, and Roscoe—who preferred fact to fantasy—accepted the results of the trial. Harley felt justice had been served in the case of Jake Dunbar vs. the State of Connecticut when the court pardoned Jake Dunbar in light of additional evidence presented by Professor Ipswitch.

All in all, everything turned out as well as could be expected. Gretchen returned to writing books, Kristin continued to sell *Heaven Scent* at her antique shop, but *Resurrection* was put on hold pending further research. Sergeant Baguette became involved in another case that he hoped wouldn't include witches and hobgoblins. Morgan is never seen nor heard from again.

At times, Harley wondered about who sent the threatening letters that caused him to buy a gun in the first place, but Gretchen was grateful to have discovered she didn't imagine her escapade into the *Netherworld*.

Epilogue

Some months later, Gretchen cleans out her closet intending to contribute clothes she no longer wears to her church. "They're out of style," she consoles herself. "I'll never wear them again." Pulling a few dresses from their hangers, she pushes back the remaining clothes to check those she hasn't worn in years. That's when she notices a pile of dirty garments on the floor—pushed way back into a corner.

"H-m-m," she says, "Wonder how long these have been here?" She pulls them out of their hiding place and sniffs. "Wow, filthy! They smell like smoke." She sniffs again. "Fireplace smoke—not cigarette smoke." *Where did I ever wear these?* She plops herself on the floor, and digs deeper into the cluttered corner of her closet.

"From another planet," she thinks inspecting a pair of weird-looking silver slippers. "I don't remember buying anything like this. And this dress...." She picks up the sheer froth of material vaguely resembling a dress and examines it. "It looks familiar...in a strange sort of way, but I'd never buy anything this flimsy. It isn't me. Where did it come from?"

She is about to toss it aside when she feels something solid in the pocket of the dress. Conscious of a smoky odor emanating from the folds of the dress, she gingerly puts her hand into a pocket and grasps the solid object. She pulls out a small vial of liquid.

"My magic potion," she says, recognizing the bottle. "I've had it all the time." She places the bottle on her dresser, and looks at the strange pile of clothes on her bedroom floor. "Now what?" Undecided what to do next, she sits down in the middle of her bedroom floor and attempts to recall the details of her adventures as a cat.

Then she smiles. She'd nearly forgotten. Picking up the pile of tacky clothes, she places them into a zippered plastic bag and tosses the bag into the farthest recesses of her closet—*in case someone else tells me it's all in my imagination.* She picks up the bottle of magic potion, looks at it, and places it in her pocket.

I promised this to Julius. She closes her closet door, gathers up the clothes she planned to give to her church and places them in the trunk of her car. The vial she takes to the backyard, digs a hole near her strawberry plants, and buries the vial for Julius to find.

I wonder if it still works.

* * *

PART III

FOR MONEY THE MONKEY DANCES

TRILOGY THREE

FOR MONEY
THE MONKEY DANCES

*Behold! What you crave shall be yours to your
uttermost dreams and beyond.*
—*Olde Irish Faery Tales*

"For money, the monkey dances," the man behind the music box invited the children as he turned the organ grinder handle and spewed out his comedic tunes. "Drop the money in the hat, and watch the monkey dance." The little man smiled his toothless smile as the crowd gathered around, and parents found coins to give their kids. In turn, the kids donated the coins to the monkey's hat.

Lauren Calloway watched from the sidelines, waiting for the crowd to disperse and for the man behind the music box to gather up his collection and climb the steps of the Capitol building. She watched as the New York senator met the music man at the top of the steps. They spoke for a few minutes, and the Senator dropped something into the monkey's hat.

Did the senator pass a message or make a contribution? Lauren couldn't be sure. The senator disappeared into the Senate Office building, and the music man gathered up his gear. He slammed a battered hat on his head and the monkey leaped onto the man's shoulder as the music man hailed a cab.

Taxi? He must have had a good morning. Lauren glanced at her watch. *He's leaving early today—before lunch.* Hating to admit defeat, she noted the cab number and headed for her car. From her car she watched for the cab carrying the music man, and found it at the next stoplight. The cab headed for the opulent Watergate district close to the Capitol, and stopped in front of an expensive-looking apartment complex. The man and his monkey exited the cab and entered the building.

"Well, what do you know," Lauren mused. "The monkey business pays more than I thought." She noted the address and drove on, returning to the Senate building to check on the senator, but he had left. She returned to her office.

Lauren had been working as an agent for the FBI for the past year, and looked forward to her assignments. She'd been detailed to this watch for the past few months--ever since the September 11th bombing in New York City, when a money trail led them in this direction. So far, her assignments had been to observe. She had no idea why she watched the music man, but that was okay. All her life she'd loved watching people.

During her teen years in Ridgecrest, Connecticut, she'd watched kids in cars watching kids on foot—keeping up on high school gossip that way. Lauren didn't tell anyone how she got her information for the school newspaper, not even her best friends, Gretchen and Kristin. She treasured her high school friendships and elated when both she and Gretchen were accepted at the University of Connecticut. They resumed their close friendship and had added Kristin, a young English emigrant from Britain, to their list of favorite people.

Gretchen, now a homemaker and married to an attorney, had recently published her third book. Kristin had bought a tiny antique shop in Ridgecrest after her college days, and built the shop into a now-thriving business. And Lauren transferred her love of people watching to her new job as FBI agent. Her sharp eye for detail helped her remember faces and numbers—and out of the ordinary phenomena—making connections older and more seasoned veterans of the force missed. That same eye for detail caused her to notice an estrangement between her two best friends. Nothing Lauren could put her finger on—more an instinct—a tone of voice when she mentioned Kristin. Then, out of the blue last week, Gretchen called to ask if she could impose on her friend for a few weeks. She needed to do some research on life in the Capitol—the setting for her next novel. She would arrive Thursday morning.

Chapter One

Love seeketh only self to please...And builds a Hell in Heaven's despite.
William Blake

Day 1, Thursday

Agent Carlton glared at the man in front of him. *What right did he have to tell him he'd done it all wrong? He wasn't there.* He could barely hide his contempt for this inferior being, his boss and head of the FBI, and from whom he took his orders. He tried to stay calm. "You would have done it differently?"

"I would. You're living in the past, Carlton. This business no longer kills for no reason. Had you used a little more *finesse* and less brute force, you would not be in the situation you're in now." Gadsden stared in the cold ice-blue eyes of the man before him. The scar on the side of his face pulsed in anger, telling Gadsden that he trod on shaky ground. Carlton, the epitome of good breeding, killed as easily as he drank his Scotch whiskey. Hard as nails, impeccably dressed in pale buckskins and Australian bush jacket, Gadsden acknowledged his attraction to the gentler sex. He also knew his weaknesses, one of them being his inability to accept criticism for his work. The guy before him seethed with rage.

"What did you do with the body?"

"Left it. It's at the morgue, now. I left my phony credentials, and took his. There's no way the police can connect that guy to this office. He doesn't exist."

Gadsden leaned back in his chair, and put his feet up on the desk. Silently, as though in deep thought, he turned and looked out of the window gazing upon the calming green of the landscape. He let the man in front of him stew. Then he turned back to Carlton and asked, "Did anyone see you?"

Carlton snorted. "No."

"You're sure of that."

Carlton didn't answer, and Gadsden continued. "My report tells me that an unidentified person gave an eye-witness account of the killer."

"No one saw me. Let me see that report."

Gadsden handed the report to Carlton who smiled his mirthless grin. "They'd never find me with that description," he assured Gadsden and handed the report back to Gadsden.

"Nevertheless, you'd need to take a long vacation for a while. Pick up your paycheck and don't come back until the coast is clear."

Carlton turned on his heel, and left the room. Gadsden pushed a button on his intercom, and said to his secretary. "Contact Calloway and get her over here."

* * *

Leaving her office at lunchtime, Lauren Calloway headed for the airport terminal to pick up her friend Gretchen. She thought about Gadsden's reaction to her surveillance report on the music man. It had certainly piqued interest at FBI headquarters, especially when she'd told her supervisor about the incident on the Capitol steps and related the senator's reactions. Perhaps she'd never learn the final results of her surveillance, or how the pieces fit together. But that's how the Bureau appeared to operate—each agent responsible for his or her own assignment. Lauren could only hope that someone in authority would connect the dots. Little did she know she'd soon find herself in the position of connecting her own dots in a senseless criminal act.

Arriving at the airport, she gunned her car into a vacant spot in the underground-parking garage and raced into the terminal. *Her plane will be landing any minute now.* In the viewing room, she watched the American Airlines plane land, then taxi into its designated docking area. Outside the secured area, Lauren spied Gretchen walking toward her, juggling her carry-on luggage. The limit of two bags and an oversize purse to boot, took some maneuvering. After passing the security area, Gretchen dropped her bags on the floor and embraced her friend.

"Ooh, it's so wonderful to see you again—it's been so-o-o long…" she gushed.

"Hey, don't overdo it, Gretchen, you'll spoil me." Lauren relieved Gretchen of one of her bags. "Why didn't you grab a cart?"

"Never saw one—or gone by the time I got there," Gretchen answered, picking up the other bag and following Lauren to the parking garage. "Some day I'm going to get one of those suitcases on little wheels and a handle, if I have to keep traveling. These old relics require a male companion."

"I agree. Speaking of male companions, where's Harley? Thought you two never traveled alone." Gretchen traveling alone surprised Lauren, as Harley had a way of keeping her on a tight leash.

Amused at the comment, Gretchen smiled. "Harley's a different animal these days," she said. "My husband has *loosed* the reins, so to speak."

Lauren popped the trunk of her Ford Focus, and the two dump the luggage into the spacious trunk. She slammed down the trunk lid before she asked, "Interesting. How so?"

Gretchen shrugged. "Who knows? Success maybe? Gives one a whole new perspective."

"You'll have to tell me about it."

"Later. First, let's find a place where I can grab a bite to eat. My treat—the airlines have become quite stingy lately—particularly on short hops." Gretchen climbed in the car, noting its newness, and remembering the *clunkers* Lauren drove in college. "Nice wheels," she comments. "New?"

"Goes with the job," Lauren maneuvers her car out of the parking garage and onto the streets of Washington, DC. "Big improvement over the days we poured ourselves into my broken down old Volkswagen, h-m-m?"

"Sure is." Gretchen turned to Lauren and smiled. "Hey, congratulations on landing the job of the Century, Lauren. You're the envy of UC grads."

"Thanks. More important, though, I love my job." Lauren steered the car to a charming little café in out-of-the-way Watergate.

"I'm impressed," Gretchen said as she viewed the café. "Almost as charming as Shaman's Pub."

"Almost," agreed Lauren. "Shaman gets the edge, though. His place is a piece of history. Watergate is young yet, by comparison." The two ordered wine and lunch, and settled down to shortening the gaps in their lives since the last visit.

"Gretchen," Lauren asked as she takes a sip from her glass of Chardonnay. "Whatever happened in Ridgecrest last year? I read all the newspapers—those that carried the story—but they left me with more questions than answers."

"Shouldn't wonder. They tossed out my testimony as irrelevant, but Kristin's the one who really shocked me—and I thought I knew her so well."

"How so?"

"Oh, we kept up our weekly luncheons after you left, but I lost a *confidante* last year." Gretchen stopped as the waitress sets lunch in front of her, and waited for her to leave before continuing. "Remember in college, that old dogma we quoted? *Never trust anyone over thirty?* " At Lauren's nod, she continued. "We thought that pretty smart, didn't we? But you know?" she shook her head as if in disbelief. "It's not funny any more."

Puzzled, Lauren broke in, "I don't follow. What did that have to do with you and Kristin?"

"Kristin and Harley betrayed my trust. I lost a whole week in my life, and the people I trusted most, let me down. We're the *soon-to-be-over-thirty* crowd, Lauren, and we're worse. We don't trust each other."

Lauren laughed. "You lost a week—a whole week? What were you drinking?"

"It's not funny."

"Sorry." Lauren struggled not to laugh. "Go on."

"Someone knows what happened, but no one's talking. Lauren, I don't trust Harley any more. We tiptoe around the subject as though we were strangers—it's like living in a box. It can't continue."

"You mean... you can't talk about it."

"Right. Harley and Kristin prefer to pretend nothing happened—that I dreamed it all—and perfectly content to leave it at that."

"And you can't?"

"I hate mysteries unless I'm writing them."

"Anything I can do?" Lauren asked.

"I don't know." She looked at Lauren, her meal momentarily forgotten. "I used research for my new novel as an excuse to get away and collect my thoughts. I never thought I'd look forward to getting away from home, but it's become my bogeyman."

Lauren, in the process of removing her napkin ring, stared at her friend...wondering if she'd slipped into her own fantasy world, when suddenly Gretchen laughed. "You should see your face, Lauren." She stifled her laugh.

Lauren, stunned by the sudden change, choked out, "I didn't know whether to laugh or cry. You had me scared." She wiped at her eyes. "I must say, though, I don't much appreciate your pulling my leg."

"H-m-m? Oh, no." Gretchen shook her head, and fiddled with her silverware. "I didn't mean to do that." She continued in a softer voice. "I really do need your honest counsel, Lauren. Goodness knows I don't get any at home any more—not now. We'll discuss it later."

They concentrated on eating—Lauren more puzzled than ever, and Gretchen hoping Lauren had answers to her puzzling questions—when Lauren's cell phone broke the silence.

Fishing in her oversized purse for her cell phone, checked the sender. "Excuse me, Gretchen. It's my office. I've got to answer it."

"Anything wrong?" Gretchen asked when Lauren snapped her phone closed. "You look as though you'd seen a ghost."

"Maybe I have. My assignment seems to have committed suicide, and I'm evidently the last person to see him alive. I've got to go by my office."

"I take it, you don't think it's a suicide?" Gretchen ventured to ask.

"I don't know, but if it's true, what happened to his monkey?"

"Monkey? Gee, Lauren, I know you can't discuss your job with me, but what's this about a monkey? Maybe I can help you worry about him."

Lauren laughed, and the two friends finished their lunch, leaving the charming little café. Lauren took Gretchen back to her small garden apartment before heading to her office.

"I'm glad you're here, Gretchen. Make yourself comfortable, and I'll see what Gadsden has on his mind. You'll be okay?"

"Sure, I'll appreciate the down time. Do what you have to do. I'll be fine." She dragged her luggage into Lauren's spare bedroom before calling out, "Oh, and good luck."

Lauren threw back a "Thanks," as she headed out the door to return to her office.

After she'd left, Gretchen toured the small, neat apartment—appreciating Lauren's taste in her selection of art. She wandered into Lauren's bedroom and spied a Siamese cat curled up among the pillows on her bed. The cat opened one eye and peered at Gretchen.

"Who are you?" she asked the blue-eyed Siamese, a replica of Einstein and Ming. "Do you have a name?" The cat rose from the pillows and strolled over to her, nuzzling her outstretched hand. Gretchen petted the gorgeous animal, and checked the collar around its neck.

"Oh, so that's who you are," Gretchen said, looking deep into the clear, blue eyes. "I'm happy to make your acquaintance, Cyrus. I'm Gretchen."

Back at the office

Lauren knew as soon as she walked into her office that trouble brewed. Mr. Gadsden waved her to a seat while he continued to talk on the phone. Lauren fidgeted, waiting for him. Something's definitely on his mind and whatever it is, it involved her. Finally, he finished his call, leaned back in his chair, and turned to look out the window behind him. Lauren waited, and wondered. *What is he thinking?*

Philip Gadsden, a Harvard graduate—an eager, young man under the age of thirty, she surmised—had an aura of success about him. A short, well-muscled young man, whose well-tailored suits camouflaged his bulkiness, and whose simplicity of language hid a well-muscled mind. *A man to be reckoned with,* Lauren knew. She watched him turn over in his mind how best to handle his latest problem—her.

When he finally turned to her, he confirmed her fears. "Lauren, I'm going to put you on administrative leave 'til we clear up this situation. At the moment, you're a marked target. If you have a place to go away from Washington, I advise you to leave."

"What happened, Gadsden?" Lauren asked. "At least I deserve the privilege of knowing why I'm being asked to leave."

"Of course, you do, but your assignment is finished. Your surveillance dug up a *can of worms,* and the brass upstairs are screaming *leak.* You know what that does to our business. The police will want to question you, but the Bureau works in secrecy. Only a handful of agents knew about your report, but when one of our undercover men is found dead shortly thereafter, the finger pointing begins. I want you out of it."

"And I don't want to go," Lauren objected. "Look, Gadsden, I agreed to take my chances when I signed on for this job. So far, I've had nothing but *baby* assignments. I want more than that." Lauren came close to begging.

"Don't take me off. Let me in on what you know. What happened to the information I dropped off? Where does it go from here?"

"I don't know, and that's the truth. It could have gone in any direction. You were not the only one to observe that little display on the Capitol steps, but a Senator can't be dragged into the public eye. Our job is to protect the President and the Congress—not to investigate them."

"Investigating Congressmen is a *no-no?* They have access to Top Security information. How do we know there isn't a traitor in Congress?" Lauren asked. "Who clears them for access?"

"We do, but it's cursory. We trust the voters who elect them. By the time a candidate goes through years of campaigning there's not much left to discover—at least that the way it's supposed to work," Gadsden offered in support of Congress.

"If I'm not involved with the Bureau, will I be free to investigate on my own?" Lauren asked. "That way, if I get into trouble, I take my own chances."

"You mean, like a double agent, Lauren?"

She pondered the question. "Never thought about it, but yes, I guess that's what I'd be."

Phil Gadsden turned back to the window behind his desk. He seemed to do his best thinking watching the monument across the square. Lauren waited.

"I'm going to recommend your release from the Bureau." He turned to face her, and grinned. "Because of your involvement in politics."

"My what…?"

"That's right," he says. "We can't have political activists in the Bureau—too dangerous." He picked up her report from his desk, and handed it to her. "Don't come near the office. Report to me by cell phone on my secure line. That's your new assignment."

Pleased, Lauren took her report. "Thanks, Phil. I'll do my best."

Later that evening

Gretchen and Lauren stretched out in the apartment prepared for a lively chat. Lauren wanted to know all about Kristin and Harley—and life back in Ridgecrest. Gretchen wanted to know more about Lauren's new assignment. She hoped Lauren didn't consider her a spy for wanting to learn every detail of her secretive job. With Cyrus vying for their attention, Gretchen told Lauren her story. Lauren questioned her, digging into aspects of Gretchen's story that she'd previously slid over.

"When did you first realize your dream had to be more than a dream?" Lauren asked. "Did you wake up one morning and say, *that wasn't a dream*, or did it hit you when you were being questioned in court?"

"You're making me analyze. Why?"

"Don't worry about *why*, answer the question. When did you first decide you were NOT dreaming?"

Sitting on the bed—her pajama-covered knees drawn to her chest—Gretchen thought back to her first suspicion. "When I met Julius at the overpass, and he warned me about Kristin. I didn't believe him, but he knew."

"Who's Julius?"

"A big, handsome, black cat I met in my dream."

"You talked to a cat *after* your dream?"

"Yes."

"And you didn't think that strange? Did you tell anyone?"

"No."

"Not good enough," Lauren decided. "You could have fallen asleep and dreamed that—or been tired enough to drop into the Delta sleep level—in which case you'd be susceptible to dreamlike thought waves." "Any other time?"

"Yes, when I found the dream potion in the pocket of a dress I never bought—stuffed in the back of my closet—along with the weirdest pair of silver slippers I'd ever seen."

Lauren came to attention. "You found what?"

"The antidote—the one I brought back from the *Netherworld*."

"Did you bring it with you?"

Gretchen laughed, enthused for the first time since the questioning began. "Yes, as a matter of fact, I did—in case I needed it."

"In case you *needed* it," Lauren repeated. "H-m-m. Why would you *need* a love potion?"

"Not *Heaven Scent*—a new potion. Professor Ipswitch calls it, *Resurrection*. It's supposed to defy the aging process," Gretchen explained. "As a matter of fact, I'm building my new novel around that potion—the one that turned me into a cat."

"Love it," Lauren laughed. "I want to try your potion." She stopped at the look of shock on Gretchen's face. "Hey, I'm thinking along the lines of solving cases and finding a missing monkey…but, if I can extend my life span in the process…"

"You'd take that chance to find a monkey?"

'He's more than a *monkey*, he's my job."

"What if you couldn't get back?"

"We'll be two this time." Lauren's enthusiasm bubbled over. "I'm *hot copy* right now. If reporters learn about me, I can't think of a better cover."

Gretchen watched her friend in amazement, loath to burst her bubble.

She doesn't think I'm crazy.

Lauren turned serious. "Besides, I'm on administrative leave—indefinitely—and advised to stay away from the Bureau. Think about it, Gretchen. We can sneak into places and observe—like mice in a corner. Come on. It'll be fun."

But Gretchen, having been a victim once, tried to dissuade her. "My little bottle won't last forever. What if we run out? We don't have the antidote."

"I thought you had a recipe."

"No, Professor Ipswitch has it."

Lauren didn't budge. "I'll take my chances. We'll get it analyzed here at the university, and if we need more, we'll make more."

"I hope you're right," a reluctant Gretchen said.

That decision reached, Gretchen and Lauren spent the rest of the evening plotting and planning. Cyrus nosed in wherever possible, and the vial of potion sat untouched on the dresser. "We'll check out the murder scene first," Lauren told Gretchen. "The newspapers never mentioned a monkey. He may have run off."

"You said, *we*. Does that mean I can come?" Gretchen asked. "I'd love to help, if I can."

"Sure. It's not as though I'm on assignment—administrative leave covers a multitude of possibilities," Lauren decided. "Let's get some sleep. We've a big day ahead."

"Looking for a monkey and testing potions? Yeah, a big day," Gretchen agreed.

Chapter Two

Day 2, Friday

The next morning after an early breakfast, the two sleuths headed for the apartment of the music man and his monkey. The place appeared vacant; no police barriers anywhere in evidence. That surprised Lauren.

"Well, what do you know?" she said. "I'll bet the FBI doesn't know this. Then again, maybe that's the reason there's no barrier." She rang the manager's office and a pleasant-looking young man opened the door. "What can I do for you?" he asked. "Looking for an apartment?"

Lauren hesitated wondering how to begin when Gretchen made a snap decision. "Yes, I am," she said. "I'll be in Washington, DC for about three months—doing research for a book I'm writing, and this looks like a nice, quiet place. Will you accept a three-month's lease?"

Lauren stepped back, puzzled. *What's she doing... asking about an apartment?*

The young man smiled at Gretchen. "You're in luck. I've had a recent vacancy. That particular apartment is being cleaned at the moment, but I can show you a similar apartment. "You two together?" he asked, looking at Lauren.

Lauren hesitated then said, "No, I'm looking for a monkey. I heard that its owner, an elderly gentleman, committed suicide. Do you know what happened to his monkey?"

"Suicide? Here?" The young man looked puzzled. "I think you have the wrong place. Mr. Alexander Dumant did have a pet monkey, but he checked out a week ago. Took his monkey with him, I suppose. It's his apartment that's for rent, but I assure you, there's been no suicide here."

He turned back to Gretchen. "Are you still interested?"

"Oh, yes, definitely," and to Lauren, "Sorry about your friend. Did you know him long?"

"No—a business associate. I'm glad he's okay." She stole a look at Gretchen, who winked. "Thanks for your help," Lauren told the young man, and left.

"When will the apartment be ready?" Gretchen asked the young man after Lauren left.

"Tomorrow. You need the furniture, too?"

"It's furnished?" Gretchen asked, surprised. "I didn't know." Then before the young man could change his mind, rushed on. "Of course, I'll need furniture. What's the matter with me?"

"I thought so. Come, I'll show you my apartment. It's identical. This way." He led her to an adjacent two-bedroom apartment.

Gretchen noted exits and entries, and asked, "Do all apartments exit into the courtyard?"

"Not all, the rear apartments open onto the pool area. Would you prefer to wait for one of those?"

"No, this is fine. I'm here to write. I'd prefer quiet to pool noises."

"Well, I'm sure you'll find this a peaceful place," he assured her as they returned to the office. "Are you ready to sign a lease?"

Gretchen signed, and received a key in return.

Leaving the office, she wandered around the apartment complex and found Lauren parked near the pool area. "Pretty slick," Lauren told her. "When did you learn to operate like that? Or does it come naturally to writers?"

"Maybe, I don't know," she said, climbing into Lauren's car. "Never know when my sixth sense will cut in—some call it intuition, some inspiration, whatever—I accept it, and don't challenge the source."

"Wow, sounds like we have a winning team."

Gretchen grinned, "Whatever. But since we seem to have no suicide, no murder, and no monkey, what's next?"

"We check the coroner's office. Maybe he can tell us what we want to know."

"Okay," agreed Gretchen. "Although without your ties to the FBI, aren't we sort of working in the dark?"

"Afraid of a little challenge, my dear?"

"Not at all. But if it's another dead end?"

"We'll try something else—like cranking up the old computer to check up on the missing Mr. Alexander Dumant. I must say, when my office cleans up a mess, they really clean it up."

"Makes one wonder, doesn't it? What if you're part of the clean up?"

"Now there's a thought. What if?"

"Sorry, Lauren, but things like that fuel the imagination of us *madcap* mystery writers. Maybe we should be watching the Senator instead of heading a manhunt."

"We'll do both," said Lauren "Now that you have your own apartment, do you plan to rent a car or do your sleuthing on foot? We've good taxi service—bus service, too."

"All of the above, as needed," Gretchen decided. "Is the coroner's office on the way?"

"No, it's across the bridge. Let's hit the senate office first, she suggested, heading out into the morning traffic. "At least we have my special parking permit. They didn't take that yet."

A few minutes later, Lauren pulled into the underground parking where they took an elevator to a balcony overlooking the Senate room. "We can talk here without interfering with the proceedings—and keep an eye out for the senator."

The two settled into plush seats at the rear of the balcony. A group of students and obvious vacationers occupied the lower seats. Lauren pulled out binoculars. "I spend a lot of my time here," she told Gretchen.

Gretchen looked down on the floor of the Senate. "What are they doing?"

"Voting on a bill. See over there?" Lauren pointed to a scoreboard on the Senate floor. "A monitor keeps you informed of how the vote's going. Sometimes it takes hours. But if you love boredom, listen to the debates before the votes. Talk about nonsense… they can discuss anything regardless of relevance."

"I know—I've watched C-Span. I can clean the entire house while they discuss some moot point," Gretchen agreed. "I get the impression it's more important to be seen on television than score a point."

"It's the name of the game. They know the outcome before they cast a vote. See that guy down there?" She indicated a young man on the floor of the Senate.

"The one who talks to everyone? Sure, why?"

"He isn't talking to them—he's polling for votes. He screens the votes for the majority leader of the Senate. If it isn't in his favor, he keeps it from coming to a vote."

Gretchen watched the scoreboard recording the votes. Republicans piled up *no* votes while the Democrats voted *yes*. "Why vote if they know the outcome?" she asked.

"A formality—to get the votes on record."

Gretchen watched the voting process. "How can they be split so perfectly? Don't they agree on anything?"

"You noticed."

"Partisan loyalty?"

"You could say that."

"After they're elected it seems they should forget party and consider what's best for the people."

"They do. They just have different ideas of what's best. It's a tossup."

"It's a logjam," decided Gretchen.

"That, too. The rules change after every election. This year, Democrats are in charge."

"It really is a game, isn't it?"

"Hey, don't knock it. The party that gets the privilege of playing the game depends on your vote. That's why everybody should vote."

"Looks more like a popularity contest than an election—like in college when we'd vote for class president."

"It's called *Checks and Balances,* and it's worked for over 200 years."

"I didn't consider the implications at the time," said Gretchen. "I will in the future." She scanned the headlines of the *Capitol News,* a paper Lauren had picked up on their way into the building. "Says here, Senator Traficante is testifying before a House Ethics Committee, today. Should be interesting."

"Personally, I think he's being railroaded, although where there's smoke..."

"He didn't follow the rules?"

Lauren laughed. "He's a cowboy—definitely not the darling of the Senate. More the Marlon Brando waterfront type—gets a kick out of shocking the Teddy Kennedy button-downs."

"You don't like him—Kennedy, that is."

"He's a letch. Are we women the only ones who see that?" She got up to leave. "Let's go. Our senator didn't show."

"Where to now? The coroner's?"

"Right."

The two left the senate office building, and headed across the bridge. The girl at the desk of the coroner's office snapped her gum, and leafed through a register she pulled up on her computer. "Don't have a suicide," she said. "Sure you have the right place?"

"No," said Lauren. "Any other place they'd send a suicide?"

"No. We did have one admission under unusual circumstances—an Alexander Dumant. That the one?"

"That's him," Lauren said. "What were the unusual circumstances?"

"No idea. You'll have to talk to the medical examiner working on him. Hold on, I'll call him." The girl punched a button on her phone, and a red light glowed. "There's someone from the FBI to talk to you about Dumant," the girl said into the telephone, then pushed the speaker button.

"Send him in," a voice answered. "I'm ready for a break."

The receptionist ushered them to a closed door. "I didn't tell him you were females," the girl explained. "He's anti-feminist. You're on your own."

"Thanks." Gretchen followed Lauren into the forensic lab in time to catch the coroner's startled expression, but he recovered quickly and introduced himself.

"Good morning," he said. "I'm Dr. Ghoul." Lauren's eyebrows shot up and the coroner explained. "I'll thank you not to give me the usual Dr. Hyde jokes." He returned back to his work. "What can I do for you today?"

"I understand you have one of our agents here, an Alexander Dumant," Lauren said. "Do you have a cause of death?"

"Not yet...your office in a hurry? Tell them I'll have a report later today."

"Any guesses?"

"Suffocation. Kind'a hard to breathe with a plastic bag over your head."

"Then, why list it as a suicide?"

"The DA called it. He wants confirmation. Likes his cases wrapped up ASAP. Since there's no next of kin to complain, that's how it gets reported." He looked at Lauren, adding, "I've an idea that suits your office, too. Never know what kind of mud can get stirred up when the press starts to dig."

"I take it you disagree," Gretchen interrupted. "Why?"

The medical examiner turned to her. "You with the press?" he asked.

"No, I'm a writer, and any *maybe/maybe not* suicide interests me. Off the record, can we work together? Strictly fictional—with a twist?"

He looked at Lauren, then back to Gretchen. "Talk to your friend here, she's the FBI agent."

"It's her fiction," said Lauren. "What will your report say? Suicide?"

"The facts, ma'am, only the facts. Let the chips fall where they may. My job is over when I submit my report. What they do with it is of no concern of mine." He grinned at Gretchen. "But writing a novel of hypotheses, that intrigues me. Always wanted to be a character in a book."

Gretchen grinned back. "I'll be talking to you," she said.

The two turned to leave when Lauren hesitates. "One more thing," she said. "Do you know what happened to his monkey?"

"Don't know anything about a monkey." He paused before adding, "If your office mopped up, maybe they know."

"I'll find out," Lauren promised.

"Evidently, the monkey's the key, Lauren," Gretchen said as they left. "Now where?"

"Let's check the zoo. He couldn't just disappear."

Delighted the first phase of their plan went so well, Gretchen suggested, "Let's have lunch first, then worry about the monkey. I've an idea we won't have to go to the zoo. That monkey's hiding out close by."

Later that day

"Gretchen, remember the summer we went out West? There were six of us who wanted to experience the spacious forests and prairies we'd only read about in history books?" The two settled down a chat, Cyrus curled between them—attentive to their conversation and accepting attention from each in turn.

"Yeah, what about it?" Gretchen asked wondering how the events of the day reminded Lauren of that particular trip. "Thought we agreed to forget what happened."

"I know, but it comes back to me every time I see a corpse. Do you realize we're the only ones remaining of that group? You, me, and Kristen?"

"No, I never really thought about it. Kristen did make a return trip last summer—to pick up some mushrooms for Professor Ipswitch. I didn't know that until the trial. She never mentioned it." Gretchen stopped peeling the orange she'd selected from a fruit basket in Lauren's kitchen. "That experience never affected her the way it did the rest of us. Makes you wonder...."

"About what?"

"Where reality ends and fantasy begins. What did happen to those kids?"

Lauren stared at Gretchen. *Why would she question what happened years ago?*

"They were accidents, Gretchen. What else could they be?"

"What if they really were abducted?"

"Not likely."

"No? They were missing all of three hours, and when authorities found them, they told fantastic stories of being abducted by aliens." She looked at her empty glass. "Do you have any more of this wine?"

"Sure." Lauren changed her comfortable position and reached for the wine bottle and emptied it into the proffered glass. She headed for the kitchen and returned carrying a freshly chilled bottle of Chardonnay.

"I happened to believe their stories. Don't you think it's odd that they all died under unusual circumstances?"

"Must I remind you again, Gretchen, accidents are not unusual circumstances?" She refilled their glasses. "I believe the police reports."

"Right."

"You're back into fantasy vs. reality again, Gretchen. "Do you get some kind of vicarious pleasure in doubting your sanity?" She chided as she returned to her comfortable place on the sofa.

"Don't I wish—I'd give anything not to be bugged by nagging doubts, but too many weird things have happened for me not to believe there's more to this universe than our small minds can comprehend—or accept."

"Okay, let's see what we can do that's constructive. To start, write down everything you dream—no matter how crazy—and we'll do our own sleuthing. Concentrate on the monkey tonight, and fantasize where he could be. And, if that doesn't work, we'll dose you with a little of that." Lauren smirked as she waved in the direction of *Resurrection*—imposed temptingly on the table after Gretchen had unpacked.

"I doubt I'll need it. It isn't my sanity that's in doubt—and it doesn't take *Resurrection* for me to drift into fantasyland." She peered into her glass thoughtfully. "Sometimes I use my dreams to plot my stories—if I can remember them. Usually, they don't make much sense unless I can straighten them out."

"Well, one thing is for sure—there's been no UFO sightings in Washington. We've a lot of weirdoes here, but they're our own weirdoes—not from outer space." She nervously twirled the chilled bottle of wine in the ice bucket.

Annoyed, Gretchen asked, "What are you doing to the wine?"

"Sorry." She pulled away. "How did we get on this subject anyway?"

"You started it… by remembering something we swore we'd forget," Gretchen reminds her. "What made you think of it?"

"We've had a strange day, and it seems to fit." Lauren avoided her steady gaze—then shrugged. "How should I know?" she finished lamely. "No, that's not true. When I heard about the *accidents*, I began to wonder if there weren't a connection."

"Yeah, me, too."

"What about Kristen…she ever mention it?"

"No, we never discussed it." Lauren refilled Gretchen's glass and her own. "She shocked me at the trial. I never knew until then that she'd returned to the scene. She never told me."

"Why?"

"I don't know. Until the incident with the potion, I had no reason to question her. She also never told me about her association with Professor Ipswitch—not even when she gave me a bottle of her *Heaven Scent*."

"*Heaven Scent?*" asked Lauren. "Is that a potion, too?"

"Yes, the Professor's first. Harley sent it to a lab to have it analyzed. I don't remember what happened to it after that." She laughed. "Too busy staying alive as a cat to worry about what Harley discovered."

Unexpectedly, Lauren switched the subject. "Are you still into reincarnation and other worlds, Gretchen?"

Startled at the sudden shift in conversation, Gretchen stared at her —then recovered enough to answer her from the heart. "No one's ever explained otherwise to my satisfaction," she answered. "Are you still an atheist?"

"Until someone proves otherwise." Lauren laughs. "I know you'll think this a stupid question, but what religion believes in reincarnation?"

"I've no idea, but it makes sense to me—in this otherwise senseless world. Why do you ask?"

"Because you accept abduction in spaceships as natural phenomena, life as an animal as a possibility, and you accept dreams as premonitions. Add a belief in reincarnation to the mix, and I wonder how you justify the whole madcap mixture. Doesn't one need to make a choice at some time between science and religion?"

"No, they're both right as far as they go." Gretchen searched her thoughts, attempting to explain her views to a non-believer. You see, I think you're an atheist because religion has never been able to justify the hereafter to your complete satisfaction; therefore, you accept the scientific version of evolution. For me, science has never been able to fully justify the beginning of life as a normal progression from the Big Bang theory—that's an elusive mystery that no one can answer specifically. I do believe that some day science and religion will merge, and become one and the same."

"And you believe reincarnation explains both religion and science?"

"Yes, even though each peers through the looking glass from different angles."

"Looking glass?"

"For want of a better word—different spectrums—if you prefer. Before my mother died, I thought like a child. After her death, I seemed to absorb some of her wisdom. Maybe she reincarnated herself through me. Isn't that crazy?"

Gretchen looked at Lauren for reassurance, but Lauren didn't answer. Instead, she picked up the empty glasses, stored the wine bottle, and headed for her room. At the door, she turned to face at Gretchen. "It does not compute," she said.

"Oh, dear," Gretchen worried. "Why do I expect others to accept my crazy theories…even if they do make sense to me."

Chapter Three

Day 3, Saturday

Next morning, the two intentionally forget their discussions of the previous evening, and set about the business of collecting items Gretchen would need to set up temporary housekeeping—dishes, towels, linens, etc., adding a few purchases from local shops. By the time they finished, Gretchen has pictures on the walls, pillows on the sofa, and food and wine chilling in the 'fridge.

"Looks great," Gretchen decided, surveying their handiwork. "Like I've lived here forever. I'll set up my computer, install a telephone, and I'm in business. What's the first order of the day?"

"Why ask me? You seem to have all the answers," said Lauren, a touch of sarcasm in her voice.

"You're upset."

"Yes, I'm upset. You never said.... I don't understand... Why did you sign that lease?"

Gretchen ignored her question. "Let's have lunch. I'll fix a salad, and break open the Chardonnay."

Lauren continued. "I did so look forward to your staying with me, especially since I won't be working for a while," she pouted as she helps Gretchen prepare the lunch. She knew that Gretchen would tell her in her own time, but later—munching on Caesar salad and croutons, she became impatient. "You didn't answer my question."

"I'm sorry, Lauren, but there's a few things I didn't tell you yesterday."

"Such as?"

Gretchen ate quietly for a time. Finally, she said, "I've left Harley."

"You? Wow! Talk about a bombshell..."

"I know. I can't believe it myself. Maybe it isn't permanent—I don't know."

"What happened?"

"Kristin. I tried to ignore it—wait it out—but it didn't go away. I felt like an intruder in my own home—so I decided to get as far away as possible, and think it through. Maybe we needed the distance. At first, I buried myself in my writing—that's supposed to be great therapy—but it didn't work, so here I am. I got the apartment because I may stay here permanently."

"I'm sorry," Lauren said. "When did it start?"

"I don't really know—I presume it blossomed during my disappearance. At least, that's when things seemed different. I think Harley was relieved when I decided to visit you."

"That does explain the apartment, and I'm not sure your being alone is good."

Gretchen grinned at her friend. "Oh, but that's not the only reason I chose this particular apartment. Call it intuition, if you wish, but I think the key to your disappearing monkey is right here in this complex. The little devil may come home when things settle down, and someone should be here when he does."

"A-h-h, the pieces are sliding into place. You do have a method to your madness. Maybe I should spend the night in case he returns to the scene of the crime. I've heard the first night in new digs is quite revealing."

"Good idea. Then we're in sync. Besides, didn't your boss advise you to get out of town? Pack a bag, bring Cyrus, and take that vacation."

"You're right. Then, you can tell me the rest of your story—about you and Harley...and Kristin."

"It's a deal—if you'll do something for me."

"Whatever it is, I agree."

Later that Evening

After revisiting Mr. Ghoul, the medical examiner, and learning that he had submitted his *suicide* report to Lauren's office, they settled down to read the revised report he'd handed Gretchen. "For your novel," he'd said with a twinkle in his eyes.

"I knew it couldn't be a suicide," Lauren said, after reviewing the report.

"It isn't the real report, Lauren," Gretchen informed her. "It's revised for fiction. What makes you think it's the real one?"

"I don't know, but I do. I think our Mr. Ghoul wants protection in case his suicide report backfires."

"That's crazy, Lauren. Official is official—and the *official* report said *suicide*. This is a fabrication created strictly for my book." She frowned. "Isn't it?"

"I don't think so. I can't outguess the agency, but I'll bet the official report doesn't even list the correct name. How do we know we saw the body of Alexander Dumant? The super at the office says he and the monkey checked out. Dead men don't check out."

"Can you call your office?" asked Gretchen.

"Sure, if I have anything to report. I don't. I've only a suspicion."

"But if the monkey shows up, you'll have proof, won't you?"

"That's a long shot."

Gretchen, sitting next to a lazy Cyrus curled up between the two girls, stroked his neck and Cyrus responded with deep purrs. "Maybe a shot of *Resurrection* will bring the monkey home?" she teased.

Lauren's eyebrows shot up. "*Resurrection!* That's it."

"Lauren, I'm only teasing."

"I know you are, but I'm not."

"Let's try something else, first," Gretchen decides. "If it doesn't work we'll try the potion, but only as a last resort."

"What do you have in mind?"

"A little hypnotism—see if you can remember a few more details of that morning on the Capitol steps."

"You can do that? I must say… you're full of surprises." She stared at Gretchen—her silence a pregnant pause before she asked, "What kind of details?"

"Details you may have missed. For instance, is the man you saw on the Capitol steps the same man we saw at the coroner's office? Or are they two different people?"

"You have doubts?"

"From what I'm hearing—it doesn't compute."

Lauren laughed out loud. "That's rich. *Touche.*"

Gretchen ignored her. "Want to try?"

"What do I have to do?"

"Relax, and follow my instructions."

"That's all?" Lauren emptied her wineglass. "Okay, I'm relaxed. Where do you want me?"

"Wherever you feel comfortable."

"Lauren sprawled, relaxed on the sofa, her eyes closed. "Okay, start your magic."

"We begin with your head and work down. As I name each part of the body, concentrate on that area and release all tension. By the time get to your feet, you should be totally relaxed and under my power. Ready?"

"I'll probably regret this," she muttered.

Lauren drifted off into a semi-hypnotic state. As Gretchen instructed her, she felt her body floating into space unattached to anything other than the voice heard as though from a distance. Cyrus, his cat eyes gigantic pools of liquid intensity, watched his mistress as though poised to protect her.

"You're moving back in time," Lauren heard the voice say. "Return to the spot where you stood in front of the Capitol steps." Immediately,

Lauren felt herself transported to the scene of the music man and his performing monkey dancing to the strains of *For Money, the Monkey Dances*.

"Tell me what you see," the voice directed. "In detail."

Engrossed in the scene evolving before her, the voice startled Lauren. She hesitated then began to speak. "It's all so hazy," she said in a voice she didn't recognize as her own. "I can't see too well."

"Move in closer. Does he look like the man at the morgue?"

Lauren tried desperately to move closer to the man on the steps, but people kept pushing her back. Finally, the man broke away and headed up the steps—a man she's seen many times at headquarters—not the man on the slab in the morgue. He stopped the Senator who turned to speak to him. Lauren could see the senator's frustration at the interruption.

"It isn't the man in the morgue," she told Gretchen.

"You're sure?"

"Yes, he's leaving. Should I follow?"

"If you can. Stay with him to where the taxi dropped him off," the voice instructed. "Keep talking—I don't want to lose contact with you."

"He won't hear me?"

"No, you don't have to whisper." Lauren listened to the soothing voice. "He can't see you or hear you—you're in my apartment, remember? Keep talking…nothing can happen to you… Tell me what you see."

"I feel so strange, Gretchen, sort of detached—as though I'm watching a scene in a play."

"Is the man talking to the cab driver?"

"No, the monkey chatters, and he answers him. Nothing that makes sense—like talking to a pet—that's all." The cabbie, music man and monkey—and the unseen Lauren—ride in silence. Occasionally, the music man, seated in the front, directed the cabbie to his destination.

"What's happening," a voice broke the silence.

"We're reaching the apartment, Gretchen, and he's arguing with the cabbie. Said he's charging too much, but he pays. The cab's leaving, and he's entering an apartment—the manager's apartment—not this one."

"Stay with him. Is he the same person we talked to yesterday?"

"No, this man's older. Oh, oh!"

"What is it?" the voice asked. "What do you see?"

"He's the man in the morgue—the one we saw yesterday."

"The manager? You sure?"

"Yes, they're arguing about something. The monkey—they're arguing about the monkey, and the monkey's getting mad—the music man does nothing." Suddenly, Lauren screamed and Gretchen awakened her. "It's all right," she soothed her. "You're safe."

Lauren returned to reality. "I think the monkey's killed him," she told Gretchen.

"Did you see him kill the old man?"

"No, but he's dead, isn't he? Now, the monkey's missing and so is the manager." She sat upright, bewildered. "What do you make of it? Maybe Alexander Dumant really did check out with his monkey."

"Doesn't make sense," Gretchen intimated. "Why must the manager die? You're sure they only fought about the monkey?"

"No, I'm not sure of anything. I watched a dream happening." She shook her head as though to clear it. "Even that's fading fast. Damn, I shouldn't have panicked. I almost had it. Great agent, I am."

"I think you did great. We know more than we did."

"Where did you learn the art of hypnosis, Gretchen?" Lauren asked. "When you were a cat?"

"No, it's nothing unusual," Gretchen assured her. "Some people are more susceptible to suggestion than others. You were easy."

"So, I'm easy. Where did you learn it?"

"It's not hypnosis, it's parapsychology. Harley uses it when he has a particularly difficult case. Sometimes I think he tries to use it on me."

"Really? He can do that?"

"Not without my consent. You consented."

"Yeah, I did, didn't I?"

"Even under hypnosis, you're in control. I couldn't get you to do anything you wouldn't do normally," Gretchen said. "And you did very well without resorting to drugs."

"*Resurrection* is a drug?"

"Has to be. How else could I lose control so easily? Kristin brings home a rare strain of Mexican LSD, and the Professor uses it in *Resurrection*. You really want a repeat of what I went through?"

"Oh, I don't know. Sounds like fun."

"You may not be so lucky."

"Anyway, we're a few steps closer to understanding what happened to the monkey. Let's get some sleep." Cyrus, already asleep and curled on the sofa, awoke instantly as the two broke for the night.

Lauren had a restless night. She tossed and turned—her mind continually returning to her hypnotic dream state. She tried desperately to recreate the scene in the apartment. What else happened that night? What did the monkey do? How did he do it? Was someone else there?

Gretchen slept peacefully certain that all answers come in time, and Cyrus stood guard over the two—spending time in each room—protecting his caretakers.

Chapter Four

Day 4, Sunday

"Today, we do tourist things," Lauren announced at breakfast as they relaxed over orange juice and coffee on Gretchen's patio. "Put your jogging clothes on, and we'll take in the local scenery. Washington is beautiful during the fall months, and the park isn't too far away—a great place to jog. We can check out the mansion, the place our local celebrity met her disastrous end, and maybe pick up some clues. Who knows, maybe all crimes lead to Washington—like all roads led to Rome."

"No one ever found out what happened to Chandra. Did your office get in on it?" asked Gretchen.

"No, strictly a local thing. They didn't want our interference," Lauren said. "It's a strange town. Things happen here, and about the time you think a mystery is about to be solved, everything closes down, and you're back to square one."

"Don't you get curious?" asked Gretchen.

"Sure. Like our suicide—someone who couldn't be disturbed needed protecting," Lauren explained. "Happens all the time. Some people hate being disturbed—have you noticed? Particularly, if it's something unpleasant—as if Washington prefers its fantasies to reality."

"Strange you should say that, considering the business you're in." Gretchen finished lacing her sneaks, and looked around for her jacket. "How do you explain it?"

"What's to explain? No one in this town can afford to get tagged with unsavory publicity or unsavory actions, as the case may be, unless it benefits someone higher up in the ranks. Case in point—the railroading of Traficante and a slap on the wrist for Torricelli—both guilty of the same misuse of public funds. Some day the real truth will emerge—as a footnote in history —when their exploits no longer affect someone's future."

"Will that happen with Chandra?"

"Already has—her senator's no longer news now that the *whodunit* won't affect Congress. Case solved, closed and yesterday's gossip—except for her parents the world forgets. Washington can keep its nails sharp and sheathed for the next crisis."

"What do you think happened to her?" Gretchen asked. "Any ideas?"

"Sure, lots of them. Why? You want the inside skinny?"

"Yeah, if you know. I have enough ideas of my own."

"Such as?"

"I think the senator's wife walked in on *kinky* sex and blew a gasket. That's enough to send any sane wife off the deep end. Tied up, Chandra had no defense, and the senator covers for his wife. How that's for phantom sleuthing?"

"Not bad...if that's what happened. Truth is, we may never find out—for another decade or so," Lauren decided. Truth is a rare commodity, buried deep in the bowels of propaganda. She tossed a jacket over her shoulders. "Come on, let's go."

The two take an apartment key and some spare cash, and head down a narrow jogger's path behind the apartment complex leading to the park.

Later that Day

On their return to the apartment, they're greeted by an upset Cyrus voicing his discontent at the new surroundings. He wanted out. Being locked up in an apartment for hours at a stretch with no relief raised the *cockles* of his ire. He eagerly leaped for the door the moment he heard a key in the lock. As Lauren entered, she felt the brush of feline fur against her legs, and realized too late what has happened. Cyrus disappeared around the corner of the apartment into the dark shrubbery and freedom.

"Cyrus, come back," called Lauren, panicking at the loss of her pet in a strange place.

"Let him go," Gretchen consoled her. "He'll be back when he's ready. Why don't we fix a sandwich, and go sit out by the pool?" She headed for the kitchen. "Cats are inquisitive creatures. Can't blame Cyrus for wanting to inspect his new territory—he's more human than you think."

"You're right." Eyeing her friend, Lauren realized the validity of her statement, and returned to the apartment, closing the door on Cyrus. "I spend far too much time worrying about creatures who can take care of themselves."

"Animals have built-in survival equipment, and no restraints on using them if backed into a corner. We think our animals are helpless little creatures that need humans to care for them. I think it's the other way round."

Startled, Lauren asked, "Really? Why?"

"Haven't you noticed?" Gretchen explained. "We're restricted by rules and regulations, and lose more of our freedoms every day. Animals only lose their freedom when they get involved with humans."

Lauren looked at her friend, realizing she's serious. "I think you miss not being a cat," she said. "Do you?"

"Sometimes. I had so much freedom as a cat, and didn't appreciate it. Although I don't regret my cat adventure and can't imagine going back, I've had nothing but problems since my return." Gretchen pondered her statement. "You know the irony of the whole thing? We do it to ourselves—build little cages around us, lock the doors—and call it freedom."

"Wow, sorry I said anything." Lauren headed for the bedroom. "Before you really start to complain, I think I'll take a shower and mull that over." She gave Gretchen a strange look. "I like your idea of eating by the pool, though. We can discuss the merits of *man vs. animal*." She disappeared.

Gretchen sat there—appalled at her outburst. "Now, I've done it. Why, should I expect others to be as crazy as I am?" She entered the cooling water of her own shower. *One thing I missed as a cat, my showers.* She let the soothing waters relax her frustrations, realizing that showers had become her defense mechanism against troubled thoughts. As a cat, she could find a quiet corner away from the other cats, groom her long, white furry exterior, and contemplate. As a *humanoid* she sought the showers.

"Mm-m-m." She laughed as the water sprayed her face. "We really are alike."

Later, munching sandwiches and snacks by the pool, Cyrus wandered into view. Trailing close behind him, the monkey in question. The two animals parked themselves on the grass a safe distance away. Lauren reached over and offered a banana to the scruffy monkey. He came close enough to grab the banana, then quickly moved to a safe distance before stuffing it into his huge mouth.

"Cyrus accomplishes, while we merely dream," Lauren mused.

"But where's his master?" Gretchen asked.

"On a slab at the morgue—the monkey's proof of that—and my hypnotic dream, a mere fantasy. So much for magic Gretchen, we're back to square one."

"He doesn't look like a killer." Gretchen eyed the monkey—her first glimpse of him. "What do we do with him?"

"Be logical, Gretchen. He isn't a killer. He's a homeless pet who's lost his master—and his master's lying on a slab in the morgue. That's reality."

"But what if he is the killer, Lauren? That in itself is reason enough for a cover-up."

"We'll have no more of your hypnotic theories, Gretchen," Lauren argued. "Nothing but the facts, ma'am, the cold, hard facts—I refuse to enter your fantasy world again."

"Okay," Gretchen acceded. "But that doesn't solve the *Case of the Errant Monkey*, does it? What do we do with him now that we've found him? Trap him? Leave him free? Or call the zoo to rescue him?"

"None of the above…for the moment. He's survived a week without our help. He'll survive another night, and we'll worry about what to do with him tomorrow. Tonight, we make friends with him." She handed the monkey another banana, and it disappeared as fast as the first one. The afternoon passed with Lauren no closer to winning over the monkey than before.

Later that night, Gretchen heard a scratching noise at her window. Looking out, she saw the monkey looking in at her expectantly. When she opened the apartment door, the monkey scooted in, heading for a space behind the sofa. She left him there, and went back to bed.

Chapter Five

Day 5, Monday

"It's been nearly a week, and I've heard nothing from my office," Lauren related at breakfast. "Have you seen our monkey this morning?"

"Not today. He came to my window last night and I let him in. Probably in his usual sleeping place—behind the sofa." Gretchen put down her coffee cup and peeked behind the sofa. "Still there," she said returning to the table. "You know, we can't keep calling him *monkey*. He needs a name. Any ideas?"

"How do you know it's a *he*? Maybe we should find out first—then name him."

Gretchen ignored the suggestion. "We could give him a neutral name, like Tony or Max."

"I know. Let's call him *Alex* after his former owner. That's neutral."

"Good idea," Gretchen agreed and tried it out on their unwelcome guest. "Hey, Alex, would you like some breakfast?"

Alex peeked out from behind the sofa, and began to chatter. "Krik-krak-kri-kri-ka."

"I'll take that for a *yes*," Gretchen said, and handed a banana to the hungry creature. Alex grabbed it and returned to his secure spot behind the sofa. "Maybe Alex really is his name."

"Could be. Not that it makes any difference, but it does conjure up questions about Alexander Dumant."

"Yeah," Gretchen agreed. "Could *Alex* be a code word, and Alexander Dumant an alias?"

"Isn't Alexander Dumant the name of a character in a book? Sounds like an alias."

"No, that's Dumas, and he's an author."

"So he is," Lauren said. "Maybe you should pay another visit to the manager, Gretchen. Tell him about the monkey coming back last night, and find out if he knows *anything* about a man who checked out with a monkey, then left him behind."

"Me? Why me? It's your case."

"We've a spooked monkey in *your* apartment. You don't know me, remember?" Lauren reminded Gretchen how she conveniently separated them when she registered.

"Okay," she agreed. "I'll do it. You see if you can get a picture of the missing agent."

"Done. Sounds like you think my hypnotic dream's a possibility."

"Worth checking out."

Lauren looked at her dismayed, her mind reeling. *So far, she's been right on target. Is she psychic?* "You may be right," she admitted, getting up from the table. "Okay, you do your thing, and I'll do mine. We'll meet here for lunch."

"Sure."

Later that morning Gretchen found herself face to face with Hunter in his office. "Hi, Hunter," she greeted the young man. "Is *Hunter* your first or last name?"

"Whichever you wish." Hunter grinned her exuberance. "What can I do for you today?"

"You'll never guess what happened last night, Hunter," Gretchen related to the eager super. "A monkey knocked on my bedroom window."

Hunter looked worried. "A monkey? Impossible."

"That's what I thought," Gretchen agreed. "But I seem to have inherited your past resident. What do you suggest I do with him?"

Hunter, eyes enlarged and mouth gaping, stuttered, "I-I d-d-don't know."

"Did your previous resident leave a forwarding address?" Gretchen probed, as Hunter continued to stare as thought in a daze.

"I d-d-don't know," the puzzled young man repeated.

"Maybe the computer…?" Gretchen waited, but Hunter did not move.

"Then, it is true," he finally said.

"What's true?" asked Gretchen. *He doesn't know.*

Hunter collected himself, and took control. "Ms. Dandrich, I can't give that out. It's privileged information."

"Okay, you take the responsibility for shipping a lost monkey to wherever it's supposed to go." She listened to the ticking clock as she awaited the dazed Hunter to make a decision. "Maybe I should call the zoo to come get him."

"N-n-no, d-d-don't do that. Let me think."

"He's made his home behind my sofa, and won't let anyone near him." Gretchen watched Hunter struggle with his conscience until he finally agreed to violate the rules.

"I guess there's no harm in it." He punched a few keys on the computer. "That's funny."

"What is?" Gretchen tried to see the face of the computer. "Don't you have a forwarding address for Mr. Dumant?"

"No, only a request to forward all mail to the Senate Office building in care of Senator Claghorn. Never heard of him, have you?"

Gretchen shook her head. "Are you sure that's all there is? I'd hate to have to call the zoo to pick up Alex."

"Alex?"

"Yeah, it's what I call him for lack of a better name. Did his owner leave his music box behind, or did he take it with him?" she asked.

"I don't know. Why?"

"Well, if he left under mysterious circumstances it may still be here, and might tell us something about our mysterious stranger."

"We could check the storage room, if you like. We hold anything we deem of value for thirty days, then dispose of it," Hunter said, finally coming to life.

"I'd like," Gretchen said.

Hunter selected a set of keys behind him, and Gretchen followed him out of the office and down a hallway. Hunter stopped at one of the doors, slid the key into the lock, and opened the door. Empty.

Gretchen came out of shock first. "But it's only been two days. Did *Good Will* come by?"

"Not that I know." Hunter turned to Gretchen. "Believe me, I know nothing of this. The maid cleaned your apartment two days ago, and picked up the key to store the stuff left behind. No one else picked up the key."

"The maid. Did she give the key back?"

"She left it on the counter."

"Did you check to see what she stored in the room?"

"No."

"Do you have a name for the maid?"

"No, she's with a cleaning company. It's not always the same one—depends."

"The name of the company? Do you have an address or phone number?"

Hunter answered her questions in a monotone, as though in shock. "Let's go back to the office," she said. A stunned Hunter locked the door, and followed Gretchen back to the office. He checked the address for *The Merry Maids Cleaning Company* and handed it to her.

"Will you let me know what you find out?" he asked.

"Sure. Call ahead first and tell them I'm coming. I may need confirmation from you."

"I'll do that. Anything else?"

"Yes, would you call me a cab? I've no transportation."

"Oh, that's right. You don't, do you? Why don't I lock up, and we'll both go?" he offered. "It's only a few blocks away."

"No need, I can walk. Tell me how to get there and call them when I'm about there. Don't want to give them time to dispose of anything."

Hunter's eyebrows formed an arch. "Why?"

"If someone went to that much trouble to cover up what happened, others might be involved. They'd have their instructions, too, don't you think?"

His mouth dropped. "Do you think? Hunter stared at her. "Th-then m-maybe I'd better go with you," he stuttered in disbelief. As she hesitated, he became resolute, turning brave. "If what you say is true, I can't let you go it alone. We'll take my car in case we find something to bring back."

Their trip to the *Merry Maids* proved futile. The FBI had beaten them to it, arriving at the precise time the *Merry Maids* picked up the key. "They insisted I give them the key," the maid told Hunter. "And they promised to drop it off with you when they finished. Did they?"

"They may have," Hunter said. "I wish you'd called me. They cleared out the entire storage room. I've no idea what they took. "You're sure they were FBI men?" he asked.

"They showed me credentials," the *Merry Maid* told them. "Why? Is there a problem?"

"The tenant left something behind. We need a forwarding address."

"Oh," said the vivacious *Merry Maid*. "That's no problem. I found this envelope behind the sofa after they left. I forgot about it—until now." She pulled a letter from her spacious pocket and handed it to Hunter. "Will this help?" she asked.

Hunter glanced at the return address on the envelope and gleefully planted a kiss on the rosy cheek of the stunned maid. "Oh, yes—and thank you. You're a doll." He handed the envelope to Gretchen. "It's all you need. The FBI can have the rest."

Later that evening

The two sleuths met at the pool to exchange findings. Gretchen related her discovery of the empty storage room to Lauren. When she'd finished, she said, "Now, it's your turn. Did you get any pictures of our mystery man?"

"No mystery. Only a picture of a corpse my boss swears is the slain FBI agent. That's a fact, Gretchen. You seem to want to turn everything into a fantasy."

"Guilty, but look who's talking," Gretchen defended herself. "You were ready to take a dose of *Resurrection*, to prove a point. Hypnosis is a proven technique, even if it's not admissible in court—and it's certainly a lot safer than any drug."

"I agree, and I don't object to using whatever facts we have, if we get the right answer." She rumpled her hair with nervous fingers.

"What's wrong, then?"

"I'm frustrated. I don't even know why I'm not working—how I earned my undeserved leave. At first, I thought it was for my own safety...."

Gretchen picked up on her thoughts. "Now, you don't. Why?"

"I think they wanted me out of the way—afraid I'll identify someone they don't want identified. Then you showed up, and threw me another idea—and confused everything."

Lauren looked so despondent.

"I'm sorry, Lauren." Gretchen realized she's stirred up a hornet's nest. "I've had a crazy year, but that's no reason for me to create doubts in your mind. Haven't you said anything to your supervisor about your suspicions?"

"No, he doesn't want to hear. He had his own problems, and I've my instructions. Unless I find something substantive to add to the investigation, I'm to stay away. Maybe he thinks I'm being followed—and maybe I am."

Her fingernail pierced the orange she held with a vengeance, and the juice spurted into her face. "Damn," she said, moving back and wiping her face with her hand.

Gretchen watched, feeling helpless. "Maybe the letter we found…" she attempted to console her.

"What about it? It gives you a return address, that's all—probably a dead end."

"Oh ye of little faith," Gretchen said. "Didn't you notice the return address? It's in Connecticut—a town close to Ridgecrest."

"Really?"

"Some farm in Redding. We could be there in a day."

Lauren hesitated. "What about the animals?"

"Take 'em with us. They seem compatible. Besides, it may be Alex's new home."

Lauren mulled it over. "It would be nice to go home for a while. She grinned mischievously. "Where would we stay? With Harley or Kristin?"

"Neither. There's a great *Bed and Breakfast* place not too far away that I've been dying to try. We could stay there."

"Like thieves in the night?"

"Why not?

Lauren laughed. "Okay, Gadsden suggested I leave town, and I'd love to meet your cat friends. When do we leave?"

"Do you need to tell him?"

Lauren considered her question. "No," she decided. "I'm following instructions. How about you? You need to tell Hunter—or Harley?"

"I don't think so."

"'Then, let's roll. Is tomorrow too soon?"

"Not for me." And the two toasted their new adventure.

Chapter Six

Day 6, Tuesday

"Looks like you plan on working." Lauren watched Gretchen pack up her computer. "Don't you ever go anywhere without that scourge of tranquil living?"

"It makes life easier," Gretchen explains. "You'll see. I can check and send messages from wherever I am without having to disclose my whereabouts. As long as my friends hear from me, they don't worry. They don't need to know where I am. That's what I like about e-mail, total secrecy."

"I never felt the need for a computer at home," Lauren replied. "I have one at the office that holds a wealth of valuable information, but I prefer to write my personal letters by hand and put a stamp on them. More personal."

"Do you have an e-mail office code?"

"Sure, one I use at the office, but...oh, oh...I see what you're getting at," she answered as she realized where Gretchen was heading. "You know, I could pull up files from my office on your computer, couldn't I?"

"Unless your office has blocked your access. Do you think they may have?"

"I don't know. I'll check it out when we get where we're going. Which is where, by the way?" Lauren asks. "Did you make reservations?"

"Yes—for the animals, too. Next problem—how do we get Alex into the car? He's used to riding, but not with us. He only comes out from behind the sofa for Cyrus. Any ideas?"

"Cyrus has a Pet Taxi. We might find another for Alex—then tempt him inside with a banana." Lauren suggested.

"I hoped we'd find one in storage, but your office cleaned out everything."

"Sorry about that."

"Yeah, sure. So far, we've only two leads—Alex and an address on an envelope."

"Time is getting short, and we haven't made much headway."

"I know, we may be on a wild goose chase," Gretchen admitted. "Think of it as a vacation, Lauren. How long since you've been home?"

"Three years. After Mom died, I never went back." She goes back to packing, amused. "This will be my first vacation since I started work, and I'm not even sure it's voluntary." She continued packing. "Do we look up Kristin…or Harley?"

"That depends," Gretchen decided, setting up her computer on the table. "What we need to do first is find out what kind of access you have on my computer before we leave. There's some reason you've been grounded and you need to know why. I suggest you check your office files now—before we leave."

"You're right. I should have done it right away—maybe I wouldn't have needed hypnotizing." She opened up the computer and began pulling up information from her office. Gretchen left to shop for a Pet Taxi for Alex and to stock up on bananas for the trip. When she returned she found Lauren still on her computer.

"I found my earlier files, Gretchen, but everything since I left is blocked. Cut off at the crucial point. Damn, I did want to find out who that guy in the morgue really was."

"Ah," teased Gretchen. "Then you do accept your hypnotic vision." She put Cyrus into her lap, and pulled at his ears. Cyrus protested and nipped her finger. "Ouch, I'm sorry, Cyrus." She kissed his injured ear and Cyrus jumped down, retreating to his basket.

"I'm not making friends with Cyrus," she said. "I think he reads my mind."

"What makes you say that?" Lauren asked absentmindedly, as she continued pulling up information from the computer. "Got it! We were right."

"About what? The body exchange, or the music man?"

"The music man is no more. He's gone—shed his identification when he left Alex behind. The old manager is now the dead agent. They did pull a switch, and your hypnosis was dead center."

"How did you break in?"

"I'll never tell. It's my secret." She printed out the information, and closed up the computer. "There's even a picture of him, but Gretchen, you know what this means."

"No, what does it mean? You're the agent—I'm only trying to write a story."

"It means we can't let on we know anything about it. I'll bet the man at this address is the missing agent who is living under the assumed name of the missing landlord."

"But who killed whom?" Gretchen asked. "The FBI? Is this the way they work? And what about the old man's family...won't he be missed? Someone's bound to ask questions."

"Evidently he's expendable. Like Chandra—people forget as soon as the next crisis hits the fan. Except for family, we really are expendable. Life goes on—with or without us."

"And yet, we all think we're so important in the world. I suppose that's the reason we have a God. Someone to care for you when no one else does," decided Gretchen. "How do you survive without that life line?"

Lauren laughed at a serious Gretchen. "You learn to live without crutches," she said. God's a crutch. People create all kinds of crutches to help them throughout their lifetime—drugs, alcohol, cigarettes, sex, politics, music, or religion—pick your poison. Religion is probably the most widely acceptable crutch. Your belief in reincarnation—that's an unusual crutch I grant you—but a crutch, nevertheless. You'd be surprised how easy life becomes when you've only yourself to depend on."

Gretchen observed her friend, recognizing her logic, but unable to accept the fact that her own deeply held faith in God could be little more than her particularly chosen crutch. "I've never heard you talk like that before, Lauren. I guess I never believed you actually viewed a world without God."

"Remember, I studied philosophy in college," Lauren reminded Gretchen. "Sort'a makes one question accepted ideologies."

"So did I, but it didn't change my conviction of a Supreme Being in charge of the Universe," Gretchen countered. "How does your philosophy explain evil, then? Do you deny evil exists? After 9/11, how can anyone doubt there isn't a Devil?

"Man is good. Man is evil. Man chooses. Face it, Gretchen. Good and evil will continue to struggle throughout mankind. But to blame some non-existent figment of the imagination with a crime is futile. Neither God nor the Devil has a thing to do with it. Some guy wants to rule the world —all in the name of Allah—and convinces a whole nation they will meet virgins in Paradise if they commit suicide by dive-bombing planes into American towers. How nutty can you get?"

"But I've met the Devil. He does exist," Gretchen said, refusing to accept Lauren's logic. "Maybe you do need to take some of my potion—and get you in touch with God."

Lauren laughed. "That'll be the day, but I accept your challenge."

"Oh, my God," Gretchen mused. "What evils have I wrought upon the earth?"

Meanwhile, at Lauren's Office

Philip Gadsden glared at the man standing before him. "You're supposed to be dead," he accused him. "What are you doing in my office?"

"We need to talk. That perfect agent of yours is getting in my way. She suspects something."

"Oh? How so?"

"She's been snooping around in what's none of her business. I thought you took care of her." Agent Archibald Carlton stood before Agent Philip Gadsden with determined fury, his dark eyes blazing with righteous indignation. His newly grown black beard barely hid a snarl beneath its sparse camouflage.

"You're paranoid. I had e-mail from her. She's out of town, and out of the way. I've told her nothing and she's never met you," Gadsden reassured him. "I don't know what kind of damage you're talking about."

"Where did she go?" asked the irate young man.

"She didn't say." Gadsden turned to look out of his window wondering at Agent Carlton's sudden paranoia. "Hey, you're the one who dreamed up this little scenario, 'the better to find the killer,' you said." He turned from the window and faced his agent. "I gave you that chance—against my better judgment—I hate subterfuge. I assure you—Lauren knows nothing."

"I left my kid in charge of the apartments, and he tells me he's leased the place for the summer. Thinking it may be your agent I went by to check.

"And…?"

"Wrong female. This one's blond, but she has my monkey. He must have come home after his scare. Damn, I hated having to give him up…"

"You didn't make arrangements for the monkey?"

"I didn't have time. He got loose and took off, and I didn't have time to search the grounds. Just as well—he'd be a dead giveaway.

Anyway, Hunter assured me the monkey has a new owner and is well taken care of. Maybe, after it's all over..."

"You're sure the old manager had no family. What if someone comes around asking questions?"

"No problem. He's a loner—no next of kin. I checked."

"You'd better find out why he was in your apartment. Did he learn of your connection to the FBI? Maybe your senate friend isn't really a friend."

"Now who's being paranoid?" The agent grinned for the first time since his entry. "Where did you say your agent comes from? Connecticut?"

"She attended school there. I believe her only remaining parent resides in New Mexico." He watched the bearded man, and tried to read his thoughts. "You planning on chasing her down?"

"Not if she really doesn't know anything."

"She doesn't, and we've cut access to her computer. You're safe."

Chapter Seven

Day 7, Wednesday

Rolling into Ridgecrest the next day, Gretchen and Lauren checked into the Red Mill Inn, a previous country residence that had been converted into a respite for weary travelers. The Inn, famous for its fabulous meals and soft piano music in the evenings, boasted a stable complete with riding academy, a fresh-water spring for the horses, and a separate home for traveling pets.

After settling the animals into their new quarters, they questioned the innkeeper in an attempt to determine the location of their quarry. She could add nothing more than they had already determined.

Later in their room, Gretchen unpacked her computer and checked road maps in the area of their destination approximately ten miles away. It appeared to cover quite a large area of land. "I think we'd better check this place out before someone recognizes me," Gretchen suggested. "You're safe, but I'm too well known here to escape detection for very long."

"Then it's time we set the stage," Lauren said, heading upstairs to their room. "You've got to let Harley know you're back. Why you insist on staying out of town, I don't understand. You've a perfectly nice home in town."

"I want to do some sleuthing on my own for a while. Then I'll let Harley know I'm here."

Lauren sensed another reason. "You suspect something. What is it?"

"I want to observe and relieve my nasty little mind, and find out for myself what's been going on in my absence." Deserting her computer, she opened her suitcase, tossed some clothes into the dresser, hung her dresses and robe in the closet, and stored her suitcase on the available floor space. Then, she turned and sat on the edge of the bed, facing Lauren.

"Do you blame me? Don't answer that. It's Friday and lunchtime, and I'm wondering who Kristin is lunching with today. Maybe Roscoe..."

"Or Harley," added Lauren. "That's why you're hiding, isn't it?"

Gretchen eyed her in silence, ignoring the question. "I'm hungry, Lauren. Let's feed the animals and check out the dining room. If I remember, they have pretty good food here."

"You aren't up to Shamans?" Lauren teased.

"Not today. I'm curious about that address we found—and how it's connected to my Washington apartment."

"Great." Lauren locked the room and they headed for the dining room downstairs. "Glad to see you've got your priorities in line."

Mrs. Warren, the young, brusque innkeeper, proved helpful and soon provided the two girls with a substantial meal of lunch leftovers—all the while entertaining them with century-old tales of the Inn. "Why, at one time," she told them, "Even the rebels took advantage of our services—right here in Ridgecrest. And George Washington and his troops stayed here...he right there in the room where you are now. My family has owned this piece of land for over two hundred years...that's how long we've been here in Connecticut. "Course, the days of affording that much land are gone forever, and it became impossible to keep the place going. We had a choice...either sell or make the place profitable. We chose the later, and we've never been sorry... such a wide array of guests we've had.... Why I could tell you stories..."

With appropriate "oohs" and "ahs," and an occasional nod of acceptance, the two girls listened and learned. Mrs. Warren, like a young actress on stage and in her element, entertained them with a running history of the Revolution—doubtless stories handed down from past generations. How much truth and how much merely a figment of a fertile imagination, Gretchen and Lauren didn't know. They didn't question her veracity, but before leaving asked her about the address on their envelope.

Checking the map and the address, she narrated another story. "The place at one time belonged to a member of the British Parliament. They returned to England some centuries ago—when they lost the war. And since then, the place had changed hands quite often. A friend of mine tells me some young Hollywood actor bought the place recently. She's never seen him, and I don't know if it's truth or rumor. But I see no reason to question the source of my information. I'm busy here at the Inn, and don't have time to check up on what never makes the newspapers." She eyed them satisfied. "Have I been of any help?"

"Enormously," the girls agreed. "You've been a tremendous help. Thanks so very much."

Back in their room, Gretchen asked Lauren, "What do you think? Are we on a wild-goose chase?"

"Could be, but it's a chase worth pursuing, don't you agree?"

"Right! Come on, let's go feed the animals."

Chapter Eight

Day 8, Thursday

The next day found them heading for the farmhouse Mrs. Warren told them about, not knowing what to expect. They'd brought Alex with them, hoping he would indicate in some way a familiarity with the surroundings. He'd become quite the conversationalist, and chattered non-stop during the ride, 'til Gretchen wished they'd left him behind.

"Sounds as if he's trying to tell us something, but I don't know what it is," Lauren said. "What do you think?"

"Maybe he can show us when we get there. Do you think an actor really does own that place?"

"Why not? I think the big question is how an envelope with his address wound up in a Washington apartment complex. That's the connection I want to make."

As they neared the farmhouse, Alex's chatter took on a new dimension increasing in volume. He began tearing back and forth across the back seat of the car.

"Look! He recognizes the place. He's been here before."

"Maybe we should have brought his Pet-Taxi," Lauren said. "What to do? Take him back?"

"No, leave him here if he wants—if it's his home. I don't particularly like taking care of a monkey who isn't ours anyway."

"Maybe you're right. That's why we're here, isn't it? I only hope we can control him long enough to complete our investigation."

As they drove into the yard, Alex went berserk, and as soon as the door opened, he darted out and rushed in the direction of the barn. Helpless, Lauren and Gretchen watched. "Let him go," Lauren said. "We'll worry about him later."

Gretchen turned her attention from the barn to the house in time to see a good-looking young man approach them. He looked as startled to see them as they were to suddenly be confronted. Dressed in an expensive riding habit complete with French-cut boots, he looked the picture of a man of leisure. The two girls stopped in their paths.

"Wow!" Lauren said.

"Cool it." Gretchen answered. "Remember, we're working."

The young man didn't appear surprised to see the visitors. "You're here early," he said. "I don't have your horses saddled yet."

"Oh," Lauren stuttered. "We're not…"

Gretchen interrupted. "Can we look around the farm while we wait? You've such a charming place here, and I've never seen a real farm in action before. Would you mind?"

Flattered and eager to show off his place, the young man agreed. "Well, it isn't really a farm. It's a riding academy now. No one's lived here for a number of years, and when it finally came on the market, I picked it up —mainly because it's within commuting distance to New York. I think you'll find the only animals here are horses."

"Did you restore the place?" Gretchen asked.

"No, I don't know who did that. Probably whoever owned it at the time." He headed for the barn. "Look around, if you wish, while I get the horses ready," he offered.

"Do you know who had the place before you?" Lauren asked.

"No, I bought it through a receivership. I paid the cash—they gave me the deed. That's all I can tell you, although I hear it has quite a history. Always planned to research what caused the fire… maybe I will some day… but you know how it is—it's in the future. Right now, I'm busy getting my academy rolling."

"Maybe we could help," Gretchen offered. "We have the time, and it looks as though it could be an interesting undertaking."

"Really? You'd do that? Why?"

"Because this place has a history, and I'm a writer. Who knows what would be uncovered during a search, don't you agree?"

"Well, yes, I suppose so." He thought it over before stating, "You're not here for riding lessons, are you?"

"No, we're interested in old historical places like this one. I'm surprised someone hasn't covered it already, especially after the fire. How did that happen?"

"The fire? I've no idea. All know is that's the reason given for restoring the place."

"Are you sure?"

"That's what they told me when I bought it." He looked at Gretchen. "You say you're a writer. Do I know you?"

"Probably not. I'm Gretchen Dandrich. And you are?"

"Christopher Martin. Are you the same one on the *Best Seller's list?*"

"Guilty," Gretchen admitted, introducing Lauren. "My friend, Lauren Calloway."

"Go ahead and do what you have to do," he told them as he sees his students arriving. "I've some horses to saddle. Where do you want to start?"

"The barn—we can help you saddle the horses since we've made you late. Lead us to them."

"Not necessary," he laughed. "That's part off the lesson today—grooming and saddling their own mounts." He led them to the barn, Lauren hoping they'd find Alex before the students did. But they needn't have worried. Alex was nowhere to be seen.

"Where do you suppose the little rascal went?" Lauren asked. "Maybe we shouldn't have brought him."

Gretchen ignored her. "What do you think about Christopher?"

"I wish he didn't have students today. There's a million questions I'd like to ask him."

"What kind of questions?"

"What relationship he is to the old man in the morgue? Do you think he could be a son or a nephew? And does he know what happened?"

"Not likely."

Entering the barn, the two helped Christopher lead out three horses from their stalls and watched as he demonstrated to the students the correct technique for preparing their mounts.

"We could help," Gretchen suggested.

"He's doing fine. Besides, those girls already know. They're taking advantage of a handsome instructor."

"Jealous?"

"Not at all. I only wish they'd step on it and get out of here so we can look for Alex."

"They're not paying any attention to us. Let's go look for him." The two disappeared into the barn, and climbed the ladder to the loft. "Reminds me of the barn in my dream," Gretchen said. "You don't suppose...? No, couldn't be."

"It burned up, didn't it?"

"Yeah, a barn in Ireland, not in Connecticut."

"Oh, Gretchen. Get real. You don't get to Ireland through a hole in the ground. You probably weren't any farther from home than next door."

"You think I made it up, too, don't you?"

"Too? Who else questions you? Harley? Kristin? Shaman?"

"Never mind. I thought you believed me."

"Let's explore the loft—maybe Alex is up there."

They find nothing in the loft except a few bats sleeping upside down on the rafters, and a few birds pecking away at the hay for seeds. They poked into corners, lifted up the hay, and eventually decided to give up the search.

"There's nothing up here," Lauren decided continuing to dig in the hay. "Maybe in the house. Any ideas, Gretchen?" But Gretchen had already started down the ladder.

"Maybe we should check the town archives," she suggested, stopping halfway down the ladder to view the spot where she last saw Elise and Shaman. "This barn looks just like the one in my dream." *Amazing, the similarity! Whatever did happen to Elise? Did Shaman bring her back with him, or did she retreat to her grave for another year?*

From her view on the ladder, Gretchen spied Alex jumping up and down and chattering wildly—as though he'd made a big discovery. She moved toward the stall to see what had excited the monkey, and called to him. "Alex, where have you been?"

Meanwhile, Lauren, having satisfied herself that nothing of importance could be gained by further investigation in the loft, started back down the ladder. She reached the bottom rung before she realized Gretchen was no longer in the barn. *Where could she have gone?* She wandered around the stalls, but couldn't see her.

"Gretchen?" she called. "Where are you?" Hearing nothing, she ran outside and called again. "Gretchen?" Racing around the perimeter of the enormous barn, she found herself back where she started. Gretchen had disappeared.

She reentered the barn, and climbed to the loft. "Gretchen? Gretchen?" Nary a sound interrupted the quiet desolation of a deserted barn.

She headed for the house and knocked on the door. A maid answered.

"Did a young, blonde woman come here within the last few minutes?" she asked.

"No," the young maid told her. "No one's been here since Mr. Martin left. Who are you?"

"Never mind. I'll go find Mr. Martin." Thinking of secret passageways and underground caches, she wondered if Gretchen had found something of interest, and returned to the barn. Empty. The quiet worried her. *What did Gretchen say as she descended the ladder? Maybe she's pulling her disappearing act again.*

Roping a horse from the corral, she saddled the gentle bay and climbed onto the English saddle. *I've got to find Chris.* Giving her mount a gentle pat on his neck, she headed in the general direction she'd seen Chris take the class. She found the group relaxing under a tree, Christopher the center of attention as he related Hollywood adventures to his attentive students.

"Come on, join us," he invited her. "Where's your friend?"

"That's why I came looking for you," Lauren said. "I can't find her. She seems to have disappeared. You don't have any secret passages or anything in that barn, do you?"

"Not that I know of," Chris laughed. "But then I haven't had much time to look around." He checked his watch. "We've got a few more miles to go before we stop," he said. "Why don't you ride along? By the time we get back, your friend will probably be waiting for us."

Lauren agreed, and the girls remounted their horses for the remainder of the lesson. An hour later they returned to the barn and unsaddled their mounts. As the stabled animals ate and drank their fill, the class, fascinated by the story Lauren told them, spread out into every corner to examine the barn. They searched in vain, but like Lauren, found nothing.

"I've got blueprints for this spread. Come on in. Maybe they'll show something," Christopher invited. The students left reluctantly, and Lauren followed Chris into the farmhouse. "Can I fix you a drink?" he asked, digging into a pile of papers in a basket near his desk.

"Yes, please. I think I need one," Lauren agreed.

"Wine okay?" At Lauren's nod, he asked his maid to bring two glasses of wine.

"She's done this before, you know," Lauren ventured.

"Who's done what before?" Chris asked automatically, still rummaging through the basket. "Oh, here's what I'm looking for." He spread the blueprints across a table, leafing through the many pages as the maid brought in a chilled bottle of wine and two glasses. Chris poured one for himself and handed one to Lauren who joined him at the table.

"Can you read those?" she asked.

"Sure, they're easy to read," he told her, explaining how the prints were set up. "This is the overall blueprint of the property. The other pages give detailed instructions for the builder to follow as he restores the buildings. Here's the one for the barn. As you can see, it required extensive work. See? It gives you the size of the beams, how they're joined, and smaller detailed sketches of the rafters, loft, stalls and manger. Everything—but I don't see any place for secret passages."

"Neither do I," Lauren agreed uncertainly. "But Gretchen and the monkey are gone. They had to go somewhere."

"Monkey? You never said anything about a monkey."

"We found him…and your address in an apartment in Washington," Lauren tried to explain. "We thought maybe the two were connected…." Her voice trailed off as she realized how foolish she sounded. "Never mind, there has to be a logical answer."

"Maybe Gretchen found the monkey and he led her astray." He grinned at her. "From my experience with monkeys, they're guilty of doing that."

"You're teasing me. Do you know anything about monkeys?"

"My uncle has a monkey. He loaned him out to children's parties and special events. Even loaned him out to an FBI agent as a cover while he staked out some low life. Smart as the dickens, that monkey."

"Your uncle doesn't happen to live in Washington, DC, does he?"

"Yeah, how'd you guess?" Chris turned to her. "Oh, FBI—the tip off. "I think we should talk," said Lauren.

"I thought we were talking." Then noticing Lauren's serious expression, he stopped bantering. "What are you saying?"

"You haven't heard? How long since you've seen your uncle?"

"Not for some time. After he learned I'd bought this place, he planned on making the trip, but it's hard for him to get away…"

"Because he managed an apartment complex in the city, was on call for the monkey, and kept a low profile?"

"That's right. You know him?"

"I guess it's time to tell you why I'm really here. As Bette Davis once said, 'Fasten your seat belt. It's going to be a bumpy ride.'" She poured herself another glass of wine, refilled his, and started her story. She begins her story with the wild tale Gretchen told her—the strange dream and unsolved murder—and ended telling him the reason for their trip to his farm.

Christopher sat stunned. "Whew," he said. "I feel like I'm in the middle of a Hollywood plot? You think my uncle is that man—the one in the morgue? And that he's not a suicide?"

"We came here hoping to find your uncle. When we learned that some actor had bought the place, we didn't make the connection."

"Maybe you should leave it be. Let it remain a suicide. I don't think I like the idea of his being murdered. Opens up all sorts of devious activities I'd rather not know about."

"We can't now—because of the monkey…and Gretchen…I think it's all tied in. Where's the monkey? Where's Gretchen? If the monkey's as smart as you say he is he's found something and took Gretchen with him to wherever he went. I wish I'd gone down the ladder when she did, instead of…"

"Don't blame yourself," Chris consoled her. "It probably had to happen the way it did."

The two sat in silence each lost in thought with only the sound the maid's activities emanating from the kitchen. Chris broke the silence.

"This friend of yours, she seems to have some kind of connection to a *Netherworld*. I've heard of people like that—highly sensitive to ethereal vibrations. Never met one before—except in the imagination of Hollywood writers. They're imaginative creatures…open to all kinds of weird fantasies…always looking for something unique and different…a new twist to a story.…"

"Tell me about them. They're imaginative creatures."

"True, now here I am—right in the middle of a real live spook movie." He laughed at the thought as its absurdity struck him.

"I must say you're taking this lightly. I can't be quite that cavalier about the supernatural. I'm an atheist, and fantasy plays no part in my life."

"This excursion may change your mind about a lot of things, Lauren. First, we wait for your friend to return. If she doesn't, then we'll decide what to do."

"You wait. I have to feed Cyrus, my cat. Call me…if Gretchen shows up on your doorstep?"

"Will do, but if she isn't here by morning, you'd better plan on staying here. Bring Cyrus with you. He'll be right at home with the other animals."

"We won't be a problem?"

"No, I'd appreciate the company. Besides, I'm fascinated. Maybe Gretchen found a lead and is following up on it. Maybe she'll be knocking on my door before morning."

After his consoling words, Lauren left the farm to return to the Inn. Once there, she managed to escape Mrs. Warren's many questions about Gretchen and their visit to the farm. She fed Cyrus and settled down for a disturbing night in her lonely room. Eventually she fell asleep—wondering what really did happen to Gretchen.

Chapter Nine

Behold! What you crave shall be yours to your uttermost dreams and beyond.

Day 9, Friday

Lauren woke up the next morning feeling as tired as if she hadn't slept. She'd dreamed about a strange Gretchen who kept trying to tell her something. Whatever it was, it eluded her this morning. She couldn't remember. *Maybe after I've had my coffee...* but coffee didn't help. As through in a haze, she seemed to recall Gretchen in an unfamiliar place having trouble returning—her lips forming words. Lauren couldn't make a connection—she seemed to be saying ... *archives—check archives.*

What archives? Land records? Early building plats? Is that what she meant? There has to be a history of landowners dating way back to the time man first laid claim to property ownership. The courthouse is open today, and I've nothing but time—*it's worth a shot.*

Lauren selected an old pair of jeans and her riding boots—*in the event, I have to ride another horse today.* Enthused, she headed downstairs for breakfast where she found Mrs. Warren presiding over the kitchen. *I'll quiz her about survey plats if I get a chance.*

"Where did you leave your friend?" Mrs. Warren asked supervising a plate of bacon and eggs. "Doesn't she eat breakfast?

"She's with friends," Gretchen lied. "I promised her I'd check out the town records on that piece of property we talked about yesterday. It's very important."

"Oh, is it now." Mrs. Warren answered filled with curiosity. "You were out there, were you? Did you find out who lives there? Is it that Hollywood character?"

"It's a riding academy...for future equestrians," Lauren said. "Do you know anything about possible hidden passages or tunnels on the place? Maybe built back in revolutionary days?"

"Why could be, you know. Come to think of it, I did hear something about them having to fill up sink holes when the old barn burned down. Nearly took the main house down, too, but they caught it in time."

"The barn burned down? When?" *Maybe Gretchen didn't dream it.* She shook her head to clear it. *No, it's a coincidence.*

"Oh, yes, about a year ago," Mrs. Warren mused. "Quite a mystery about it at the time. You know, they never did learn how the fire started."

"Really?" Lauren pressed the woman to keep talking. "Wasn't there an investigation?"

"Oh sure, but then...it was Halloween...probably kids...."

"No doubt." *She doesn't know.* "Now, about the archives...."

"Oh yes, the courthouse. Go on into town. You can't miss the building—it's off the main drag and quite impressive...some two hundred years old...an old historical landmark so to speak. I believe they store the old records in the basement, if I remember... The women will steer you in the right direction. They're real helpful, but inquisitive... I have to warn you."

"That okay. I've no secrets. Gretchen has them all." She left the old lady gaping after her. *That should keep her occupied for a day or so.* She hurried down the steps to her car.

Later that day

The women in the archives department were more than helpful to Lauren. They insisted on furnishing her with copies at no cost. Armed with copies of old land plats and loads of lore about its history, Lauren returned to the academy. The nippy weather told her that winter would be early this year. *I'll need warmer clothes soon—wherever I decide to live.*

When Lauren knocked on his door, Christopher gave her the unwelcome news. Gretchen hadn't made an appearance. He'd heard nothing unusual during his restless night. Lauren surmised that Gretchen must be hungry as well as cold by this time.

"Did you bring your suitcase?" he asked.

"No, I'm giving us one more day to find her. My restless night gave me a new lead, and I've brought something you might be interested in—even if it doesn't lead us to Gretchen." She laid copies of the old plats out on a table.

Ecstatic, Chris viewed the collection. "Why didn't I think of this?" Together they spread out the copies on the table. Choosing the one for the barn, they poured over it, looking for anything different about the barn that didn't now exist.

"Something else I found out this morning," Lauren told him. "Your barn is a restored version of the original—the one that burned down. When Gretchen returned from her disappearing act a year ago, she talked about a barn that burned down, but didn't know the location of the barn. She got it mixed up with weird dream fantasies that sounded too surreal to be authentic."

"And you think the two incidents are tied together? The fire and her dream?"

"Not exactly…maybe…I don't really know." Lauren hesitated, not wanting to make the connection yet.

"Exactly…what did happen to Gretchen? Maybe you'd better tell me the entire story…from beginning to end. Better yet…" he glanced at his watch. "Have you had lunch?"

"No, and I'm really hungry."

"Then let's go out. It's the maid's day off, and I'm not a cook."

"Could we lunch at Shaman's? That's where the story starts."

"Shaman's? Hey, I've heard about that place. Weren't they involved in some big *hush-hush* murder trial a while back?"

"Yes, that's the one where Gretchen testified and no one believed her —not the jury nor her husband. I'm afraid I don't believe her either."

"Ah, a mystery. Gretchen lives her own stories, h-m-m?"

"You don't believe it either."

"I think I'll hold my beliefs in reserve," he answered. "But since Gretchen isn't here to lead the way, we'll start—as you say—where it all began." He helped Lauren with her coat, got his own, and pulled on an English-style golf cap. "Great disguise," he told her as he directed her to his Jeep.

"What? The cap?"

"And the Jeep." He laughed. "People ignore both."

Lauren understood. Ridgecrest had its share of celebrities, and paid little attention to them, but occasionally it did happen and a crowd would form. At two in the afternoon, they found Shaman's Pub nearly deserted. The regulars had gone back to work, and the once roaring fire burned low.

Einstein and Ming stretched and welcomed the newcomers, then returned to their job of gracing the hearth. A nippy day, Shaman directed his guests to a table near the fire so they could capture the heat from the fireplace.

Chris glanced at the two cats—curled like bookends on the warm stone hearth. "Beautiful decoration for your fireplace, Shaman," he commented.

Shaman grinned. "That they are," he said. "Names's Eintein and Ming. But they're more than decoration."

"I don't doubt," Chris answered. Turning, he glimpsed Shaman staring at Lauren.

"You've been here before, have you not?" Shaman asks her.

"Yes, back in my college days—with Gretchen and Kristen. You remember?"

"Never forget a pretty face. Three of the prettiest *colleens* at the University."

"Thanks, Shaman. You've quite a memory." He helps her off with her coat and hangs it on a wooden peg on the far wall. Chris adds his to another peg and returns to the table. "We did hang out here a lot in those day," she tells Chris, and to Shaman, "You've become a landmark. Glad to see you're still in business."

Shaman looks pleased and accepts her compliment. Lauren introduces Chris to Shaman as he takes their order. Returning with their wine, he diplomatically leaves them to their private conversation.

"A landmark?" Chris asks. "How do you figure that?"

"Historically speaking," Lauren explains. "This town dates back to Revolutionary days, and a lot of the buildings are that old. Like the place where Gretchen and I are staying—*The Red Mill*. According to Mrs. Warren, the innkeeper, *The Red Mill* housed British soldiers at one time. A private residence then, it later became a refuge for the patriots on their way to fight the British—and a stopover for General George Washington and his troops."

"And this place? A watering spot for troops?"

"As far as I know, it's always been a tavern. Shaman seems to have been here for an eternity, which goes back to my story. Gretchen claims he's been reincarnated many times. I know he spins yarns as though he has first-hand knowledge of history—even as far back as the 1500's. Most customers accept them merely as entertainment, and give them their due.

"And, Gretchen? How does she accept his yarns?"

Gretchen tells a story about his meeting an old-time love at an Irish graveyard once a year—on Halloween night—the only time they can meet since Elise through some twist of fate, is destined to spend eternity until Shaman can rescue her."

"And how does he do that?"

"Through Magus, according to the story."

"Magus—isn't he the fictional character who travels the *Netherworld* chasing Evil?"

"You've heard of him?"

"As an actor, you learn all kinds of useless information. Gretchen claims to have been to this *Netherworld?*" Lauren begins to laugh watching the expression on Chris' face. "What's funny?" he asks.

"Your expression—your eyes—they're like saucers. You're a skeptic who wants to believe," she accuses him.

"Hiding one's expression isn't something you learn in acting class. Sorry about that."

"It's okay. I like it. Better than having to guess people's motives—as happens in my profession."

"Ah yes, your profession. We only got as far as Gretchen and her career as a writer, I've no idea what you do." He waits for her to answer. When she ignores him, he repeats his request. "What do you do—when you're not sleuthing?"

"That's what I do. Sleuth."

"Must I dig it out of you? What do you sleuth?"

Lauren hesitates wondering if she should say any more, then answers cautiously. "I work as an investigator for the FBI. At the moment, I seem to be on administrative leave. Somehow your uncle's death is connected to my extended vacation, and how I happen to be here." She pulls out an envelope from her purse. "Gretchen found this in her apartment in Washington—with your return address on it."

"I see. That's why you two came sleuthing?"

"Yes, to find out if there's a connection between my investigation and your uncle's death. We were about to give up, when Gretchen disappears."

"And you think there's a connection."

"I don't know. Why didn't anyone notify you of your uncle's death?"

"I've no idea, except…"

"Except what?"

"I changed my name. My given name is Alexander Dumant, the same as my uncle's. I did it for anonymity in the theater world… as well as to protect my uncle."

"I understand the theater reasoning, but why your uncle?"

"He's mixed up in *stooging* for some senator. I don't know the details, but that's how he uses the monkey. In his last letter, the one I answered, he said something about pulling out and returning to Redding. 'Too risky,' is how he put it. That's the last I heard."

"Maybe they don't know you exist. No *next-of-kin* to notify—that type of thing—happens all the time. People do get lost, you know. Particularly in my business."

"Your business—spying on an old man?" Chris asks.

"Not me, my office. I'm trying to find out why they cut me off, put me on indefinite leave, and refuse to tell me why."

Shaman brings their order of pastrami on rye, replenishes their glasses, and disappears. Chris takes this interval to study Lauren. *A no-nonsense type—embroiled in something she can't define logically. And she can't afford to be illogical.*

"I'm curious when things don't make sense," Lauren continues. "Gretchen may stretch the truth and believe in fantasies, but I deal with facts. That's why I'm here. To make sense out of nonsense, so to speak."

Chris stops eating and roars with laughter.

"I'm glad it amuses you," Lauren says. "Look, you've awakened the cats. I don't think they appreciate your humor."

"You're afraid," he accuses her. "Afraid that cats can really talk, that Einstein is a *familiar*, and you're out to—as you say—make sense out of nonsense." He glances at the two cats on the hearth. "I do believe they are listening," he teases. "Maybe they have the answers."

"Oh, come off it. You refuse to take me seriously. Look, it's getting late and this place is filling up. Have you learned enough?" As she speaks, the door opens, and a particularly cold breeze fills the room. The two shiver, and Lauren turns in time to see Professor Ipswitch take his usual place at the end of Shaman's bar.

"*Déjà vu*," she tells Chris. "Speak of the devil. That weird little man who caused the draught is the esteemed Professor Ipswitch—and nemesis of Gretchen's fantasies. I wonder if he and Kristin are still in business?"

"I think we should stick around and get to know the old coot," Chris says. "He's the inventor of weird potions, h-m-m? You pique my interest, my dear. He looks harmless enough."

Lauren laughs. "Chris, you look absolutely rapt. It would serve you right..." she stops as she realizes he isn't listening. "What are you thinking?"

"Let's have a nightcap with the professor," he says—a roguish expression on his face.

"Be careful, Chris, you may be his next victim," Lauren muses, gathering up her things and following him to the bar. Chris props himself next to the eminent professor and Lauren next to him.

"Shaman," he says, "How about a *crème de cocoa* for the two of us before we leave." He turns to the professor. "How about you? Will you join us?"

"Be delighted," says Professor Ipswitch. "By the way, I don't believe we've met. I'm Professor Ipswitch from the University—and you...?"

"Christopher Martin, and this is Lauren Calloway. We've heard about your inventions."

"If it's a nightcap you're seeking," the professor says. "I've the perfect aphrodisiac. It's my latest invention—guaranteed to make dreams come true." He hands a small vial to Chris. "One drop is all it takes for peaceful, undisturbed rest."

"Why, thanks.". Chris examines the vial the professor hands him. His eyebrows rise to a question mark, as he reads the inscription on the vial. *"Behold! What you crave shall be yours, To your uttermost dreams and beyond."*

As Shaman sets the drinks before them, Chris asks, "Is this guy for real?"

Shaman shrugs. "Hasn't killed anyone yet."

Chris holds the vial as though poison, and looks at Lauren. "Are you game?" he asks.

"Why not? Looks harmless." He adds a drop to Lauren's drink, and pockets the vial.

"You don't want to dream?" she asks.

"Someone has to stay sane to pick up the pieces," he tells her.

Chapter Ten

Day 10, Saturday

Lauren feels rather than sees the escape route Gretchen has taken. Vaguely aware of her encounter with Professor Ipswitch at Shaman's Pub the night before, she seems to hear his voice in the distance. *"Sweet dreams, my dear. May you find all the happiness you crave beyond."*

"Where's Chris?" she wonders, looking around and floating on what looks like a giant lily pad. A frog croaks at her invasion of his property. "What are you doing on my lily pad?" the frog asks.

"I'm sorry. I seem to be lost. You didn't by chance see a tall, blonde female wandering around here, did you?" Lauren asks the frog.

"You mean that intruder Alex brought back with him?" He looks towards the shoreline. "She's over there. Evidently, she likes our mortal enemy, the cat, more than she does us frogs. Take her away."

Lauren turns and notices a giant playground built offshore for animals. There were swings and chutes, ladders and sandboxes, and weird-looking buildings giving shelter to various animals, each separating various species of animals—reminding Lauren of a giant zoo.

What catches her eye is a monkey hanging on a banana tree contentedly peeling its fruit. *He's too big for Alex.* Next to the monkey, she sees Einstein and Ming, the Siamese cats from Shaman's hearth, curled around a huge cauldron. Einstein raises his head and opens his big blue eyes as she comes out of the water. Satisfied she presents no eminent danger, he returns to his sleeping position.

Where does Gretchen fit into this scene? And, Einstein, is he the talking cat Gretchen told me about? As she walks around the outside perimeter of the playground, she notices the wide assortment of various wild animals. *Must be some type of invisible barrier separating them; otherwise, they'd all be fighting.* She moves from one animal to another—from the lion perched on a grassy mound to a lamb nursing at his mother's side. *No barriers—how is that possible?*

Seeing neither Gretchen nor Alex, she returns to the sleeping Siamese on the hearth—a hearth that looks very much like the one in Shaman's Pub.

"Einstein," she asks the sleeping cat. "Have you seen Gretchen?" Lauren wonders why she thinks it's possible to talk to a cat as if it were human. Einstein is mute, but looks in the direction of the forest. "She's in the forest. Where? Could you show me?"

Einstein gets up, stretches his magnificent loins and after sniffing in his companion's ear, glides towards a path leading into the foliage. Lauren follows. In the darkness, she hears loud animal noises. They mute as Einstein approaches the opening of the glade ahead. There he pauses, his nose directing Lauren to a structure that appears to be an entrance to a mine.

Lauren looks at Einstein, puzzled by his meaning, but sensing that he expects her to enter the opening. "You want me to go in there?" she asks, her skin starting to crawl in fear. She looks ahead at the darkness. *Wish I'd thought to bring a flashlight!* But as she enters the opening, the passageway becomes as light as day. She finds herself in a room furnished in early Colonial, and adequately appointed as though ready for occupancy at any time. *Have I slipped into the Seventeenth Century?*

She turned back towards the entrance and sees a door close. She is alone. Attempting to return, she found the wall solid and impassable. Apprehension growing, she is about to scream when Gretchen appeared at her side.

"Lauren, when did you get here?"

"What's going on, Gretchen? Where is this place?"

"You shouldn't be here," Gretchen told her. "But I'm glad you came."

"I'm dreaming, but how did you get here?"

"I followed Alex. I saw him in the barn, and caught hold of him at the same time he disappeared. I must have lost consciousness for a while, and when I came to, I found myself in this room. Alex seems familiar with the place, but can't get me out 'til it's over."

"What do you mean? "Til what's over?"

"It's an underground movement to change the world. Your outfit is mixed up in this whether they know it or not."

"How can that be? I heard nothing."

"Think about it, Lauren—the senator, the FBI agent and the mix-up of bodies in the morgue—all part of a gigantic plot for global control. *A new beginning,* they call it. New books printed to replace war-infested history books. Peaceful coexistence taught in schools to students. Think of it, Lauren—the world a safer place to live—peace for all eternity."

"I don't know, Gretchen. Who are the good guys and who are the bad ones? It doesn't make sense to me." Lauren sat on one of the uncomfortable antique chairs, and Gretchen perched on the hearth beside her. She looks at the old-time spinning wheel by the fireside, and the huge, black cauldron hanging over a fire burning low in the massive stone fireplace. It's as though she had stepped back in time.

"Must there be good guys and bad guys?" Gretchen queries. "Peace doesn't involve good or bad when aggression is erased. If we know nothing about violence, it doesn't exist. It's that simple."

"Denial doesn't change history, Gretchen. Better to face reality. I rather like the world I live in, don't you?" Lauren asks.

"Well, I must admit, it does sound like a movie plot, but isn't it a great idea?"

"No, it isn't. Perfection is a bore. Achieving perfection makes life worth living. Who's in charge of this nefarious plot? Do you know?"

"There you go again—being rational, Lauren. I think it's a blast. "

"You didn't answer my question. Who's in charge?"

"I've no idea. They call themselves, *The New Americans.* They're in the process of sending out letters calling for new members who want to live in a peaceful land," Gretchen says. "I think it's a great movement. *Give Peace a Chance.* We have demonstrations and everything."

"But Gretchen, you've never been politically active before. Why now?"

"It's so exciting. Besides it makes me feel part of something—something worthwhile—and I like that." Lauren watches as Gretchen talks of her new feelings, her involvement, and her acceptance.

"You've no intention of returning, have you?" Lauren asks.

Gretchen looks guilty. "There's no reason to return. Not 'til there's a better world."

"That's my job, Gretchen," Lauren says. "And it can be done—but not by abolishing the past in exchange for some *Alice in Wonderland* philosophy. I ask you again, Gretchen. Who's in charge?"

"I've no idea."

"Can I see a copy of the letter—the one drumming up new membership?"

"Sure." Gretchen leaves the room and returns with a four-page letter, written in closely typed copy, and entitled, *The American Way of Life,* (AWOL.) "See? Even the acronym is synonymous to Peace."

"So it is. AWOL from the world—underground—it's all there, isn't it?"

"I'm so glad you understand, Lauren. In some way, your organization is involved. I haven't figured out how, but I'm sure it is." As Lauren reads the proffered letter, Gretchen writes. When she finishes, Gretchen hands her the note she has written.

We're being monitored. Be careful what you say. Pretend to accept their philosophy or we'll never get out of here. Lauren tosses the note into the fire and stares at the flames as the note burns. As she wonders how to proceed, she hears a knock on her door and Mrs. Warren's voice floats into the room.

"Time to get up," the voice says.

* * *

"You left a *wake up* call on the downstairs counter, Ms. Calloway," Mrs. Warren calls through Lauren's door, "Time to get up."

Lauren struggles to open her eyes. Instead of staring into a fire, she faces a brilliant morning sunbeam burning through her bedroom window and into her room. As she comes to life, she remembers her dream. At the farmhouse, Chris also awakens, and remembers the previous evening. He calls Lauren. "I slept the sleep of the dead last night. What do you suppose that professor puts in his potions?"

"Gretchen calls him *evil*. Maybe she's right."

"Yeah, maybe, but I haven't slept like that in years." He changes the subject abruptly. "Dream anything exciting last night? I'm assuming you did dream, even if I didn't."

"Yes, and I'm trying to interpret it. In my dream, Gretchen spies Alex in the barn and grabs him, then disappears into thin air—along with Alex. What happens next is sort of like an old *Star Trek* movie. Chris, I think she's in danger and can't get back."

"Alex? Who's Alex?"

"Your uncle's monkey. We didn't know what else to call him. Do you know his name?"

"No, never heard Uncle Alex call him by name. Sounds as good as any other name. What else?"

"There has to be an opening somewhere in the barn for them to disappear like that."

"We've looked."

"We'll look again."

"Why didn't she come back for us?"

"I don't think she can."

"Come on over. I'm not going in that barn alone. I may find the rabbit hole and disappear, too."

Lauren laughs. "Not much like a scripted Hollywood scene, is it? No prepared lines or logical endings."

"You make us sound like a bunch of puppets."

"Sorry," Lauren answers. "It's the public's general concept of Hollywood actors. They tend to believe their inflated press releases."

"You sound like Uncle Alex."

"That why you changed your name?"

"Could be," he agrees. "How long will it take you to get here?"

"As soon as I have breakfast. I've some ideas I want to discuss with Mrs. Warren first."

"Mrs. Warren?"

"Our local historian. I'll fill you in when I get there. It's in the maps I brought over yesterday, and we both missed it," Lauren explains.

Chris hangs up the phone and grabs the maps. He pours over them, trying to figure out what Lauren meant, matching the old maps with the more recent ones. By the time Lauren arrived, he thinks he has it figured out.

Late Afternoon

"Did you see it?" Lauren asks as soon as she enters Chris's study.

"I think so. The new barn didn't follow the same plans, but there is a tunnel under the barn." Chris looks at Lauren as though to verify his finding. "The entrance appears to have been covered over. How could Gretchen disappear through a hole that is no more?"

"It isn't sealed up," Lauren assures him. "And it's been there since before the Civil War. At one time, this barn housed slaves escaping from the South. If they could get to Washington, and link up with underground railroads they had a good chance of making it to Canada and freedom. This barn served as a refuge and halfway point."

"Where did you learn all that?" Chris asks.

"From the horses mouth, so to speak. Mrs. Warren—her ancestors lived in this part of the country—and she has records…"

"And she remembers the barn before its restoration, right?"

"Right," says Lauren giving Chris her *are-you-with-me-or-against-me* look as he opines, giving full credence to the lines on the map and the vague possibility of a tunnel under his barn.

"All well and good," Chris finally agrees. "Now what do we do? Turn the barn upside down looking for an opening that may not exist?"

"But it has to be there. Else how could Gretchen and Alex disappear?"

"Good question, and one that needs an answer. Let's go." He gathers up the maps, grabs a jacket, and pulls Lauren out the door. They head for the barn.

"We're not riding today," he tells the spirited horses expecting a gallop on the range. He pats them on their rumps and gives them an extra ration of oats in their feeders. Then he moves them away from the area of the barn where Gretchen presumably disappeared. "If Hollywood could see me now…" he grumbles.

Lauren heads for the manger, pulling back the hay in each compartment. "There's nothing here, Chris," she says reaching the last stall. She turns to him, puzzled.

"Over by the door, Lauren. They didn't rebuild as many stalls as previously. The last stall is now the back door." Chris strides over to the door, and as he does, he accidentally touches a wall near the door. An opening appears in the floor. Chris finds himself straddling a trap door in the ground. "I found it," he calls out to Lauren, struggling to keep his balance and not fall as he tries to figure out what exactly he touched.

Lauren rushes to Chris, nearly tumbling into the opening before pulling back in time to avoid the same fate as Gretchen. "What did you do?" she asks, peering over the side of the hole, and seeing only darkness.

"I'm not sure," Chris answers. "I'm lucky I'm not down in the hole, too. I grabbed the doorknob to keep my balance. Anyway, we solved the riddle. Except…." His voice trails off as he questions his find. He moves away from the opening and the door springs shut again.

Lauren looks puzzled. "Didn't this area burn up along with the barn?" she asks.

"It's been rebuilt by someone who knew its original intent—and no doubt capitalized on that knowledge, but for what purpose? Why is the tunnel still in use?" A puzzled Chris turns to Lauren. "Did you know about this?"

"Me? I don't know who or why—or even how, where, or when—I'm as lost as you are." She plops down on a bale of hay, looking defeated.

"Okay, have it your way, but let's go back to that first day you and Gretchen came snooping around my farm. You say you found an envelope in your apartment with my address on it, and you followed the trail. Are you trying to prove that the death of my uncle and the envelope you found are somehow linked—that your office is engaged in a cover up?"

Lauren is silent, listening as Chris continues his third degree.

"How long has it been since you last contacted your office, Lauren, and asked about that FBI agent you claim is posing as my uncle? See how he fits into this cops and robbers story?"

"I've told you everything I know. We were following the money trail."

"And that led you here?"

"No, we got sidetracked when we found the envelope and saw the return address. A long shot, but we decided to check it out and make a trip here since it's our home. But to answer your first question, 'No, I haven't contacted my office.' This may sound strange, but I don't trust my office…at least, not everyone there."

"You think there is a cover up—that it's all connected?"

"I don't know how, but yes, I do. The fire, your uncle, Alex, my office, they're all connected in some strange way," she explains. "Gretchen and I decide to play it cool—and try to solve a mystery we knew nothing about. As for Alex—we thought maybe the monkey knew this place, and would find a home here. Otherwise, I'm as lost as you are."

"You think she's in danger?"

"Yes, because she knows now, and we need to find her."

"Good Lord, I've gotten myself smack dab in the middle of a gosh-darned sci-fi movie," Chris says. "Maybe I should be writing a book."

"Lauren grins. "Gretchen beat you to it, but you can play the lead."

"Okay, let's set up the next scene and get back to business. When did a secret passageway for escaping slaves become a secret tunnel?"

"Recently, I believe, and there has to be another way to get back and forth. If we go down this way, we may not get back. We've got to find the other end, and I don't know how to do that."

"Another entrance—or exit," Chris ponders. "Alex knows this one—he came back, but monkeys can jump—and climb—and Gretchen can't. She may not be able to get back, and I doubt Alex would be of much help in that area."

"How deep is the tunnel? How far does it extend? Where does it end? Do we have a ladder if this is the only entrance?" Lauren has only questions and no answers.

"Well, we have to find a way back or we'll get lost, too." They head for the house, back to the maps and to plan strategy. "Your Mrs. Warren gives us hearsay, the archives give us maps. What we need is someone who's been there."

"A hundred and fifty years ago?"

"A historian, maybe. The public library?"

"Or, Shaman," suggests Lauren. "Shaman? The man at the Pub?"

"Why not? We need dinner. He likes to talk, and claims to be hundreds of years old. What more do you want?" She looks at Chris with an impish grin, as though to test his courage, and waits for his answer. "Afraid of what he'll say?"

"Maybe." He hesitates, mulling over her suggestion. "We do need dinner. Shaman does like to talk, and it won't hurt to test him."

"Yes, he closes on Sunday, so it's either today or wait 'til Monday."

"Let's go. Maybe we can lead the conversation to whatever he knows about the old barn." Chris looks elated as he prepares to leave. Lauren notices his exhilaration and is inwardly pleased.

Saturday Evening

They find Shaman at his usual place behind the bar mixing his special drinks. Chris gets right to the point, watching for his reaction. "Shaman, do you know anything about an underground rail road in these parts?" Shaman didn't disappoint him, and stops in midair pouring one of his special drinks.

"Well, that's a right grizzly subject for a Saturday eve," he says, fast recovering. "What brings that old business to mind? You located one of those old tunnels?" He looks at Chris and Lauren grinning impishly at his side, and pours each of them a glass of Chardonnay.

"Could be," Chris says. "Lauren tells me you've been here forever. We were hoping you could help us locate someone who has disappeared."

"Why not call Roscoe or one of the other coppers? Why come here looking for a lost person?"

"Because of the person lost," says Lauren. "It's Gretchen. She disappeared into an underground tunnel, and we can't find a way to get her back. We're looking for another way."

"You must be at the old Grange Farm," Shaman tells Chris. "That where she disappeared?"

"Yes, one minute she's here, the next minute she's gone. First the monkey, then Gretchen—we think she followed him. Now they're both gone."

"A monkey? What kind of monkey?" Shaman looks at Chris.

"An organ grinder type monkey, I don't know the species. Is it important?"

"It is. Some are capable of instruction. Others are not. Which is it?"

"Alex is as capable a monkey as there is and can follow instructions, if need be," Lauren interrupts. "If he could talk, he could tell us what we need to know. He's witness to a murder."

"Murder?" Shaman glanced at Einstein, curled on the hearth, his ears alert. The door opens and Professor Ipswitch enters. Shaman mixes a Rob Roy for the professor and puts it in front of him. The professor concentrates on his drink, ignoring Shaman. "Your table's ready," he tells them leading them to a vacant table. He does not return to their original conversation, but in *soto voce* tells them. "Check back tomorrow."

"You're closed."

"I'll be here."

A weird feeling comes over Chris as he and Lauren wait for their order. "I think the other entrance is here—in this building," he says. "Maybe we shouldn't wait until tomorrow."

"You feel it, too."

"Strange happenings take place in this establishment, Lauren. Shaman's long since disappeared from the world of men—filled with secrets, experiences, and knowledge that far exceeds our understanding."

Lauren smiles as though amused by his comment. "That's what Gretchen tries to tell me, but I don't believe her tales of a *Netherworld*. You think there is such a place?"

"Nothing's impossible. Did Gretchen tell you anything that could give us a lead?" Chris asked. "Like, how she got back?"

"I didn't take her story seriously. It was Halloween. I looked on it as a ghost story, like Ichabod Crane." Lauren tries to remember. "Maybe I should have listened closer."

"You don't remember a Halloween ghost story?" he asks, amused.

"Okay, you decide. She mentioned something about a forest—by the university—and thought of it as an old mining camp. An underground tunnel with tracks, although at the time I'd never heard of a mine in Connecticut."

"A story, h-m-m? You still think so?"

"It's becoming reality, isn't it? The underground track is evidently common knowledge by those who've lived here many years—Mrs. Warren, Shaman, to name a few, and Professor Ipswitch—although for other reasons."

"Speaking of the professor, why do you suppose Shaman gave us that brush-off as soon as the professor came in?"

Lauren laughs. "I've no idea. Maybe he keeps secrets from the professor."

They bat suspicions back and forth, enjoying Shaman's specialty. The professor leaves as they finish and they hear his motorcycle skid on the gravel driveway, Shaman returns to their table. "You need another entrance to the tunnels, do you?"

Lauren looks at Chris, then says. "You know where one is?"

"I know of one, there may be others."

"Do you remember Gretchen?" Lauren asks. At Shaman's nod, she continues. "We believe she unintentionally stumbled into the tunnel, and can't find her way back."

"Where? How?"

"At the ranch—in the barn."

"But the barn's been rebuilt. There's no entrance there now." Shaman looks at the bewildered faces before him, "Is there?"

"We found it—a bottomless pit. Anyway, our ladder didn't reach to the bottom. We can't go down the same way Gretchen did without knowing we have a way out. We don't know if she's alive down there or wandering around lost. We need to find an entrance from another direction—and find out what happened."

Shaman shook his shaggy head. "That girl—she can get into trouble more without half trying...how long has she been missing this time?"

"Since Friday afternoon."

They watch Shaman digest the information, then hesitantly says, "I can get you in, but the tunnel is active again—a haven and headquarters for—at the moment, war protesters."

Chris looks stunned—in disbelief. "Hm-m-m? More of your Irish lore, Shaman?"

"Not at all. You're sure that's where she is?" "We're sure. Can you help us?" Lauren pleads.

Shaman grins at her. He's not beyond appreciating attractive young ladies. "Be here in the morning and I'll take you there."

"You think she's safe?" Lauren asks. "They won't hurt her?"

"No, they'll try to recruit her. If she's smart, she'll go along with them, and wait her chance to get away."

"That could take months."

"Or years. Those people believe in their causes. Do you have the necessary protection—in case?"

"We will," Chris assures him. He looks at Lauren, "And to think, I was sitting around minding my own business...."

"When real life hit you," Lauren grins at him. "You'll get used to it."

Chapter Eleven

Day 11, Sunday morning

Sunday morning starts out as a beautiful day with brilliant sunshine and few clouds, but as Chris and Lauren approach Shaman's, the clouds suddenly amass, the sky darkens, and thunder resounds in the distance. Rains pour onto the foothills, soon making puddles on the road.

Shaman opens the door, and they duck into the shelter, shaking off the rain.

"Did you bring this on?" Chris teases Shaman, as he seats them at a table by the fireplace, then takes off to prepare hot toddies while they dry themselves off before a cheery fire.

"If I tell you, you won't believe me," Shaman says.

"Probably not," Chris agrees.

"The storm keeps people from wandering around the pub," Shaman explains. "They tend to become a little crazy if confronted with something they don't understand."

"Can't say I blame them," Chris agrees, accepting the hot drink. "Now, getting down to business, Shaman. What do you have to offer a novice in the realm of the supernatural?"

Shaman sits on the hearth next to Einstein and Ming. He strokes Einstein, his hands moving to the rhythm of the rain that beats on the windows as he collects his thoughts. He chooses his words carefully.

"There's a difference between this world and the *Netherworld*," he begins. "Everything that is here is there, but better. All things are brighter, the sun more golden, the flowers smell sweeter, and there is peace in the world. That's because of Magus who is vigilant in his crusade against evil. Today, evil is again attempting to take control of the world, and going underground to hide its nefarious ways. It is more than Magus can handle and he is requesting assistance." He stops, noticing the perplexed faces of his visitors. "The *Netherworld* is being compromised," he explains.

"Compromised? Where's the *Netherworld*?" asks Chris. "And what does it have to do with Gretchen and a missing monkey?"

"My sources tell me they're connected." Shaman strokes Einstein and Ming as he waits for a reaction.

Chris looks at Lauren, puzzled, then back to Shaman. "Your source?" he asks. Cats?"

"A very special breed of cat," he replies. "A source of wisdom from the ages." He continues stroking Einstein. "I've never told anyone the story of how Einstein came into my life, but I assure you, his wisdom never fails."

His listeners are silent, looking slightly confused. Finally, Lauren asks, "Why don't you tell us the story? Let us decide."

"Gretchen wouldn't hesitate. She understands," Shaman tells them.

"Then we can do no less," agrees Chris. He turns to Lauren, "Why do I feel as though I'm entering a movie in the middle of a scene?"

"Maybe because you are," says Shaman, and Chris has to be satisfied. "Ready, Einstein?"

Einstein rises to his full height and stretches languidly before heading for the storeroom. Chris and Lauren follow, Shaman brings up the rear. Einstein pauses before a locked door, and Shaman brings forth a key. "Don't be surprised at anything you encounter," Shaman tells them returning the key to his pocket. "Sometimes you have to return to the past to understand the present."

Einstein leads them down a dark tunnel towards a brilliant light that shines in the distance. Occasionally, he turns to Shaman, and at Shaman's nod would continue. Approaching the light, Lauren becomes aware of a peaceful aura surrounding them. She sniffs the balmy fragrant air, and looks at Shaman. He, too, seems to relish the change of atmosphere. Chris seems not to have noticed.

"Where are we?" she asks.

Shaman doesn't answer, letting the surroundings speak for him. Towering shapes of pine trees come into view and he heads for a lovely cottage hidden in their depth. The roof of the cottage is thatched and low. The windows, small panels of glass set into a larger pane, open to a panorama of verdant forest. Uneven cobblestones lead to a rustic door, held in place with huge brass hinges. Shaman leads them through the cottage door into a warm great room boasting an enormous black, stone fireplace. An inviting room, full of peace and light, its atmosphere enhanced by a cozy blazing fire. Dark leather chairs, each with a footstool placed before it, and an inviting rocker face the blazing fireplace. A quiet lamp glows on an ancient oak desk.

"Is this your home?" Lauren asks, looking around the cottage and thinking it similar to the cottage in her dream. Unexpectedly, she asks, "Gretchen says you've lived for centuries, but that's impossible, isn't it?"

"What else does Gretchen say?"

"I never believed her, now I wonder…" Lauren settles into a cozy rocking chair by the fireside, absorbing the peaceful vibrations in the room. She'd never felt so much at peace.

Shaman raids the small icebox in the pantry, and returns with refreshing drinks. "You're going to need this before your journey," he tells them pouring each of them a small glass of lemonade. As they partake of their refreshments, he begins to speak. "Gretchen knows from whence she speaks," he says, in his deeply sonorous Irish brogue—a delight to hear. "You are in the *Netherworld,* a world where Gretchen could wander at will if she so desired, but rather than accept her ability to traverse in two worlds, she struggles to find meaning behind her strange adventures."

"That sounds logical," Lauren interjects.

Shaman smiles. "Ah yes, but sometimes logic creates its own barriers. Gretchen questions and gets wiser for the asking. A thoughtful question carries its answer on its back, as a snail carries its shell." He then proceeds to tell them the story of his encounter with the fisherman and Fionne, and they listen attentively. When he finishes, an eerie silence reigns, broken only by the monotonous ticking of an old grandfather clock in the corner.

Chris is first to break the quiet. "That's a beautiful story," he says. "But I don't understand how your dream can help us find Gretchen."

"I don't think of it as a dream. At first, I thought I'd had too much of my own spirits the night before. Then I hear a scratching at the front door. When I open the door, a shadow darts in. I turn around, and Einstein is sitting next to Ming on the hearth. But that wasn't all. Something else happened. Instead of the spirits leaving me with a terrific hangover, I have this overwhelming feeling of peace and tranquility—and from that day on, I've had no desire to partake of my spirits."

"A strange story," Lauren comments. She looks deep into Einstein's eyes. "Einstein may be a special cat, but I'm more inclined to believe a homeless animal found a home on your hearth."

"Oh, ye, of little imagination," Chris teases. "I'd much prefer it were a premonition."

Lauren ignores him, remembering something else Gretchen had said. "Who is Elise, Shaman? Gretchen mentioned someone by that name. Does she exist?"

"Elise? Yes, she exists. Many centuries ago—when logic as we know it today did not exist—a belief in many worlds existed—but one world or many worlds, wherever there is life there is good and evil, joy and sorrow. And wherever there is life there is action, and many fates determined by councils of learned men. At one such council, the fate of a young woman held sway while they determined her punishment for no more serious a transgression than that she dared to escape an unkind husband.

"Tongues clacked at the gall of a woman who elected to live on her own. A council met to determine her fate, and they sentenced her to banishment from Earth. They placed her in a boat filled with food and a few of her earthly belongings, and pushed her off into the sea—destined to sail alone until such time as she repents sufficiently to be forgiven by her husband.

"When the woman hears her sentence she does not weep or wail, but puts on her best clothes in preparation for the ritual that would be her funeral. After the keening ends and the mourners return home, she drifts for centuries from one world to another refusing to repent. One day she finds an island with no people, and there she makes her home. She survives by catching fish and eating of the bountiful fruit provided by bushes and shrubs.

"After partaking of the annual Feast of Shaman, a great wish came upon me to walk along the sea, to gaze out onto the desolate waters and listen to the breakers crashing against the coast. As I wander along the seashore, a vision appears before me—a woman so beautiful I quail in wonder and amazement. Her long golden hair floating around her, her milk-white skin and ruby lips, and sparkling and flashing dark eyes enchant me. When she tells me her story—how the fates determined her banishment from Earth, and how only Morgan, the Magician, has the power to release her, I want only to be her Savior. I meet with her every day and every night and come to know her. When next I see Fionne, my contact in the *Netherworld*, I implore his assistance.

"'Fionne, do you know this Morgan who has the power to reverse banishment of the undeserved?' I ask him. He admits knowledge of the great man, but cautions me to beware of such beauty for 'one who is lovely can bewitch you into believing she is good as well. Even a magician can be fooled. You may have fallen in love with a mortal that can no longer enter the world of man.'

"But I could not be dissuaded. 'I have heard much of Morgan,' Fionne tells me. 'He can help you, but his price is exorbitant.'

"I assure him I will pay whatever the cost, but he must find a way whereby she is mine. 'I'll tell you on the morrow,' he promises, and true to his word, the next evening he returns. 'You must put yourself in the hands of Morgan, and follow his instructions. Are you prepared?' I follow Morgan demands, and they are difficult. He allows me one day a year—one day that my beloved Elise may return to Earth."

At that moment, the cottage door opens and a beautiful woman appears on the threshold—her arms filled with the bounty of the forest—nuts, grapes, berries, roots and herbs. Shaman greets her and taking her by the arm, he leads her to his guests.

"This is Elise," he tells his guests admiring her with adoring eyes. He pauses a moment—as though wondering if he should say more—then continues. "Last year, thanks to Professor Ipswitch and his contacts in the *Netherworld*, Elise need no longer return to the grave, but may remain with me through all eternity."

Leaving the two skeptics to believe what they will, he bids them adieu and taking Elise by the hand, the two return down the path from whence they came.

"Why do you suppose he told us those stories?"

"I've no idea."

"They're Irish fairy tales, nothing more."

"Oh, I don't know. I like to believe that Einstein is a unique animal—destined to solve the problems of the world."

"You fell for his story."

"It ties into what Gretchen told you. How else could Shaman have known about this particular cottage? It looks ancient—like a stage set for a Seventeenth Century scene." Chris looks around the cottage as though seeing it for the first time. "Does it look like the cottage in your dream? The one where you saw Gretchen?"

"Hm-m? My dream?" She finishes the last of her lemonade, and laughs as she remembers. "I fell onto a lily pad and had to swim ashore.

"They do look very much alike. Do you suppose it's the cottage where Shaman met the fisherman and Einstein, or the cottage of the banished woman?"

"Maybe neither," Chris says. "Now that the players are gone, what say we take a tour of the area?" He starts to rise, then sits back down. "I'm beginning to feel a little strange. How about you?"

Lauren looks at Chris. "No wonder. You've shrunk!"

"That drink!" Chris stares at the oversized doll sitting on a mammoth chair. "We've both shrunk!"

"Did you notice, Chris? This didn't happen 'til Shaman and Elise left."

"Why the old coot. That's why he didn't join us. He knew." Only Einstein remains the same, their new size giving him the appearance of being a young tiger cub. "We're bloomin' Irish leprechauns. Shades of Professor Ipswitch—at least we didn't become animals." Chris accepts his transformation as part of an adventure. "Always did want to be a mouse in a corner."

"I don't mind shrinking providing I don't regress intellectually," Lauren agrees. "We'll need all our faculties to survive. What did Shaman call this place?"

"The *Netherworld*."

"At least, we didn't regress in time the way Gretchen did."

"I'm not so sure," Chris says. "This cottage is definitely Seventeenth Century Ireland, but you may be right. At least, I don't feel it's something we can't handle." Wandering outside, they find everything in direct proportion to their reduced size—a land of little people.

"We're like everyone else now."

Chris jumps up and clicks his heels to test his agility. "Always did want to be a leprechaun, and live in a forest with the animals."

"Aren't you ever serious?" Lauren asks. "We've got to find Gretchen and Alex."

"We can do both," he says as he rushes to keep up with Einstein bouncing down the cobbled stones. "Come on, Lauren. I haaven't had so much fun since I played *Huckleberry Finn* in high school."

Lauren gets into the spirit, trailing along behind him, but stops at the river's bend as she recognizes the frog on the lily pad. "Can you tell me where Gretchen is?" she asks him.

The frog looks as her, but directs his remarks to Einstein. "Tell her the proper procedure for requesting information," the frog directs Einstein.

Lauren turns to Einstein and asks him the same question. "Can you help me find Gretchen?" *I'm as bad as Gretchen—talking to a cat!*

Einstein turns and walks away. Chris watches the by-play, amused at Lauren's confusion. When he turns and follows Einstein, Lauren follows. "The frog speaks only to animals," he tells her. "Einstein wants us to follow him."

The two hold hands and follow the arrogant monster cat through dense undergrowth. As he reaches the edge of the forest, he stops and sits. Lauren and Chris catch up with him and observe an open glade where people seem wholly absorbed in creating piles of paper scraps. No one notices the intruders.

"I wonder if we're invisible," Lauren asks Chris.

"There's one way to find out," he says, venturing with caution toward one of the tables. No one notices him. A scrap of paper floats from a table close to him. He picks it up and returns to the forest. "Do you think they can't see me or am I just lucky?" he asks Lauren.

"They can't see you," Lauren assures him. "But they did see Einstein. One pointed him out and I stood right beside him. They didn't see me."

"No wonder he stopped at the edge of the forest. He may need a quick exit."

"What did you pick up?" Lauren asks.

Chris looks at the paper in his hand. "My God," he says, looking at the tables loaded with similar bills. "It's a hundred-dollar bill. What did you say about 'following the money?' It's here—millions and millions of dollars —they're turning them out like confetti on New Years' Eve. Is this a counterfeiting station?"

Lauren looks at the bill. "The mystery deepens. Now we know *what and how,* but *why* is another question. *Who* benefits?"

"The elusive *why*—and *who.* And don't forget *where. Where* does the money go?" Chris, scrutinizing the scene before him, spies Alex dancing on one of the table. "Look," he points out the monkey to Lauren. "It's Alex, isn't it?"

Lauren follows his gaze, sure enough, Alex is dancing and entertaining the workers—moving from table to table as if right at home. Lauren remembers the organ grinder's sign, *For money, the monkey dances,* where she first saw the dancing Alex on the Capitol steps. "If Alex is here, Gretchen can't be too far behind."

"What do we do?" Chris asks. "Grab the monkey?"

"No, not yet. We'll let him lead us to Gretchen. Someone has to feed him, and my guess is that's Gretchen." They wait beside Einstein as workers place boxes of cash on a railway tram, and prepare to close up shop for the day. "I wonder where they stay."

"Let's follow the tram," Chris says. "Gretchen isn't going anywhere, but the money is."

"I'm concerned about Gretchen, not the money," Lauren argues. "We've got to get her out of here."

"We will," argues Chris. "No one can see us, but they can see Gretchen. We can work like mice in a corner, but she can't—not without a dose of Shaman's *lemonade.* Even then, they may suspect something if she disappears."

"You're right, although I hate to admit it," Lauren agrees. "We'll do what we can before the *lemonade* wears off, as I'm sure it will eventually."

"Didn't think of that," Chris says.

"Shaman never tells us the consequences of his actions," Lauren adds.

"We follow the tram," they decide and scurry down the track after the disappearing tram. They soon see its blinking lights up ahead. Einstein has disappeared.

"If we catch up, we can hitch a ride," Chris suggests, sprinting faster down the track with Lauren in close pursuit. They catch the slow-moving tram, and hop onto the tailgate. The clickity-clack of the tram wheels makes talking difficult, and the two watch the rails in silence as the miles disappear beneath them. The tunnel is cold—a cold penetrating cold, and lights flicker at intervals—other than that, they travel in total darkness. Lauren shivers and moves closer to Chris. *What if something happens and we can never return?* The tram rattles on as though the only reality.

Chapter Twelve

To imagine is everything, to know is nothing at all
—Anatole France

Day 12, Monday

Chris and Lauren spend the first night taking advantage of their unique situation. As the workers revel in the success of their endeavor, the two intruders investigate the surroundings. Uncertain as to how long they would remain in their present state of invisibility, the two fight weariness, seeking an explanation for the hidden enterprise.

"Records have to exist somewhere," Chris says digging into any place looking like a possible storage area. "Where are we, anyway?"

"Don't ask me," Lauren answers. "Einstein appears to have deserted us. Gretchen is nowhere to be seen, and we appear to have entered a sort of no-man's land for animals."

"Anyway, everyone's asleep. This may be our only opportunity to find out what's going on."

"I don't really care right now. I want to find Gretchen. Everything else takes second place."

"You've forgotten your *follow the money* theory?" Chris needles.

"No, but priority is priority. Gretchen first."

"I don't think she's here. If she is, I doubt she knows what's going on," Chris says opening boxes and digging into anything that looks as though it might give him a clue. "Who is that senator you say my uncle worked with?"

"I didn't say. That's privileged information."

"Really—couldn't by chance be old Senator Claghorn, could it?"

Surprised, Lauren asks, "How'd you come up with that name?"

"It's on this box," he explains reading the caption on the box. "EXCLUSIVE PROPERTY OF SENATOR EDWARD CLAGHORN—DO NOT OPEN—CONTAINS DOCUMENTS INVOLVING NATIONAL SECURITY. Looks like your office, the state department and my uncle were mixed up in counterfeiting—maybe mailing huge donations to God knows who for whatever purpose."

"Don't jump to conclusions," Lauren cautions. " I'm sure there's a logical explanation. We don't know if it's counterfeit money—could be legitimate currency."

"And I'm a monkey's uncle. You saw Alex dancing on the Senate steps—and again today—dancing as though he belongs here. I'm opening this box." He pulls out his penknife.

"No, not here." Lauren stops him. "Let's get it to the tram while everyone's asleep. We can go through it at our leisure if we can get it back to the cottage."

"Good idea. I think I'll take a box of this money, too."

They look around for one of the small flatcars they'd seen the workers using to load and unload the boxes of money. Locating an empty one, they tip the box over onto the flatcar—no small achievement for two elfin creatures—and drag the flatcar to the tram. Not even the squeaking wheels of the cart disturb the grog-filled crew. No one stirs except for one or two bodies that turn over and continue to snore—the grog they drank acting like an aphrodisiac to the tired crew.

"How do we turn the tram around?" Lauren asks.

"We don't need to, it goes in either direction, but we have to find the switch that reverses the power." He looks around the mechanism, and sees Einstein curled up on the tram surrounded by a motley crew of ragtag cats. "Are you here to help?" Chris asks.

Einstein looks at him in silence, and speaks to the group beside him. "Show him how it's done," Einstein advises his crew of cats. Together, they disengage a hook that hangs over the tram, snags the box on the flatcar, and lifts it onto the tram. Then they sit back looking smug.

Chris laughs. "Well done," he tells Einstein. "Now find the switch that reverses direction." And Einstein did. Cats and all pile onto the tram and head back to the cottage in the forest.

"Do you know where Gretchen is?" Lauren asks Einstein.

He shakes his head, but speaks to the cats behind him. A large, black cat steps out from the pack and heads back down the tracks. Lauren watches him. "That looks like Julius," she says to Einstein.

Einstein nods as though to say, *Julius will find her.*

When they reach to glade, the ragtag cats help load the boxes onto a flatcar, then assist in pulling them across the glade, and into the forest to the cottage. When Lauren and Chris are safely deposited at the cottage, Einstein gives the cats a nod of thanks, and they disappear into the forest. Weary for sleep, they find comfortable beds in the two little bedrooms and lie down to catch a few hours of shut-eye. They awaken to find themselves their original size.

"I suppose we're no longer invisible, either," Lauren laments. "Now what?"

"We drink more lemonade," Chris says, "But not 'til it's necessary. We'll have to conserve unless you have that potion with you. Do you?"

"No. I don't know where… Oh, yes, I do. Gretchen had it with her the day she disappeared." She stares at Chris. "Do you suppose?"

"What?"

"Oh, Chris, she might have taken some of the potion, and could be any one of these animals around here."

"She'd let us know, wouldn't she?" Chris looks puzzled. "You know her better than I do. What do you think? Would she use it?"

Lauren recalls Gretchen's reaction when she wanted to test the potion on herself—*a fear of not returning to her human form the next time?* "No, I don't believe so—not unless she were cornered and had no other means of escape."

"Forget that, then," Chris decides. "We wait for Julius' report. In the meantime, let's dig into that box we brought back. " He drags out the box and opens it. "Damn, I sure wish Shaman would show up with one of his famous steak burgers. I'm starved."

"Just like a man. He wants it all spread in front of him. I'll see what I can rustle up." Lauren checks the cupboard and finds it well stocked. She chooses a can of soup and a box of crackers. "It's soup and crackers for lunch," she tells Chris. "Shaman didn't intend for us to starve. You get started on that box of goodies and I'll take care of the meals. I've an idea Elise has a garden outside, or maybe we can catch a fish from the stream."

"Sure, and maybe you can find the old fisherman and catch the special fish that eats of the special bush. Now, wouldn't that be a kick?"

"You never know. This is the *Netherworld.*"

"It's catching."

"What is?"

"Life in the world of unreality, I suppose," Chris says, his voice fading as he digs into the first box. Lauren concentrates on building a fire in the small fireplace. She finds an ancient pot in which to heat the soup, and hangs it on spit over the fire. Soon the room is filled with aromatic orders as the pot bubbles invitingly."

Meanwhile, Julius is having his own problems. He finds Alex faithfully guarding Gretchen in a small cottage in the forest. Although he tries to entice him away, Alex has his orders. He doesn't budge. Julius leaves. *This will take strategy. Einstein will know what to do.* And Einstein does.

For money, the monkey dances, he reminds Julius. *Entice him with money. He knows his place.* But Julius doesn't need to entice Alex as movement begins again. The tram, back in its rightful place after taking Lauren and Chris to their cottage, returns the workers to the glade and the printing press. Alex, not realizing Julius has usurped his spot guarding Gretchen, climbs on board the tram with his buddies. As they disappear around the bend, Julius trots off to the cottage. He parks himself on the hearth waiting for her to notice him. She doesn't, and he waits.

Is she deliberately ignoring me?

Gretchen sighs, her mind on her seemingly inescapable situation. As she sits in the chair by the fireplace, she wonders whether her telepathic thoughts ever reached Lauren, or if she's destined to remain in the underground cottage for the rest of her life. Julius jumps on her lap to get attention. She automatically begins to stroke him. Startled, she recognizes him.

"Julius? Is it you?" Julius snuggles against her, purring his delight.

She smiles and hugs him to her as she hears: *We could make such beautiful music together.* "It is you. Oh, Julius, can you help me find my way out of the forest? I'm being treated like a prisoner and I don't know why. Alex moves freely, but he's so afraid of losing his *status* with the others he's absolutely no help to me at all."

Your friends look for you, and Einstein sends me to find you. He and your feline friends return at midnight. Can you be ready?

"Oh, yes, yes I can." She grabs Julius, and whirls and dances around the room. "Oh, I love you, I love you, I love you." She kisses Julius on the tip of his nose. "I can't believe I'm really going home." She stops and sits down on the rug, suddenly disheartened. "But Julius, there's no exit to this place. I'm not a cat any more."

Ah, but you could be. You have only to drink of the potion. The black feline nuzzles against her, purring lasciviously. *You'd rather stay here?*

"I'm sorry, Julius, I dropped my purse when I fell down the rabbit hole. I don't have it." She runs her hand along the animal's arched back and Julius responds. He nuzzles her hand "Does that mean I can't return?" she asks.

Julius moves to the door of the cottage. *I must report to Einstein.*

Gretchen watches him leave, dismayed, but at the door, he turns to her.

There's lemonade in the fridge. I'll return at midnight. And he was gone.

Delaying his meeting with Einstein, Julius moves to the rabbit hole located under Chris' barn. He examines the grass under the opening, and spies a handbag hidden nearby in the tall grass. Dragging the purse by its handle, he returns to the cottage, leaves the purse on the hearth, and heads for his rendezvous with Einstein.

Meanwhile, Lauren and Chris investigate the contents of the box. "Just what was your office working on?" he asks, digging into the box. "And I wonder how many more are involved besides my uncle, and your FBI agent?"

"I'm not the one who connects the dots," Lauren says. "We were trying to find the money trail. At least, that's what I was told. Everything's so secretive in the FBI. Each agent has his own part in the program, and only a very few top-secret intellects have authorization to put it together."

"What happens if those few connect the wrong dots?"

"I don't know. It's how they work. The idea is, if everyone does his job, the pieces all fall into place, and the result is the solution. Mission accomplished."

Lauren watches Chris digest this piece of information. "You accept that?" he asks.

"Mine is not to question why..." Lauren quotes, "But to answer your inquiry, yes. We take an oath to uphold the laws of the agency."

"Don't you realize that one monkey wrench could skew the entire mission?" he asks, pawing through the contents of the box. "Like this box, for instance. How did it get here? It's got information that should have been processed long ago. Maybe if the Senator had forewarned the President, he could have put the CIA and SEC on the alert and into the mix—and there may not have been a 9-11 at all."

"You can't be sure of that," Lauren answers.

"No, I can't, Lauren, but this looks mighty suspicious. What else am I to think? Why else is my uncle dead and his body buried under false pretenses? Why else are you on administrative leave if not to get you out of the way? We've run into a situation that has no explanation. Who needs all that fake money? What is it funding? The war or campaign funds for the next election?"

"What you're thinking is impossible, Chris. They'd never get away with it, she argues. "Counterfeiting is against the law. There'd be an investigation."

"In a perfect world, Lauren, that would be true. But we're not living in a perfect world. We're living in a world of liars, cheats and thieves—those who'll do anything for power. No, I don't put it past our politicians to play a power game in exchange for votes. Winning is the name of the game."

"I guess I prefer to see the best in people, not the worst," Lauren answers. "I need an explanation before I condemn anyone."

"A noble gesture. Crooks love that philosophy, and have more than enough explanations to suit the casual administrator. But you're an agent for the FBI, Lauren. You need to be continually vigilant for interlopers—despite your inner feelings."

"I am vigilant, as you say," Lauren retorts. "Why else would I be in this position? Certainly, not out of choice. You're the one I had to convince. You treated my story like another scene on your imaginary stage. You didn't want any part of it—your uncle notwithstanding—even after we told you about the body switch."

Chris stops and looks at her, taken back by her outburst. "You're right. *Mea culpa*. I stand corrected. I didn't believe you. And you have every right to chastise me. "

Lauren grins inwardly, knowing she's bested him on this round. Now that she'd convinced him, maybe they could concentrate on getting Gretchen back. And with the evidence in the box, they could turn Washington on its heels. She sits back and gloats.

Chris glances at her. "You don't have to look so superior."

She laughs, looking very much like a smug Cheshire cat who'd eaten the last of the cream.

Chapter Thirteen

Day 13, Tuesday

True to his word, a few minutes after midnight, Julius appears at the cottage. Gretchen is beside herself in frustration realizing the purpose of the lemonade. Julius grins smugly. *Aha, you drank of the lemonade, I see.*

"Why, Julius?" she asks the grinning feline. "Why did you shrink me?"

You're also invisible, except to me.

"I am?" She climbs on a stool and looks in the mirror on the wall. No face stares back at her. Gretchen isn't appeased. "You tricked me, Julius." She jumps down from the stool and a thought strikes her. "Is that why everyone is so tiny here? Do they all drink lemonade?"

Julius says nothing, and Gretchen continues her inquisition. "Has that lemonade been there all this time? Who'd have thought that a tiny glass of lemonade would do this to me? I feel like Gulliver—when the little people capture him and hundreds of tiny hands tie him down."

It's the best I could do.

"I feel like a museum piece."

Julius exhibits his facetious cat smirk, and warns her. *It's temporary—we must work fast.*

"Should we take it with us?"

No, follow me. Julius leads the way from the cottage, down the mining track, heading for the cottage on the other side of the forest. On the way, they meet Alex returning to check on Gretchen. He takes one look at the pair and leaps for the nearest tree. Using his long arms for leverage, he swings himself back toward the camp and his cronies.

"What'll we do, Julius? He's gone to warn the others."

He doesn't know about Magus' cottage on the edge of the Netherworld. We need to hurry.

Arriving at the clearing, Einstein meets with his renegade pals. They appear a ragtag bunch—street cats that live by their wits—not the domestic breed Gretchen knew from past encounters. Einstein takes immediate charge of his cat crew, directing them to head the enemy off at the pass. *You know what to do. Keep them busy.*

To Julius, Einstein tells him, *You know the way from here, Julius. You go on ahead. We'll stay and guard the entrance to the mine. They have to return this way.*

Gretchen runs as fast as her short legs can carry her, across the clearing heading for the forest on the other side. *If only I hadn't drunk so much of that lemonade, but I was thirsty.* She races alongside Julius who suddenly stops in midfield. *Would you perhaps like a ride? Climb on me. I can run like the wind, if need be.*

Gretchen accepts the offer, and climbs on the back of the black cat, leaning forward the length of his body with her arms encircling his neck. Julius seems unencumbered by the extra weight, heading with exhilarating speed towards the special opening in the forest. As they near the opening, they hear a loud bang and stop to look back.

"Oh, look what they did, Julius," Gretchen says, sliding off his back. " The entrance to the mine disappeared—it's covered by rocks. "Is that what Einstein asked his cats to do?"

Watch.

Einstein, his ragtag army swarming around him, gives them the special *tails up* message. Pointing their long tails towards the rocks that cover the mine entrance, the *mission accomplished* message, signifying success in pinning the little people on the tracks inside the tunnel. It would be quite a while before they could dig out from under those heavy rocks.

"We're safe, Julius. They can't get to us now."

We're safe unless they return and loose the animals from their cages.

"The animals? You mean the animals I saw when I first came here? They aren't dangerous, Julius. They were helpful to me. Why do you say they are dangerous?"

They haven't been fed today. You and your friends may be their next meal. He turns and leads Gretchen away from the scene and into the forest.

"Will Einstein be safe?

Einstein has many lives. He has eaten of the sacred bush. We ordinary cats have only nine and must be careful how we use them.

Approaching the cottage, Gretchen stops and stares—bewildered. "Why didn't I find this cottage? It looks just like the one the other side of the forest."

You were not meant to find this one. Only Magus can approve entry —or exit.

"Magus? Where am I, Julius? Who are those people? Why are they here?"

They pay penance to Magus, and destined to repeat their vices for all Eternity unless given a chance to redeem themselves. They may be here for all Eternity.

"When will that be?"

If they return to earth, and do good, instead of evil, they earn points to Heaven.

"Why don't they return?"

They refuse to believe.

Approaching the cottage, Julius prepares to leave. She stops him. "No, Julius, don't go. I need you here."

Enter the cottage. Your friends are here. I must check on Einstein.

Lauren catches sight of Gretchen outside the cottage window and rushes to greet her. "Oh, Chris, look who's here!" Amid hugs and kisses, she pulls Gretchen into the cottage. When she sees Lauren, all thoughts of Julius leave, and she follows Lauren into the cottage.

"I'm so hungry, Lauren. Do you have anything to eat here?" Then she sees the opened box and its contents littering the floor. "What's this?" she asks forgetting about food.

"It's what we were looking for—in Washington, remember? We don't know how it got here from the storage room at your apartment complex."

"Strange."

"Yes, isn't it?"

"Have you forgotten about me?" Chris asks from the sidelines, waiting patiently to be noticed. "I take it this is Gretchen, the missing sleuth?"

"I'm sorry, Chris. Yes, this is Gretchen."

"I'm so glad you're all right. You had us worried when you disappeared without a trace."

"No more worried than I," Gretchen answers. "How are you, Chris? We met briefly, I believe, at your farm. You were not too friendly."

"Sorry about that. I'm not used to having beautiful women telling fantastic tales show up on my doorstep. And, I admit to being less than cordial. Lauren straightened me out." His apology amuses Gretchen no end.

Gretchen looks down at herself. "I'm not usually this small, Chris, but it seems the accepted style in *Netherworld*."

"We had our introduction to that elixir. Standard equipment in cottages here, I presume. What happened when you disappeared?"

Gretchen looks puzzled. "Disappeared?"

"Chris has been helping me since you disappeared from the barn. You remember—the barn on Chris' property?"

"Yes, you were in the loft when I fell down the rabbit hole. How did you know where to find me?"

"After you disappeared, we got hold of some pre-Civil War building plans, and discovered an underground railway used by slaves escaping into Canada. They ran right under the barn. We found your exit, but didn't want your fate to happen to us, so we enlisted Shaman's support. He led us here."

"He's evidently been here before," Chris adds.

"Yes, Julius told me I'd been here before, too."

"Julius?" Chris asks.

"Oh, dear. Now I've done it. Never mind." She looks at Lauren and then at the box in the middle of the living room. "Can we get the evidence out with us? There isn't much time."

"Why?" asks Lauren and Chris in unison.

"They may already have opened the animal cages. You don't want to be their dinner tonight, do you?"

"What are you talking about?" Chris asks.

"The animals—the ones who guarded me. Magus controls the forest, but sometimes the animals are uncontrollable. I'll feel better when we get out of here."

"Chris and I took the tramway to the other side of the forest, found the box and took the tramway back. Where were they holding you? We didn't even see Alex. Have you seen him?"

"Yes, but I don't recommend we wait for him. He's their spy, now."

"What happened?"

"Nothing, that's just it, Alex does as he's told. They're his masters. Can we get out of here?"

"Not until Shaman and Elise return. In the meantime, I'm fixing dinner."

"Elise is here? Shaman did bring her back with him. I'm so glad."

"Yes, this is her cottage. You did say you were hungry, didn't you?"

"I'm more afraid than hungry. You sure we're safe?" Gretchen wants to believe, but remembers Julius' warning.

"It's not safe to enter the glade, but the forest is Shaman's territory." Chris explains this to her as though now an authority on the laws of *Netherworld*. "Elise wanders the forest gathering flowers and berries. She feels perfectly safe. Shaman will return for us when we're ready."

Gretchen spies her purse on the hearth where Julius placed it. "That's my purse," she asks. "Where did it come from? Did you find it?"

Lauren and Chris look puzzled. "It wasn't here when we came," Chris says. "Someone must have brought it while we slept. Lauren?"

She shrugs. "Did you tell anyone you'd lost it?"

"Julius. Maybe he found it and brought it here."

"Who is Julius?"

"A black cat," Lauren answers, "And I'll thank you not to ask too many questions. Accept it on faith, that's what I've learned to do."

Gretchen looks at the two skeptics, and sighs. "What can I say?" she asks.

They sit down to Lauren's quickly prepared dinner, and for the rest of the evening discuss the contents in the box and what it could mean to their future.

* * *

"We've been compromised," Archibald Carlton tells Philip Gadsden. "I can't get any response to my calls."

"How?" Gadsden answers. "There's no way. The plan is foolproof." He looks at the agitated individual facing him in his office. "What have you done?"

"What have I done?" Carlton answers. "I've tried to get hold of Senator Claghorn. "He's unavailable for comments. I've called the professor, and he's noncommittal. Says he's not involved. He furnishes a place of operation—other than that he wipes his hands of all responsibility. He knows nothing."

Gadsden laughs. "Aha, the professor. Slippery as an eel, isn't he? I warned you. He builds in escape hatches at every turn. How do you think he's survived centuries of turmoil and comes out unscathed. If you've figured him as a fall guy, you've stepped into deep *doo doo*."

"It's that female agent," Carlton fumes. "You lost touch with her, and somehow she's stumbled onto the whole damned operation."

"You give a novice too much credit. She knows nothing."

"She's the only wild card. It has to be her."

"If what you say is true, she's found professional help. There's no way she knew enough to act alone."

"Can you contact her? Find out where she is? I've tried all morning to contact my sources, and all lines are down in that area—an absolute blackout. Cell phones, computers—all down. It's as though the operation dropped off the face of the earth." Carlton sank into the one chair in Gadsden's office and puts his head in his hands, looking the epitomy of utter defeat.

Gadsden looks at him, feeling sympathy to only a small degree. He'd never thought much about the plan at its onset—pouring counterfeit money onto the economy in an attempt to smoke out recipients of the real money being used to finance terrorist organizations. He had no sympathy for trickery. *If it blows up in their faces, they have it coming.* He particularly didn't like having to pull his agents out of the fire when their stupid plans went awry.

"You lost control and your fantastic plot backfired," Gadsden chides him. "Now, you need someone to blame. Look in the mirror, Archie. You've been outmaneuvered. I've an idea Agent Calloway did your job for you, and deserves your thanks, not your censure."

Chapter Fourteen

Day 14, Wednesday

Gretchen resumed her normal size after sleeping off the effects of the lemonade, and appeared no worse the wear after her experience. Waiting for Shaman to arrive and accompany them to civilization, Gretchen and Lauren busy themselves in the kitchen preparing breakfast. Chris digs again into Senator Claghorn's mystery box.

"Well, whatta you know." He pulls out a bill of lading signed by Senator Claghorn listing the items in the box. He sees a yellow plastic package with the words HEROIN printed in black letters. He glances towards the kitchen. *Now what do I do? Bury it and not tell anyone, or wait for Shaman?* He closes the box and pushes it into the back room. *We need to get rid of this.*

He returns and Lauren offers him a cup of coffee, her eyes questioning. *What did you find?* He accepts the coffee, but ignores her raised eyebrows, his mind struggling with his own questions. *What did my uncle have to do with this?*

Shaman enters the cottage, and observes the silent by-play. "You've found something?" Chris nods. "What is it?" And Chris takes him to the back room. Shaman lifts up a few of the packages, and discovers something else. Tucked under the packets of heroin, one package labeled URANIUM.

"Oh, oh, I didn't dig deep enough. Now what do we do?"

"Bury it—deep in the forest," Shaman decides. "It's better the world never knows. Let time work its magic." He removes the correspondence, hands it to Chris, and reseals the box. They rejoin the others. Gretchen is setting out plates of food on the rustic maple table.

"Can't it wait?" she asks, eyeing the box under Shaman's arm. "Let's eat, then you can tell us what we're about to bury."

"Join us, Shaman?" Chris selects a seat, ignoring her comment. "Shaman?" Gretchen persists. "Did we miss something?"

Shaman looks at the box under his arm. "Well, your friends did help save the free world, at least for the time being. I'll let Chris explain. I've no time to lose."

"Chris?" Two sets of questioning eyes turn on him after Shaman leaves, heading for the forest. "Remember those unburned poppy fields in Afghanistan?" he asks. "Why weren't they burned instead of left for harvesting?"

"It's their survival," Gretchen says. "At least, that's what I thought. Am I wrong?"

"Not really," Lauren says. "The poppy fields fund the war on terrorism."

"Then they should be burned. If we're to fight terrorism, why not cut off their money supply?" Gretchen looks at Lauren for an explanation.

"Depends on who needs the funds. Congress isn't too generous with the taxpayer's money in that department; hence, the Senator's intense interest in money, the by-play he engaged in with Alex, and the implication that my office is involved. A tricky game, isn't it?"

"A clever game," Chris agrees. "Like the old New York shell game—three-card Monte. 'Which card covers the booty?' I've an idea old Senator Claghorn hit the jackpot on his last visit with the troops, and looking for a safe place to hide the booty, got my uncle involved. Dropping that box into *Netherworld,* must have been like frosting on his yellow cake. He knew nothing of a thriving underground community already holding the world hostage. That old excavation under my uncle's barn must have seemed a safe haven."

"You mean, we accidentally fell into a *pot of jam*?"

"Well, Gretchen evidently did. We'd never have discovered that underground railway if she hadn't fallen down the shaft."

"How could the senator get it out of Iraq?" Chris asks.

"Senators have immunity," Lauren explains. "Can even hook rides on Air Force One if it's available—the perfect cover. No one suspects a senator."

"But why? To hold until after the election?"

"Maybe, or maybe the president knows and plans to release the information at the appropriate time. That's possible, too, isn't it?"

"Anything's possible. It's being used as political leverage. Dissenters don't want that box found until after the next election."

The three ponder the enormity of the power that has dropped into their laps until Chris, holding his cup out for a refill, muses with a grin. "We could play politics, too, Lauren, and hold your office hostage until they tell us what really happened to my uncle."

"I've an idea your uncle discovered the senator's find and refused to go along with the plan. When that happened, he knew too much and had to go. Our agent used him as a cover, and my boss fell for his story."

"And your uncle isn't a suicide." says Gretchen. "Anyone for more coffee? I can make another pot." They decline and she pours the last of the coffee in her cup. "What are your plans now, Lauren?"

"Take pictures of our find, and pass the information on to Security. Let the President use it for leverage, if he needs to. I'm sure Senator Claghorn is already aware all is not rosy."

"There she goes, taking all the fun out of our discovery," Chris comments. "I had visions of money and virgins at my beck and call. You busted my bubble." Lauren laughs, and Gretchen teases him. "As though you need it—with all those gorgeous babes in Hollywood...."

Chapter Sixteen

Day 17, Saturday

"Now that we're home, Lauren, what are your plans?" The two girls had settled into Lauren's apartment in Washington, and over glasses of wine review their success. Cyrus is happy to be home and seems none the worse for wear after his lone vigil at the farm. Alex had not surfaced, but then, he alone knew the location of the escape hatch in the barn. They could only hope he survived.

"You know," Lauren says, sipping her wine. "After having exposed a nefarious plot to intercept money intended to fight terrorism, I'm no longer on administrative leave. I'm sure some heads will roll and others will be crowned, but that's no longer my responsibility. I leave that to the top honchos in Security."

"What do you think would have happened if we hadn't been so nosy?" Gretchen speaks absentmindedly as though it's no longer important. She caresses Cyrus who is cuddled beside her, and her thoughts are on Julius. "Would their plan have worked?"

"We'll never know." Then, as though reading her mind, asks,"For a while there, I thought Julius would come with us. What changed his mind?"

"As much as he likes to visit, he says he's a field cat, and would go stir-crazy as a pampered, petted house cat. Says we *humanoids* build our own cages, and he wants no part of that—might as well be underground with the rest of the little people. He didn't like that much, either."

"Strange how things eventually work out to the good, isn't it?"

"Not strange at all. You don't really believe we did that alone, do you Lauren, with no help from a higher power?"

Lauren views her friend with empathy. "We had help from Shaman, and the plat books. Other than that, *we* did it. When will you realize that nothing happens without physical energy? You're not logical, Gretchen."

"You're wrong, my dear. God creates true logic. Man's logic is egotistical and flawed. He believes he can destroy and recreate the world to be a better place, but then screws up everything he touches. God creates harmony—the stars, the sun, the moon, the tides, the weather—all he touches achieves perfection. He wastes nothing—everything is recycled—even man's soul after his body fails. With man in control, it's a continual struggle to destroy the perfection that God creates. You'd settle for a world like that, Lauren?"

"Sure, rather than believe Magus programs the world's events. You read too many fairy tales. Reality says you'd never have known about Harley and Kristin if you hadn't accidentally walked in on them at lunch. When you heard Kristin mention divorce, how did you feel?"

"Harley didn't agree, did he? Kristin can be quite persuasive, but Harley expects me home at the end of summer." Gretchen finishes her wine and gets up to refill her glass. "Strange, isn't it? I never realized how easily Kristin pulls my strings. She's my friend, but she does try to manipulate people's lives." She puts her hand up as though to stop Lauren's self-proclaimed comment. "Don't preach. I know. She couldn't do it without my consent."

"Logic says you can remain friends, and be stronger for the experience," Lauren says facetiously.

"Maybe. I did get some good material for my novel, though, and gave Harley something to think about." She grins at a sudden thought. "Sometimes I think we don't solve anything, Lauren. We only rearrange the mystery."

The End

Special Thank You:

To my only daughter for editing the final galleys for this book and helping to market it after I am gone.
To my granddaughter, Brette Boockvor and her husband for helping to develop the idea for this book's cover.
To my great nieces, Erin and Heather Vanderhoof who kept me writing until the book's completion.

Lightning Source UK Ltd.
Milton Keynes UK
UKHW011830090721
386917UK00001B/16